Praise
Feline Detec

'Original and intriguing
lovers will en

'Deliciously clever and

'**I loved it.** The whole concept is just so "real"!'
Barbara Erskine

'Mandy Morton's Feline Detective Agency instigates a new
genre, both **wonderful and surreal.**' Maddy Prior

'The world that Morton has created
is **irresistible.**' *Publishers Weekly*

'Witty and smart. **Prepare to be besotted.**' M.K. Graff

'Mandy Morton's series is both **charming and whimsical.**'
Barry Forshaw

'Hettie Bagshot might be a new face at the scene of a crime,
but already **she could teach most fictional detectives a
thing or two.**' *The Hunts Post*

What readers are saying
about the series:

'This series is **the perfect warm, fluffy cosy mystery
read** for fans of Agatha Crispy-style mysteries and
cat-lovers alike.'

'**True escapism into a world of pies, cakes and cats** while
somehow smuggling a truer reflection of the real world than
much human detective fiction.'

'A deceptively nasty murder wrapped up in a cardigan,
and served by the fire with tea and cake. **A delight from
beginning to end.**'

'**Hilarious and captivating.**'

'**The cat world's answer to the cosy crime novel**, with bags
of charm and characters you don't want to leave behind.'

'**I love this series** and am waiting with a warmed pastry, a hot
mug of something, and a crackling fire for the next in the series.'

By Mandy Morton
The No. 2 Feline Detective Agency
Cat Among the Pumpkins
The Death of Downton Tabby
The Ghost of Christmas Paws
The Michaelmas Murders
Magical Mystery Paws
Beyond the Gravy
The Ice Maid's Tail
A Pocket Full of Pie
The Cat and the Pendulum

THE WINDMILL MURDERS

THE NO. 2 FELINE DETECTIVE AGENCY

Mandy Morton

This edition published in 2023 by Farrago,
an imprint of Duckworth Books Ltd
1 Golden Court, Richmond TW9 1EU, United Kingdom

www.farragobooks.com

Print ISBN: 978-1-78842-433-2
Ebook ISBN: 978-1-78842-434-9

To all the would be Shield Maidens and
for Nicola my own Peace-Weaver

Chapter One

The cats in the town had had a very good Christmas. In fact, they had unanimously agreed to carry the festivities on until Candlemas. The Pawlights drama group had extended the run of its annual pantomime and a number of rewrites kept the performances fresh, although the costumes suffered from several backstage parties during the panto season. By the last night, on 1st February, Cinderella wasn't the only character in the cast dressed in rags.

The magnificent Christmas tree that had stood proudly at the entrance to Malkin and Sprinkle's department store now leaned in a northerly direction, having received several batterings from the January winds. The baubles had long since escaped, blown into shop doorways to be collected by kittens as treasure to carry home, but the principal beacon of Christmas still stood *almost* tall as the January sale seekers rushed past.

The No. 2 Feline Detective Agency had closed its doors to any form of work at least two weeks before Christmas and the proprietors, Hettie Bagshot and Tilly Jenkins, had made a calculated decision not to engage in any cases until the new year was at least a month old. It made perfect sense to hibernate in their bedsitter behind Betty and Beryl Butter's bakery, where pies and pastries were on tap and a roaring fire kept the cold away.

The weather had been kind, offering a seasonal sprinkling of snow on Christmas Eve, followed by a bout of wet and windy weather which quickly gave way to a series of frosty but sunny early February days. Hettie sat in her armchair by the fire, waiting for Tilly to return from the library. There was a sadness about their room: the paper chains they'd had such fun draping about the place now lay in a heap on the floor with the discarded Christmas cards; the pretend snow that Tilly had excitedly sprayed all over their small window now looked like a bad case of dandruff; and the tree they'd carried home so joyfully from Meridian Hambone's hardware store stood belligerently in the space by the sideboard, shedding its needles in hope that some would get stuck in unsuspecting paws. The tree was sulking, and – as Hettie took in the desolation that the end of Christmas brings – so was she.

She was now tired of the party season, and had reached her limit as far as cheese straws, mince pies and even roast dinners were concerned. Tilly's idea of holding on to Christmas for as long as possible was all very well – she had a mountain of books to read, jigsaws to do, and now her new-found hobby at the library – but Hettie had no interest in such things.

She'd restrung her guitar, thinking that she might take it up again, but had discovered that it held no joy for her without an audience. Her days on the road with her band were long gone – to compensate, she'd dug out one of her records to play on Tilly's Dansette, but she'd got no further than the end of side one before forcing it back into its sleeve and returning it to the sideboard. Rediscovering her youth had only made her feel worse, and, as she sat waiting for Tilly to come home, boredom began to engulf her.

Since giving up her music and subsequently starting a detective agency, life had certainly not been short on excitement. With Tilly as her redoubtable sidekick, and their friends Bruiser and Poppa lending a paw when required, their business had gone from strength to strength. They had successfully solved a number of high-profile murder cases that brought them national acclaim, and the charmed life they enjoyed in their bedsitter was a far cry from the days when both cats had been homeless. Betty and Beryl Butter had offered them the security of four walls, a fire and their pie of the day for a very small rent during leaner times, and now, in spite of their growing success, Hettie and Tilly saw no point in seeking pastures new, even though they could easily afford it.

Hettie glanced at the clock on the staff sideboard, a place where they kept the business of life, both commercial and domestic, but the hands had hardly moved since the last time she'd looked. In hindsight, she should have gone to the library with Tilly, if only to stretch her legs, but the thought of joining Turner Page's genealogy group filled her with dread. She had no interest in tracing her own Bagshot family and was a firm believer in leaving the past where it belonged. Tilly, however, possessed a spirit of adventure in all things. She loved digging and delving, was never happier than when she was surrounded by books, maps and documents, and her thirst for knowledge made her the perfect partner in their detective agency.

The monotony was suddenly broken by a knock at the door. Grateful for the interruption, Hettie sprang from her chair, delighted to see her two landladies bearing gifts as they forced their way into the room. 'Mind yourself!' warned Betty. 'Hot casserole coming through!'

The pot was banged down with great urgency on Hettie's table as Betty blew on her paws to cool them down. Her sister followed with a plate piled high with freshly baked cheese scones and a lemon meringue pie.

'These scones are nice dipped in the casserole,' said Beryl. 'Even nicer split with a scraping of butter first. You've got enough there for a couple of days.'

Hettie stared in amazement. She was more than used to baps and pies from the Butters' bakery, and she and Tilly occasionally dined with their landladies in their flat upstairs, but a home-cooked casserole was a little out of the ordinary. 'That's lovely,' she said, 'but you really shouldn't have gone to all that trouble.'

'Ah well,' said Betty, 'it's us that's got the trouble, on account of unforeseen circumstances of a critical nature, isn't it, sister?'

Beryl nodded and took up the subject. 'Our distant cousin, Clematis Wilt, runs a garden centre in our home town of Prickly Brook, up in Lancashire. She was overseeing her bargain basement section when she slipped on one of her aquatic plant bundles.'

'She slid the length of the compost section and ended up in the café, where she collided with a cat carrying a tray of the daily special and a passion fruit milkshake,' continued Betty. 'They managed to save the sausages, but the mash went everywhere. She won't be wearing that twinset again.'

Hettie was about to ask what all this had to do with the casserole and the cheese scones, but Beryl was too quick for her and continued the story. 'One of Clematis's assistants came to her rescue and managed to wipe her down with a dish cloth, but she couldn't get up so they called a nurse, who happened to be shopping in the pest and fertiliser section. It appears that she's slipped a disc and has got to lie on an old door in her bed for a week, so sister and I are off up to Lancashire to run her garden centre till she gets back on her feet.'

'So who will run the bakery while you're away?' asked Hettie.

'Well, that's where the casserole comes in,' said Betty. 'It's an inducement.'

Hettie was confused for a moment until the penny finally dropped. 'You mean you want me to run the bakery?' she said, horrified.

'You, Tilly and Bruiser to be exact,' corrected Beryl. 'No need to panic – we've written it all down for you.'

'But none of us would know where to start,' Hettie protested.

'Well, Tilly has retail experience,' Betty pointed out. 'She often helps Jessie in her charity shop, and Bruiser is good with deliveries in Miss Scarlet, and you could... er...'

Beryl came to Betty's rescue. 'Bake the pies and pastries.'

'But I've never baked a pie in my life and I really wouldn't know my self-raising from my plain flour!' said Hettie, getting more anxious by the second.

Betty and Beryl exchanged glances before offering some words of reassurance. 'You've nothing to worry about,' said Betty. 'Sister and I have filled our freezer with bread and pies galore, all labelled and ready to bake. All you have to do is stick them in the ovens each day. As long as you start early, all will be well.'

'What do you mean by early?' asked Hettie, dreading the answer.

'Four o'clock should give you plenty of time,' said Beryl. 'You'll be glad of those ovens on these cold, dark winter mornings.'

Hettie was about to point out that to get up at four o'clock in the morning was, for her, completely impossible, let alone the time to start a working day, but the conversation was lost in Tilly's arrival home from the library.

The Butter sisters repeated the details of Clematis Wilt's accident for Tilly's benefit, outlining the contingency plans for the bakery, and were delighted with Tilly's response. 'How exciting!' she said. 'When do we start?'

'Well, as long as the Morris Convertible passes all the checks Bruiser's doing on her at the moment, we thought we'd leave as early as possible tomorrow morning,' said Beryl, 'but we'll have some time to set you on with the baking.'

'Anyway, we'll leave you to your casserole now, as we've got to write up the delivery lists for Bruiser, and sister has still got the lemon drizzles to ice. We're having a run on them at the moment so we've done enough to last you the week out,' said Betty, moving towards the door, swiftly followed by her sister.

The Butters had barely closed the door behind them before Hettie exploded. 'What a bloody nightmare!' she began as Tilly put the kettle on, sensing that a hot, sweet, milky tea was needed. 'Four o'clock in the morning!' Hettie continued. 'What sort of time is that? No cat should be up at that ungodly hour. Who in their right mind would even *consider* getting out of a warm chair at that time of night?'

'Well, strictly speaking it's the morning by then,' Tilly pointed out gently, spooning two extra sugars into Hettie's mug, 'and the Butters do it six days a week all year round so that we can enjoy their lovely pies and cakes.'

'That's no reason for the rest of us to suffer. If I'd wanted to open a bakery, I'd have done it by now. I just can't believe we've been lumbered with this.'

'It's only for a week,' said Tilly, 'and it *is* an emergency. The Butters have been so kind, letting us live here, sharing their coal stack in the yard, not to mention all the pies, baps and frothy coffees they give us as part of our rent. It's nice to do something for them for a change.'

Hettie could see she was fighting a losing battle, and in her heart she knew that Tilly was right. The sweet tea and the thought of a casserole for dinner was gradually defusing the situation, and an air of calm descended – for the moment. Tilly sipped her own tea thoughtfully on her blanket by the fire, choosing her moment to bring Hettie up to date with her day at the library. The excitement of running the Butters' bakery had eclipsed her own news, but she couldn't contain herself any longer. 'I made some progress today with my family tree,' she began. 'I might be descended from what Mr Page calls "landed gentry". If he's right, my ancestors go at least as far back as the sixteen hundreds and the time of the witch trials. He thinks that Matthew Katkins might have been related to my family!'

'Matthew Katkins?' said Hettie. 'Who the hell is, or was, Matthew Katkins?'

'He was the Witchfinder General. Look, I found a book about him – isn't he the one you sang about in one of your songs?'

'I made that up,' protested Hettie. 'It wasn't about this Katkins character of yours. Witches were all the rage back in my music days. How do you know he was related, anyway? I'm not sure all this genealogy is good for you. Those witchfinders were murderers, tricking cats into confessing to things they hadn't done and then hanging, drowning or burning them. Why would you want to be related to cats like that?'

'I wouldn't, but Mr Page says it's a real breakthrough in my tree and will give me lots of lines of investigation to follow.'

'Turner Page fell out of his own tree years ago,' mumbled Hettie. 'Since he got his paws on Furcross House and turned it into a library, there's no stopping him. That literary festival he held was a disaster, and he hasn't looked back since.'

'We did manage to solve the murders at it,' Tilly pointed out. 'He's thinking of having another one later this year.'

Hettie choked on her final mouthful of tea, making no attempt to conceal her dismay. 'As soon as you have the dates, I'll book us in to Marley Toke's guesthouse in Southwool for a week. There's no way I'm going through another of Turner Page's book festivals. We need to be as far away as possible. Anyone attending will be taking their life in their paws.'

Tilly was disappointed by Hettie's attitude, but knew she had a point: Turner's festival had been a disaster from start to finish. Even by their detective agency's standards, the body count had been unusually high: the death of Downton Tabby was particularly high profile, not to mention the Brontës of Teethly, which nobody did any more.

'I haven't told you the really exciting bit,' Tilly continued, deciding not to mention the book festival again. 'I've got two great-aunts and they might still be alive. According to Mr Page's *Who's Who* book, they live in a big house with lots of land in Norfolk. It's called Skrimshaw Priory, and I've decided to write to them.'

'Well, that does sound a bit more interesting,' admitted Hettie, 'but you'll have to write your letter after supper. I'm starving, and we may as well tuck into that casserole before it gets cold. We're going to need all the strength we can get if we're going to run the bakery for a week.'

The casserole was exceptional, and – in spite of the Butters' suggestion that it might last for two nights – Hettie and Tilly went back for second and third helpings until the pot was empty and only two cheese scones remained. They decided on just half the lemon meringue, as Tilly declared that a bigger slice might make her sick in the night. Contented and very full, Hettie settled to a pipe of catnip in her chair by the fire. Tilly pulled a sheet of her best business notepaper out of the top drawer of the filing cabinet, and, after much deliberation, in which she managed to chew the rubber off the top of her pencil, she composed her letter to her great-aunts.

'Dear Aunts Skrimshaw,

I think I am your great-niece, Matilda Jenkins. I have been trying to trace my family tree and, if you are still alive, I would love to hear from you. If you are dead, then I am very sorry for bothering you.

With best wishes,

Matilda Jenkins (Tilly)'

Satisfied that her letter had just the right tone to it, she addressed the envelope to Skrimshaw Priory and settled down in her blankets to read all about Matthew Katkins. She read on well into the night and finally closed her eyes, only to discover that the witchfinder had followed her into her dreams.

****

August 12th 1647

The hooves splashed through the reed beds, the cloaked figure paying no attention to the driving rain as his horse drew ever closer to the Priory. Matilda watched from the window as her uncle clattered in across the cobbled yard, fearful of the news he might bring and knowing what she must do. The cat threw himself off his horse, leaving the stable cat to lead the animal away. Matthew Katkins was pleased to be home and was looking forward to his own fireside. The trip had been successful – six hags despatched, all with credible confessions and the satisfaction of knowing that his determination had paid off. Their cries as the flames consumed them still rang in his ears, their fur and flesh melting in the heat until there was nothing left but the scorched earth they sprang from. 'Earth to earth' the stupid parson had chanted, hoping to absolve them of their sins, but Katkins knew that the devil had claimed them in death as he had in life.

Throwing off his wet cloak, he strode into the Great Hall. His servants scurried around him, pulling off his muddy boots, filling his tankard with ale and laying a table by the fire. Within minutes it groaned with meat, bread and fruit.

Matilda knew she would soon be called; he would want her to sit with him, to listen to his hateful stories of cruelty and death and praise him for his work. Yes, that's what he called it – his life's work: the relentless killing of female cats condemned as witches by their neighbours. Those who pointed the claw, the accusers, watched as Matthew Katkins went about his work, crushing his victims' paws, pulling their teeth and pricking them with hot needles until they screamed for mercy and confessed to being practitioners of the black arts.

She chose the blue muslin dress he'd brought her back from Colchester and hurried down the staircase, making sure to conceal the bitter root powder in the pocket of her gown. She would wait until he had eaten and called for his Malmsey wine. The sweetness would hide her deception and very soon the nightmare would be over and her sisters would be free from his tyranny.

He was still breathing when she left him, but by morning she would be a murderer.

Chapter Two

Tilly had made the mistake of reading her book on Matthew Katkins before she went to sleep. He'd entered her dreams and turned them into a nightmare she couldn't escape from, and now the hammering on the door meant she'd been found out. They were coming for her.

'Come on you two, rise and shine!' bellowed Betty. 'There's pies to be baked and horns to be creamed. Get yourselves up – we've a lot to get through before we leave you in charge.'

Tilly was relieved to be bucketed back into reality and gratefully sprang out of her blankets to put the kettle on, leaving her night's terrors behind her. Hettie just turned over in her chair, sinking deeper into her covers, and Tilly knew that her first job of the day would be a difficult one: coaxing Hettie Bagshot out of her chair at any time of day was a potential problem, but at a quarter to four in the morning it was going to take more than a milky cup of tea.

Beryl Butter came to the rescue by barging into their room without knocking, carrying a laden tray. 'Good morning all,' she boomed. 'Sister and I thought you might like a light breakfast before we get underway. There's bacon rolls and frothy coffees. Bruiser's had his and he's shovelling coal into the ovens to fire them up. Betty has sorted some bakers' whites, caps and snoods for you to wear, as we can't have our standards lowering. You might need to stick them in the twin-tub each day when you've finished – baking can be messy.'

Beryl left their breakfast on the table and returned to help her sister with the first batch of bloomers and baps. Tilly selected the biggest bacon roll and padded over to Hettie's chair. There was a very small gap in the bundle of blankets, so she pushed the roll into the hole and waited. The tangle of cat and covers began to move and gradually Hettie emerged, her whiskers twitching with interest at the smell of bacon. Tilly bided her time, then snatched the roll away, forcing Hettie to sit up properly.

'Why did you do that?' Hettie grumbled, licking her paws and rubbing the sleep from her eyes. 'I was wide awake and just resting.'

Tilly giggled. 'Of course you were, but now we've got to get up and face the day. It's going to be really exciting, playing at baking, and Betty has got us some outfits to wear.'

Hettie groaned and grudgingly accepted the roll Tilly proffered. She took a bite out of it and suddenly life was worth living again as the combination of bacon washed down with frothy coffee did the trick. Tilly finished her breakfast in record time. She pulled some thermal tops and bottoms they'd bought from Jessie's charity shop out of the bottom drawer of the filing cabinet and dressed herself.

Hettie was sorely tempted to turn over and go back to sleep, but the roar of the bread ovens outside their door and Betty's rendition of the 'Toreador Song' as she injected jam into her first batch of doughnuts made that impossible. Hettie stumbled from her covers and pulled on the thermals Tilly had chosen for her, and the two cats struggled out into the hallway, which was the main preparation area for the bakery.

Betty and Beryl were stationed at either end of a long trestle table. Beryl was egg-washing pastry pie lids, while her sister – having finished the doughnuts – had moved on to cream horns.

Beryl rested her pastry brush for a moment to instruct the new recruits. 'Now get those whites on and don't forget the nets. We don't want that long tabby fur of yours turning up in the custard slices, do we?'

It was too early in the morning to argue, so Hettie and Tilly did as they were told. Hettie was rather pleased with her new work clothes; Tilly felt a little swamped by hers but Betty solved the problem by turning the legs and sleeves up. She fixed the snoods on both their heads then forced the caps on to hold them in place.

'Right!' said Beryl to Hettie. 'I'm putting you on savouries, and Tilly can work with Betty on the sweet stuff. I am now going to demonstrate the crimping technique. If you look closely, you will be able to spot the difference between a chicken and ham pie and a steak and kidney. There's plenty finished in the freezer, but you might get a rush and have to make some more up.'

Hettie's interest in pies was limited to eating them but, as she watched Beryl marking the edge of the pies with her claw – right to left for chicken and ham, left to right for steak and kidney – she was, for the moment, fascinated.

Tilly, however, was never slow at coming forward to try a new skill. Under Betty's instruction, she was making headway with piping the cream into the horn pastry cases, until she got a little too confident and blasted Betty full in the face. Hettie and Beryl were helpless with laughter as Tilly did her best to mop up the mess, while Betty wiped herself down and decided to move on strategically to the fudge brownie tray bakes.

The Butters made everything look so easy. They had been born into pastry and pies, inheriting all their skills from their mother, who had left them enough money to move south from Lancashire to set up a bakery in the town. They had been an overnight success: cats now travelled from miles around, shunning their own local outlets for a Butters' pie. Even Malkin and Sprinkle's food hall featured their products as bestsellers in the 'Extra Lovely' range.

The enormity of what they were taking on suddenly hit Hettie as Beryl moved on from pies to pasties, speedily filling the pastry with a meat and vegetable mix before magically knotting and sealing the pasties ready for the oven.

'If your gravy leaks, you're in trouble,' she said. 'Dries 'em up, see. It's bad enough competing with the Cornish bakers, but a dry pasty leads to a disappointed customer, and we can't have that, can we, sister?'

Betty nodded in agreement and continued the discussion regarding the merits of local foods. 'I'd like to see those Cornish cats knock up a Lancashire Lardy cake, or an Eccles for that matter. They might have the pasty sown up, but lardies and Eccles belong to us!'

'What's so special about a Lancashire Lardy cake?' Tilly asked, as she wiped her paw round the bowl that had held the brownie mixture and licked it clean.

'Bless you,' said Betty. 'You've put your claw on it, because they *are* special, and there's the sticky factor, of course. Lancashire lardies have to be extra sticky.'

'And what about Eccles cakes?' Hettie asked, having never favoured anything that consisted of just currants and pastry.

'Ah well,' responded Beryl, 'your Eccles is real Lancashire. It's all down to soaking your currants, and if you've any sense at all, you'll have a nice bit of soft Lancashire cheese with it – sets it off a treat.'

Hettie wasn't convinced, but was pleased to be given the task of filling pastry cases with an egg and cheese mix. The Butters' quiche was a particular favourite of hers, and if this day ever came to an end, it would be her choice for supper.

Two hours later, a wonderland of pies, breads, pastries and cakes had been created and Betty announced a tea break before moving on to set up the bakery for the day's business. Bruiser, who'd been loading his first batch of pie deliveries into Miss Scarlet's sidecar, joined them for a hot chocolate and a sausage roll. Miss Scarlet was his pride and joy. Strictly speaking, the motorbike belonged to Hettie, but she had never mastered it and much preferred to ride with Tilly in the sidecar if they were out on a job, as they could close the lid to keep warm and dry and hear one another to discuss the case. It was the main transport for the detective agency and Bruiser had joyfully given up his days of wandering the highways and byways to become a permanent member of The No. 2 FDA, as it was affectionately known. He had also proved to be invaluable to the Butter sisters for any heavy work around the garden and bakery, and was well rewarded with a dry, warm shed to live in at the bottom of the garden, where Miss Scarlet also lived.

Tea break over, Betty and Beryl presented a masterclass in how to stock the fixtures in the shop. Betty started with the window display. 'Breads to the left, cakes to the right,' she began, as Hettie and Tilly dutifully carried trays of baked goods to the window. 'Baps at the front, with the baguettes building to a crescendo of large bloomers and brown and white farmhouse at the back.'

Tilly marvelled at the artistry that went into setting out the bakery window. It was her favourite shopfront in the town, and now she fully appreciated the care and passion that went into it.

Next came the cakes. 'I like to colour code the iced fancies,' Betty continued. 'Pink at the front, then yellow, then white. Next come the brownies, fudge squares, doughnuts, lardies, Eccles and Chelseas, with the Victoria and chocolate sponges at the back. I like to think of them being on parade, like on our dear Queen's birthday – rows and rows of little soldiers.'

'What about the cream horns?' asked Tilly, as they were her favourites.

'Good question,' said Betty. 'No fresh cream in the window in case the sun comes out. I made that mistake once and we were up to our necks in melted cream. It ran all over the fudge squares and we had to sell them off half price. We keep the fresh cream cakes in the cabinet under the till now. We can keep an eye on them there and it tempts the customers into an extra treat when they're waiting to pay up.'

Betty unbolted the shop door and stepped out into the high street to check her work. Tilly was about to follow but suddenly remembered she had a letter to post. She ran back through the shop to their room, narrowly missing Hettie who was carrying a tray of pies, picked up her letter from the sideboard and bounded back out into the street with it. Betty was making some adjustments to the row of yellow iced fancies, so Tilly crossed the road to Lavender Stamp's post office and pushed her letter into the box just in time. The red mail van skidded to a halt and a rather portly cat got out, wheezed his way across to the letter box and emptied the contents into a sack. Tilly watched as he glanced nervously up at the first-floor window of the post office; there was a notable twitch of the curtains and the post cat reacted by hurriedly throwing his sack into his van and driving off at speed.

Most cats would have found his behaviour a little strange, but those who frequented Lavender Stamp's post office would know that encounters with the postmistress were to be avoided at all costs. To say that Lavender was a difficult cat would be an understatement. She had issues: her fondness for sherry, her ability to humiliate any cat who crossed her threshold, and her naturally spiteful character were just the tips of her very own iceberg. The town's gossips put her unpleasant behaviour down to her being ditched by Laxton Spratt after a brief fling back in the day, but that was probably only half the story.

Satisfied that her letter was now on its way to her great-aunts, Tilly stood with Betty to admire the window display before both cats returned to the shop, where Hettie was getting the hang of the hot pie cabinet. 'Always ask if they want hot or cold,' said Beryl. 'You'll get a rush on hot at lunchtime, but some like hot pies for breakfast. There's nothing more disappointing than a cold pie when you were hoping for a hot one, is there, sister?'

Betty nodded enthusiastically. 'And speaking of hot, which one of you is going to run our breakfast griddle?' she asked. 'They'll be beating the door down at eight o'clock for sausage, bacon and egg baps. Sister and me take it in turns usually – one on the hot filled baps, the other on the till.'

Hettie and Tilly were becoming a little overwhelmed by the growing list of jobs involved in running the sisters' bakery, and they were very relieved when Bruiser stepped forward. 'I can do the griddle if yer want,' he said, as all eyes turned to him. 'In me days sleepin' under the stars, I used ta rustle up a nice supper – eggs, bacon, sausages and even a nice bit of fried bread in me old fryin' pan. I'm sure I can 'andle a griddle for a few days just ta 'elp out.'

Betty hugged him and Beryl went off in search of another set of whites for him to wear. 'You'll have to get your deliveries to Malkin and Sprinkle's done before the bakery opens at eight,' Betty pointed out. 'We keep the griddle going until ten, but they'll want their pies and breads long before that. Sister usually runs them down in the Morris at about seven-thirty.'

'Well, I'd better be gettin' on then,' he said. 'It's nearly seven, so I'll fetch Miss Scarlet and load up the rest of the stuff. Is there anyone I should ask for at Malkin's?'

'Doris Lean is in charge of the pie section. She'll be tapping her paw at the back door of the food hall and she can be diffi-cult, insisting on counting the pies before she'll let you go so just make sure your numbers are right. Here's the order form for the week. She'll insist on signing it each day.' Betty pulled a piece of paper out from the drawer underneath the service counter and Bruiser took charge of it, cramming it in to his waistcoat pocket.

'And don't forget to drop off the baps for Elsie Haddock's chip butties. No chip shop's complete without baps, and then there's Molly Bloom's bread order for her café. It's all written down on these bits of paper by the till. Hang on to them – we have to file them so we can send out the invoices at the end of the month.'

Bruiser tapped his pocket with his paw, acknowledging the importance of his task, and went off to fire up Miss Scarlet.

Hettie was rather proud of her display in the hot cabinet, and moved on to the cold pie and quiche fixture. Tilly, realising by now that presentation was everything, applied herself to the cream cake section, feeling a great pride in arranging the cream horns that she had filled herself. By the time Bruiser returned from his deliveries, the bakery shop was full to bursting and the Butters had changed out of their bakery whites into their 'going out clothes', as Beryl called them.

'Just time to show you the till,' said Betty. 'The price list is next to it and if you get stuck just make it up. If you're clever enough to solve all those murders, I'm sure you'll manage the bakery for a few days. Now, the thing about the till is it has a mind of its own. You put the price in on the keys, pull this handle at the side, and wait.'

Hettie, Tilly and Bruiser waited as instructed, but nothing happened.

'I find if it's having an off day that it works if you turn your back on it,' Beryl continued. 'A useful tip is to ignore it and bag up your customers' purchases.' She acted out putting a custard slice into a bag and sure enough, while her back was turned, the till drawer opened.

Tilly was tempted to applaud, appreciating the trick, but was suddenly distracted by a queue forming at the bakery door. 'You'd better get that griddle on,' suggested Betty. 'It's ten to eight, and that lot out there are breakfast regulars from the building site by the recreation ground. I'm off to fetch the Morris, as it's time sister and I were heading north. Be sure to help yourselves to anything you fancy. Running a bakery is hungry work.'

'I'll fetch the cases down,' said Beryl, leaving Hettie, Tilly and Bruiser to fend for themselves. Bruiser struggled into the chef's whites that Beryl had thrown at him, switched on the griddle and put a row of sausages and bacon rashers on to get things started. Tilly positioned herself by the till to take the orders and Hettie thought she'd get ahead by splitting some baps for Bruiser. It all seemed so easy without customers, but the three cats knew that as soon as the bolts on the shop door were drawn across they would be tested to their limits.

Chapter Three

The Butter sisters left with very little ceremony. Their Morris Minor Convertible chugged down the high street and out onto the open road, leaving their newly acquired assistants to face a stampede of construction workers, all keen to get their teeth into a breakfast bap. Bruiser put in a command performance worthy of any griddle chef, and Tilly gave as good as she got in reply to several cheeky remarks from the cats in the queue as she bagged up their orders. Hettie, who'd been elected to add up and handle the till end of things, had clearly drawn the short straw. She'd always been good at sums, but anything mechanical was beyond her and the till was proving to be her nemesis. Not only did it refuse to open half the time but, when it did, it turned nasty by trapping Hettie's paw every time she tried to extract a customer's change.

By the time the breakfast rush was over, Hettie had had enough. Nursing a very sore paw, she made a declaration. 'Tomorrow I'm putting myself on bagging up. That till is a nightmare. Five more days of this and I'll never play my guitar again.'

She was settling in for a rant but her rhetoric was curtailed by the appearance of Lavender Stamp, who was making a beeline for the bakery. 'Well, that's all we need on our first day,' said

Hettie. 'I'll leave this one to you two. I'm going to put another batch of pies in the oven.'

Bruiser took one look at Lavender's face as she approached and decided on the spur of the moment to go and check something on Miss Scarlet, leaving Tilly to deal with the town's harridan on her own. Tilly greeted the postmistress with one of her best smiles, but Lavender was in no mood for niceties. She had seen Betty and Beryl drive off, and – in her capacity as self-appointed queen of the high street – felt she was owed an explanation. 'Perhaps you'd be good enough to explain to me where the Butters have gone, and why they seem to have left you and your acquaintances, for want of a better word, in charge?'

Tilly's hackles were up, but a confrontation with Lavender Stamp was the last thing she was looking for. Through gritted teeth she gave what she thought was a comprehensive reply. 'They've had to go up north to Prickly Brook to run their cousin's garden centre for a few days as she's had an accident. She slipped on an aquatic bundle and has to lie on an old door until she feels better. They left us in charge of the bakery, as it was all a bit last minute.'

'Well, I've never heard anything more ridiculous in my life,' Lavender spat out. 'What do they know about running a garden centre? And what do you know about running a bakery? You, Miss Bagshot and that scruffy stray who drives that motorbike are only good for delving into criminals and their sordid lives. I hardly think that sort of work equips you for running a high-street bakery. You'll be attracting the wrong sort of cats, and every thief and murderer will be turning up here before we know it.'

Hettie had been listening to the conversation and couldn't help coming to Tilly's defence. She burst through from the back of the bakery with all guns blazing. 'Ah, Miss Stamp – could I just point out that in my experience thieves and murderers enjoy a good pie the same as any other cat. Like you at the post office, we are here to serve, and the only thing we are investigating at the moment is what brings *you* here today. We are very busy, so if you'd like to place an order we can help. If not, perhaps you'd like to return to your own counter. And on the subject of murderers, you wouldn't recognise one if it bit you on the b…'

Hilda Dabbit's arrival saved the day and brought Hettie's sentence to an abrupt conclusion. Without another word, Lavender flounced out and returned to her post office. Hilda, however, settled in for a chat, making herself comfortable on the chair that the Butters kept for less able cats. Hilda Dabbit ran the town's dry-cleaning and mending service further along the high street, but she was also the main purveyor of tittle-tattle and gossip. What Hilda didn't know about the townsfolk wasn't worth knowing and her first port of call every day was the bakery, where she picked up any news that was going.

'This is a bit of a change round, I must say,' she began, keen to establish the facts regarding the Butter sisters' absence from their counter. 'Has there been a murder or something? I see we have The No. 2 Feline Detective Agency out in full force and no sign of Betty and Beryl, although rumour has it that they drove off at eight o'clock this morning, obviously going somewhere, and Doris Lean informed me that Mr Bruiser was doing the bakery deliveries this morning when she popped in to collect the casual slacks I'd mended for her. They needed a new zip, but between you and me she needs to shed a few pounds – those slacks are under great strain, and things have got much worse since Christmas. I put it down to her working on the pre-packed meat counter – all that ham and corned beef, not to mention the pork pies, and it's next to the cheese counter. She had hopes of moving to haberdashery, but Lotus Ping has no plans to give up her button drawers and bolts of cloth any time soon. I suggested that she ask Mr Sprinkle for a trial week in kitchenware, but she pointed out that since the accident with her sister's pressure cooker she's had no interest in gadgets of any sort and was sticking to saucepans and a gas ring.'

Hettie was astonished by the way Hilda could present a monologue without even considering taking a breath. After the breakfast rush and their encounter with Lavender Stamp, Hilda was a pleasant distraction. Just like a toy with a flat battery, Hilda's round-up of Doris Lean's job prospects finally came to an end, offering Tilly an opportunity to explain the situation regarding the Butters.

Taking up the new subject, Hilda offered her thoughts on garden centres. 'Aquatic bundle, you say? Well, that's typical – what's fish got to do with gardening? I mean, when did you last see a stickleback with a trowel in its fin? If this Clematis had stuck to plants and compost, she wouldn't be in this mess. That's the trouble these days – every cat in retail wants to turn themselves into a department store instead of sticking to what they know best. A cat came into my dry cleaner's the other day and asked if he could have a key cut. I showed him the door and sent him across to Meridian Hambone's, pointing out that it was a hardware shop he needed. Mind you, Meridian overstretches herself. I hear she's starting up a fashion strand next to her white goods department – hot pants or some such nonsense. You can rely on them coming off the back of a lorry, just like the fridges and the TVs her son Lazarus comes by, for want of a better description. Don't get me wrong, we all like a bargain with no questions asked. I like a good sort through Mr Page's rejected library books from time to time. If you don't mind the covers missing and the odd tooth mark on the spines, you can pick up a nice thriller or even a cookery book. I bought a genuine Delia Sniff off him just before Christmas. Some of the recipes were missing and it smelt of catnip, and there were a few nasty stains here and there, but I cleaned it up with some of my fluids and it's almost as good as new. Delia keeps her cheese in her car boot, of course.'

The last comment hung in the air for a moment before Tilly seized the opportunity to steer Hilda back to the bakery. 'What can we help you with today?' she asked as Hettie, now rejoined by Bruiser, fell about in fits of laughter behind the counter.

'I'll have my usual,' said Hilda, getting to her feet. 'Actually that was a silly thing to say, wasn't it? I mean, how would you know what my usual was? I'll have a Bakewell tart and one of those small pasties.'

Tilly reached for the tart and Hettie made the mistake of prolonging the transaction. 'Hot or cold, Miss Dabbit?'

'Well, it's not going to warm up at this time of year, is it?' Hilda replied, missing the point entirely. 'I thought I might get away with what was left in my coal bin but – as I was saying to Nutty Slack on the phone this morning – February can be a cruel month. Do you remember that big freeze we had a couple of years ago, all snowed in we were, and you were trying to sort out those missing kittens up at Wither-Fork Hall. Bad business, that. I was only saying to...'

'No!' said Hettie, raising her voice more than she meant to. 'I meant would you like a hot or cold pasty?'

'Oh I see,' said Hilda, pulling her purse out of her coat pocket. 'Hot, please – you need something hot at this time of year, don't you?'

Hettie put a hot pasty in a bag and the Bakewell tart in another one, leaving Tilly to take the money Hilda had counted out. It was exact down to the last penny. Tilly moved to the till, punched in the total, pulled the handle and – to Hettie's surprise – the till drawer opened immediately.

Hilda gathered her purchases, pushed her purse back into her pocket and headed for the door, offering an apology. 'Sorry I can't stay and chat,' she said, 'but I really must get on.'

No sooner had Hilda Dabbit bustled out into the high street than the lunchtime rush began. Bruiser, who'd been up since three, excused himself to put his feet up in his shed with a hot steak and kidney pie and a cold pasty for his supper. Now his griddle work was over for the day, he felt he could be of little help behind the counter and decided to leave Hettie and Tilly to it.

As Tilly seemed to have developed a positive way forward regarding the till, Hettie took over selecting and bagging up the customers' orders. Tilly was a little slow at adding up, but their teamwork got them through their first lunchtime rush. The cats in the bakery queue were unusually animated at the prospect of being served by the town's detectives, and were quite forgiving about the odd mix-up over whose bags were whose. Hettie and Tilly had reached celebrity status and the locals had heralded them as heroes over and over again.

The busy lunch hour came to an end as quickly as it had begun, leaving Hettie and Tilly completely exhausted and with barely a cake or a pie left to sell. Tilly gathered all the leftovers together and put them on one tray in the window, making sure there were no cream cakes among them. Hettie had already secured the last quiche for their supper and put it in their room with two bags of crisps, which was just as well as she could have sold it ten times over. It was clear to her that they should put their own choice to one side as a priority each day to avoid disappointment.

'I can't believe that we've got to do this all over again tomorrow,' she said, slumping down on the chair and taking in the empty cabinets. 'I don't know how Betty and Beryl do it. They're always so cheerful, too – all that singing first thing in the morning and they never stop laughing and joking with the customers.'

'I think it's because they love what they do,' Tilly pointed out. 'When we have one of their cakes or pies it makes us happy. Just think how many customers we've made happy today – not many cats can say that.'

'It's a refreshing change from murder I suppose,' said Hettie, secretly marvelling at Tilly's train of thought. Since they'd met, Tilly had brought the sunshine into Hettie's life: she always looked on the bright side, even on the darkest of days, and there had been plenty of those since they'd started their detective agency. Hettie was naturally pessimistic, mainly because other cats often disappointed her. She could count her true friends on one paw: Tilly, Bruiser, the Butters and Poppa, the town's plumber, who had been her roadie during her music days. These cats accepted her temper tantrums for what they were and knew that underneath the bluster was an astute and often very kind cat trying to get out. Hettie and Tilly were the perfect match, Tilly for her optimism and Hettie for her humanity and determination to put things right. It was the ideal combination for a detective agency, although perhaps not the best qualification for running a high-street bakery.

'So what do we do now?' Hettie asked, counting the cakes Tilly had put in the window. 'It's just gone three and we only have two custard tarts, an Eccles cake, a pink iced fancy and a minced beef pie with half the crust missing to sell.'

Tilly checked the list of dos and don'ts that Betty had pinned up for them behind the till. 'It says we should shut up for the day when the stock has run out, but to make sure we wipe all the surfaces down thoroughly, including the window, and we must mop the floor.'

'Well, that's the best news I've heard all day,' said Hettie. 'Chuck me a dish cloth and I'll get cracking in the window.'

The two cats busied themselves in cleaning the fixtures and cabinets ready for another day. Hettie created quite a spectacle, wedged into the window with her cloth, and a crowd of kittens on their way home from school stood and giggled at her. Tilly could see that her friend wasn't enjoying the attention and came to her rescue by sharing out the final tray of cakes among the small spectators, who soon skipped off home with their unexpected treats.

When the bakery shone like a new pin, Hettie shot the bolt across the door and elected to light a fire in their room while Tilly mopped the shop floor.

Now that the busy part of the day was over, Tilly's thoughts returned to her new hobby. She had thought that tracing her family history would be fun, but as she sloshed the mop across the bakery floor, the terrors of last night came back to her. The book on Matthew Katkins was by no means as vivid as her nightmare had been; there was a great deal of detail about the witch trials, but very little on the cat himself. Tilly felt she had been drawn in as a character in Katkins' story, and he was inhabiting her thoughts in a very visceral way. She remembered every detail of her nightmare: the bleakness of her room in the priory; the smell of the food in the Great Hall; the mud-stained boots and travelling cloak, discarded on the flagstone floor; the intense heat from the log burning in the fireplace; and most of all Katkins himself, as he detailed every act of cruelty he'd performed with such relish.

The nightmare had ended badly for her and for Matthew Katkins, but she still had to read the final chapter in the book, which would surely reveal how Katkins had really died. Pulling herself together, she plunged the mop back into the bucket and joined Hettie in front of a blazing fire. Their room was cosy in the late afternoon and Hettie had even managed to put the kettle on and prepare two mugs ready for Tilly's return. They were both very tired and hungry and agreed to have an early supper before settling down for the night.

The quiche was good, and so was the leftover lemon meringue pie, but Hettie had hardly finished her final mouthful before she fell into a deep sleep in her armchair. Tilly stoked up the fire, set her alarm clock for half past three, and settled down in her blankets to finish her book on Matthew Katkins.

It came as a surprise to her that Katkins' death was a bit of a mystery. Some sources said that he had become a witch himself and was subjected to his own methods of torture, tied up and thrown into the pond at Skrimshaw Priory, where he floated, proving he was indeed a witch. Other accounts suggested that he was taken to Skrimshaw Mill and hanged on one of the sails or had died from lung disease, but the final offering made Tilly's blood run cold. Documents discovered at the priory in the eighteen hundreds suggested that his niece Matilda had poisoned him on August 12th 1647 and that the servants had fed his body to the pigs on the priory's farm to protect her from arrest.

Tilly threw the book down as if it had burnt her, feeling suddenly very alone and frightened. She glanced across at Hettie, sleeping in her tangle of blankets, and wanted to shake her awake, but she knew that wouldn't be fair. She was being irrational. What could a murder that might have happened back in the seventeenth century possibly have to do with her? Matilda was surely a common enough name at the time and she *wasn't* Matilda – she was Tilly. And even if Katkins was related to her, he was long dead anyway, so what harm could he do to her now?

She knew that she should settle down to sleep. They had another busy day ahead of them in the bakery, but she was too frightened to shut her eyes in case the nightmare returned. Eventually, her tiredness overwhelmed her.

****

February 14th 1651

Matilda watched from the arch as her kitten played in the mud. Little Matilda was barely three, but she was as bold and inquisitive as her father had been. The years of war had dragged on, a war that had beheaded a king and slaughtered so many of the cats who had been loyal to him. The love of her life had died by a Roundhead's sword in front of her, on the spot where Matilda now played. He had never known the joy of fatherhood, nor had he been particularly loyal to the king. She thought back to their wedding – a joyous occasion, and a chance for her to shake off the shackles imposed by her hateful uncle, the witchfinder, as he was now known. His death had freed her to make her own choices, and she had always loved the miller's son. As kittens, they had climbed to the very top of the windmill and clambered out to ride the giant sails. They had fished in the pond, gathered bluebells in the woods, and played hide and seek in every nook and cranny the Priory could offer. They took lessons together, grew together and eventually loved together, until Matilda's mother died and her brother Matthew Katkins moved in.

Gone were the happy days. She remembered how Katkins had banished the miller's son from the Priory, and the way she was kept as a prisoner in all but name. Her mother had brought her up to believe that the Priory and all the land surrounding it was hers by birth through the female line. She had learnt in her history lessons that no male cat had been allowed to inherit since the monks left after a Viking raid. The first Matilda had been a Viking Lord's mistress and a formidable warrior; she and her female descendants had fought to keep the Priory and all its lands. Katkins had set out to change that but he had failed – she'd made sure of that.

The miller's son returned, and for a brief time they were happy, but now she must raise this kitten on her own and pass the land on to her. It was Valentine's Day. She would take Matilda's muddy little paw and the two of them would walk to the burial ground by the mill, where they would lay flowers on his grave and she would weep for him.

****

Tilly woke up sobbing, her blankets soaked with her tears. It was a few moments before she could adjust to her surroundings, taking in the familiar sights and sounds of their room. Hettie lay on her back in her armchair, snoring. The fire smouldered in the grate, sulking from a lack of coal, and the roar of the Butter sisters' ovens was music to Tilly's ears. She reached for her alarm clock; it was a quarter past three and she was thankful that the night was over.

She crawled from her blankets and shivered as she added sticks and coal to the fire. It responded immediately and she padded across to fill the kettle and switch it on. She could hear Bruiser shovelling coal and was pleased to know that someone else was awake. Her dream had left her with a feeling of desperate sadness and the only cure was to face the day.

There was a polite knock on the door just as the kettle was coming to the boil and Tilly ran to answer it. Bruiser's cheerful face brought her back from the night's terrors and she had to try very hard not to hug him. 'We're all up an' runnin',' he whispered, 'an' I got the first batch of pies out o' the freezer. Shall I shove 'em in the oven?'

'That would be lovely,' said Tilly. 'I'm making tea and toast, so come in when you're done and we'll have some breakfast.'

Bruiser returned to the ovens and Tilly threw on her thermals before attempting to wake Hettie. It wasn't as difficult as she thought it would be, as the alarm clock did the job for her. The heap of tangled blankets and tabby cat reacted immediately to the harsh and piercing sound. Hettie leapt off her armchair in a blind panic, her heart almost beating out of her chest. 'What's happening?' she shouted, looking for the emergency that had woken her so abruptly.

'It's only the alarm clock,' said Tilly, trying not to laugh. 'It's time to get up. There are pies to bake and a shop to stock.'

The realisation of another day in the bakery hit Hettie hard. She gathered her blankets around her and stumbled back to her armchair, too cross even to speak. Bruiser arrived as the first round of toast was being buttered and Tilly made much of sitting him down at the table. 'There you are,' she said, lifting her voice. 'A nice mug of hot milky tea and a buttery slice of toast for you. As you can see, Hettie doesn't want any breakfast, so I'll make some more toast and join you at the table.'

Bruiser nodded, catching Tilly's wink and playing along with the conspiracy. Hettie peeped out of her blankets and watched as he devoured the toast and licked his paws appreciatively, before receiving another slice which went the same way. By now, she was wide awake. The smell of toast was irresistible, and it was more than she could bear to watch Bruiser – and now Tilly – tucking in with such relish. 'I could manage some toast,' she said eventually, 'if there's any left?'

'Oh, I thought you'd gone back to bed,' said Tilly, pretending to be surprised. 'I'm afraid breakfast in bed isn't possible this morning, as I've got to deep fry some doughnuts and cream up my horns.'

It was a rare thing for Tilly to be sarcastic, but she had learnt from the master. Hettie was left with no choice but to struggle from her blankets and embrace the day.

Fortified, Bruiser returned to the ovens. Hettie pulled on her thermals and Tilly produced two slices of buttered toast and a hot mug of milky tea for her. Hettie made short work of the toast and, now in a much better frame of mind, put on her baker's whites and joined Tilly and Bruiser by the ovens.

The three cats did their best to follow the Butters' guidelines regarding the preparation of the day's baked goods. Tilly had a bit of a problem icing the fancies, on account of her paws being too big. Hettie had a run-in with a rather overbaked batch of bloomers, and Bruiser managed to drop a dozen eggs. As the floor was clean, Tilly scooped them up and decided to offer scrumbled egg and bacon baps as a new line on the breakfast menu. Scrumbled eggs were her own invention, as she liked to see white bits as well as yellow on her plate.

The stocking of the bakery was Tilly's favourite job. Leaving Hettie and Bruiser to carry the items through for her, she set about the window display. It took longer than she'd expected, as nothing seemed to go according to plan. The newly iced fancies insisted on sticking together in a solid lump; the breads looked like a hurricane had recently passed through them; and the coconut haystacks had completely collapsed and assumed biscuit status.

Tilly, Hettie and Bruiser all briefly ventured into the high street to view the window from a customer's point of view, and all agreed that the overall effect was a catastrophic mountain of misshapen cakes, pastries and breads. 'It looks like a jumble sale after everyone has gone home,' Tilly commented as she stamped back into the bakery, hotly followed by Hettie and Bruiser, who were unable to disagree.

'The thing is, we can't be expected to become bakers overnight,' Hettie pointed out, loading up the hot pie cabinet. 'It takes years to be as good as Betty and Beryl. Each to their own and all that – I bet the Butters couldn't solve a murder.'

'We'll be investigating our own murders when they get back. They'd kill us if they could see that window display,' Tilly pointed out, 'and these cream cakes aren't much better.'

Bruiser decided not to comment, but excused himself to go about his deliveries, happy to escape from the bakery, if only briefly. Hettie absent-mindedly chewed on a sausage roll, hot from her cabinet, while Tilly stood with her head in her paws behind the till. 'I don't think we can do this,' she said. 'We'd be better off closing for the day while we sort this mess out. Maybe Molly Bloom would help? She's used to running her café and it always looks nice in there.'

'That's because she knows what she's doing,' responded Hettie through a mouthful of flaky pastry, 'and she's got Dolly Scollop to help her. I'm sure Betty and Beryl's regulars will put up with us for a few days. There's nothing wrong with the actual stuff we're turning out. It's just the presentation that's a bit random.'

'A bit random?' Tilly protested. 'The iced fancies look like a welded together tray bake. The doughnuts are more jam than dough, and my cream horns resemble every instrument in an orchestra except the horn section.'

Tilly was tired and very irritable and Hettie could see that there was nothing she could say to make things better. They were stuck with the bakery, whether they liked it or not, and Betty and Beryl would soon have things back to normal when they got back.

Bruiser's deliveries proved uneventful, as he'd chosen the best-looking pies and breads to take out in Miss Scarlet. On his return, he fired up the griddle and filled three baps with bacon and scrumbled eggs for them to enjoy before they opened the bakery. Tilly managed to make three not-quite-as-frothy-as-usual coffees to go with the baps, and they sat on the floor by the ovens to eat their second breakfast of the day.

By eight o'clock, when Hettie unbolted the bakery door, a much happier atmosphere had descended on the three friends, who'd unanimously decided to make the best of a bad job. Tilly assumed her position on the till and presided over the cream cakes. Bruiser was on hot filled baps, and Hettie fetched and bagged bread and cakes from the window, while reigning supreme over the hot pie cabinet. She had weeded out the worst casualties, deeming them unsaleable, and had put them to one side for lunch later. There was no time to do anything more creative with the shop window.

The construction workers barely looked at the window display as they lined up for their breakfast baps, and Bruiser did a roaring trade until he switched off his griddle at ten o'clock. He retreated to his shed with a slightly burnt beef and onion pie and a very strangely shaped cream horn that Tilly had pressed on him, just to get it out of her sight.

Meridian Hambone saved the day with the iced fancies, barging her way into the bakery on her mobility scooter. Meridian was probably the oldest cat in the town and – although she could walk perfectly well – the scooter that her son Lazarus had built for her was her pride and joy. 'I've got meself in a fix,' she said, as she rammed the crisp carrousel. 'I needs a birthday

33

cake quick, on account of it bein' Lazarus's birthday. Don't ask me 'ow old 'e is, as it was a long time ago, but e's got a likin' for one of them fancies in pink.'

Tilly leapt at the opportunity to rid the bakery window of the items that troubled her most. 'We've got a special iced fancy tray bake cake that he might like,' she said, putting a positive spin on the disaster that sat in full view of the high street. 'We call it a fusion cake, made up of individual iced fancies all stuck together in lemon, pink and white. You're in luck – we have one left in the window.'

Meridian clapped her paws together, delighted with Tilly's suggestion. 'Sounds perfect! Could you pipe 'is name on it if I come back in ten minutes? I got to brave the post office for me penshin, so wish me luck.'

Tilly bounded to the door to see Meridian safely off the premises and lifted the fancies en masse out of the window. She struggled through to the preparation area and made up a cup of icing, adding a squirt of red food dye. She filled a piping bag and proceeded to pipe the top of the cake with 'Lazarus' in bold, bright red letters. She was tempted to add 'happy birthday', but didn't want to push her luck. She found a box that was only just big enough and forced the cake into it.

Meridian returned from the post office a little older and greyer after Lavender Stamp's own brand of customer service, and was delighted with Tilly's efforts. She paid up, adding two very jammy doughnuts to her bill, and took off at speed back to her hardware store.

There was no doubt that the day was improving, but Hilda Dabbit brought some sad news with her when she popped in ahead of the lunchtime rush. 'The grim reaper has struck!' she announced, before she was hardly over the threshold. Shutting the door behind her, she looked from left to right in a covert manner, even though there were no other customers in the bakery, and approached Hettie and Tilly at the counter.

'It's her own fault, really,' she began, 'always trying out these new-fangled things – electric tin opener, pressure cooker, video, a roving phone as big as a brick. Always popping in to Habicat for the latest invention, she was. That electric typewriter set her back a bob or two, although she called it – wait for it – a "word processor". I mean, I ask you, you don't process words, do you? You speak them or write them down, although most of what she wrote down was nonsense anyway – not that I'm one to speak ill of the dead.'

Tilly was about to join the conversation, but Hilda batted on. 'Morbid Balm popped her head round the door to see if her best mourning suit was ready. Rome wasn't built in a day, I said, and that's when she told me. The cat who does her cleaning found her – still in her bed, with the Teasmade switched on and boiled dry. She'd been moisturising her paws, evidently, and got a shock off the Teasmade. Killed her stone dead, by all accounts. She hadn't even drunk her tea, and there was a half-eaten ginger biscuit on her bedside table. I said to Morbid, you just don't know what's round the corner, do you? Morbid's used to it, I suppose, what with her working for Shroud and Trestle. Someone's got to do it, but that sort of work wouldn't suit me. No happy ending for an undertaker, surrounded by all those grieving cats day in and day out – although I think she'll get a good send-off.'

Hettie felt it was definitely time to interject. Not only was she curious about who had actually died, but she was aware that the lunchtime rush would be starting at any minute. Hilda needed to be moved along as quickly as possible. 'Who has died?' Hettie asked, adopting the forceful tone she used during interrogations.

Hilda moved even closer to the counter to serve up the best bit of gossip she'd collected all week. 'Marmite Spratt,' she whispered, 'but keep that to yourselves.'

Tilly had taken the trouble to bag up Hilda's usual during her commentary on the pros and cons of gadgets and undertakers, which she exchanged for cash before opening the door to release the dry cleaner into the high street, where no doubt she would find plenty more cats to pass on the details of the demise of Marmite Spratt.

'Well, that's a turn-up for the books,' said Hettie. 'The queen of social history snuffed out by her own Teasmade – you couldn't make it up.'

'I only saw her the other day at the library,' said Tilly. 'She was arranging a book launch with Turner Page for her latest *Strange But True*. There's ten of them now. She had her own shelf in the library and it was labelled.'

'Miserable cat, really,' said Hettie. 'No wonder Laxton Spratt left home when he did. Just think – if he'd stayed, Marmite might have ended up as Lavender Stamp's mother-in-law.'

On that happy note the lunchtime onslaught began. In spite of the unfortunate visual quality of much of the stock, the customers were undaunted and filled their baskets, one of them even offering a compliment regarding the rustic appearance of her wholemeal cob. By two o'clock, there was barely a crumb left. The two cats made short work of cleaning the fixtures and the floor and retired to their room for a late lunch and a well-earned rest.

Chapter Four

At Hettie's insistence, their telephone was kept in the staff sideboard, swathed in cushions. The sideboard was Tilly's domain and, as she was very much the homemaker of the two, she used the space to store all of life's necessities inside it. It was an Aladdin's cave of blankets, cushions, tools, bits of string, Hettie's record collection, and anything Tilly deemed suitable for putting by for a rainy day. The fact that it also offered accommodation for the telephone and answer machine was down to one of Hettie's irrational phobias. She hated the thought of not knowing who was on the end of the line when the telephone rang, regarding it as an infringement of her privacy. She insisted that when it did ring Tilly would answer it, and she would only engage once she knew who was calling. Tilly had fought hard to get the telephone installed at all, pointing out that a detective agency without a phone was like a cardigan without buttons. Hettie had finally given way when Tilly offered to stow the telephone in the sideboard and – while Hettie wasn't looking – Tilly had added an answer machine.

Tilly regarded the answer machine as magical. For the first few months after it had been installed, she would insist on ringing it and leaving a message for herself when she was away from home, all for the sheer joy of hearing her own voice on her return. The novelty eventually wore off, but the answer phone had proved invaluable to their business.

The machine was bleeping away merrily to itself when they returned to their room and Tilly dived into the sideboard, keen to retrieve the messages while Hettie sorted through the bag of misshapen goods she'd rescued from the bakery. 'For lunch, I can offer a very flat pasty with very little filling, a slightly burnt chicken and ham pie, or a sausage quiche which I forgot to put the sausage in – or we could have half of everything each. I've saved a couple of decent steak and kidney pies for supper later, and I've made up a bag for Bruiser.'

Tilly wasn't really listening. She was too busy hauling the telephone and answer machine out of the sideboard, clapping her paws in excitement when she discovered that there were six messages. 'Oooh look! I wonder who they're all from? Maybe Marmite Spratt was murdered and they want us to investigate,' said Tilly, hardly able to contain herself.

'It sounds like an open and shut case if you believe Hilda Dabbit,' Hettie pointed out, 'and Morbid Balm would have come to see us if she suspected foul play. I suggest you listen to the messages instead of guessing who left them.'

Tilly settled down on her blanket and pressed the play button. The machine announced the first message and a familiar voice boomed out of the small speaker. 'Hello you two – Betty and Beryl here. I expect you're busy in the bakery, but this is just to say that Clematis has taken a turn for the worse. The old door she was sleeping on slipped on her sheets and shot her out of bed and onto the floor. So we're now looking at the possibility of two slipped discs, a sprained paw and a reoccurring headache every time someone mentions her coming back to work. Oh, just a minute, I've got to put this wheelbarrow through the till. We've got a customer kicking off here. We'll phone you back.'

There was a clunk as Betty replaced the receiver and the machine moved on to the next message while Hettie seethed at the thought of having to run the bakery for even longer.

'Hello – us again, although sister is helping a customer with some ornamental gravel chips at the moment, so it's just me. I'm not sure where I'd got to but... oh dear! I'll have to call you back. We've got a split bag on our paws and gravel spilling everywhere.'

The third message was just a series of noises, crackles and bangs. Beryl's voice was audible in the distance, and she seemed to be having some sort of altercation, with Betty adding the odd helpful word like 'faulty plastic' and 'refund'.

The next took Hettie and Tilly by surprise. 'Hello! Molly Bloom here. I don't know if you've heard, but Marmite Spratt has passed on, so she has, and Bugs Anderton is arranging the wake. She wants to have it at Bloomers and I know that the Butters are away, but if they get in touch, could you ask if they're happy to supply pies, pasties and funeral cakes? Dolly and me can handle the sandwiches. We haven't got a date yet. Anyway, I'll catch up with you both soon. Bye for now.'

The fifth message returned to the chaos in Prickly Brook Garden Centre. 'Back again, sorry for the interruptions – it's what comes of having the phone next to the till,' Betty pointed out. 'Well, what a time we've had up here. It's clear to sister and me that Clematis does not run a tight ship – more like a beached rowing boat, really. Her staff, for want of a better word, are all too old for the job. It seems that none of them can lift a bag of compost, add up, or even find a plant if asked. The winter pansies look like they haven't flowered for weeks, and the grow-your-own mushroom kits have broken out and are dropping their spores everywhere. Her indoor plant section is now outdoors, as the tin roof took off the night before we got here and is awaiting collection at the local lido five miles away in Prickly Bottom. I said to sister, that won't fit in the Morris, not that we'd have time to fetch it anyway, and to make matters worse...'

The machine cut Betty off in mid-sentence, having allowed her the allotted time. The final message was from Beryl and caused Hettie and Tilly to link arms and dance around their table. 'Beryl here,' she began, 'sister has gone off to put our cases in the car. What she was about to tell you was that Clematis's sister Wisteria arrived last night – fresh from her Spanish hideaway, complete with veranda and swimming pool – to run the garden centre until further notice. She seemed to think that sister and me would be staying to do the dirty work while she sat in the café, painting her claws and hoping to scrape the daily takings into her fake leather *bolso* – that's Spanish for bag. Sister told her to *vete a la porra* – that's sod off, in Spanish. So we are about to leave. Morris willing, we should be back in time to fire up the ovens for tomorrow. In short, you're stood down, so you can all have a lie-in in the morning. That's sister hooting her horn, so I'd better get on.'

'Thank goodness,' said Hettie, slightly out of breath from dancing round the table. 'I'll go and take Bruiser's food down to his shed and give him the good news. Build that fire up and we'll have a slap-up lunch when I get back.'

Tilly put the kettle on, adding coal and sticks to the fire and changing into her pyjamas. Although it was only the middle of the afternoon, she wanted to be cosy and, after such an early start, she felt that she deserved some home comforts. She was exhausted. They'd been so busy with the bakery that she'd had no time even to think about her recent nightmares, but now she was beginning to wish she'd never tried to trace her family history. The nightmares had taken her to dark places, and she was becoming more than a little concerned about the letter she'd written to her great-aunts – if, indeed, they were her great-aunts. Life was good, and on reflection she was starting to think that digging up the past wasn't one of her best ideas.

When Hettie returned from delivering the glad tidings to Bruiser, she too changed into her pyjamas. The two cats sat by their fire, drinking tea and chewing their way through some of the rescued pies and pastries. When they were both full to bursting, Hettie settled to a pipe of catnip and Tilly fell asleep on her blanket.

****

Lavender Stamp hated receiving telegrams in her post office. In fact, when she heard the machine starting up behind her counter, she did her best to ignore it. The messages were mostly birthday greetings and other celebratory events, like the birth of kittens or weddings. Lavender was of the opinion that if cats were too lazy to send a proper card through the post, she wasn't obliged to be in any hurry to deliver their telegrams. A telegram meant that she had to close the post office and struggle out to deliver the clipped message to the recipient in all weathers, at any time of the day or night.

Today she was in no mood to go anywhere. It was pension day, and she'd spent the morning shouting at elderly cats over her counter as she counted out their weekly allowances. She'd given herself an extra half an hour for lunch in her kitchen at the back of the post office, where she'd eaten a frugal sardine sandwich and completed her crossword from the day before. Her lunch had done nothing to improve her mood, and when Molly Bloom called in later to buy a stamp and casually impart the news that Marmite Spratt had breathed her last, the day suddenly got a whole lot worse. It wasn't the fact that Marmite had died that upset Lavender; it was more the notion of what could have been if her son Laxton Spratt had continued his courtship of her all those years ago.

Lavender's late mother had run the post office in those days. Laxton had taken on a holiday job as a post cat, and had sweet-talked the young, attractive postmistress's daughter into walking out with him. It was a summer romance that came to nothing and ended abruptly when Laxton took off to pastures new, leaving Lavender with a nasty dose of fleas and a sad and solitary life ahead of her. Laxton had been the biggest disappointment in Lavender's life, and she had never recovered from his rejection of her. She had loved him and he had deserted her.

She allowed her mind to wander back to that hot summer, with memories of cream teas, visits to the pictures and country walks, paw in paw. He'd made her laugh, and she'd never doubted him until he left without a word of explanation. On that day, Lavender's life had changed forever. The bitterness she felt had consumed her to such an extent that it became her life's mission to make everyone around her as miserable as she was.

The spluttering of the telegram machine brought her back from her musings and she copied down the message, tutting as she stared across at the bakery; it was shut up for the day. She folded the paper and pushed it into an envelope, then strode out into the high street, locking the post office door behind her. She crossed the road and made her way down the alleyway that ran down the side of the bakery and into the Butters' yard, wasting no time in hammering on the back door. Eventually a very sleepy-looking Tilly answered, and Lavender pushed the envelope into her paw.

'Well, this is a fine time of day to be wearing your night clothes,' she spat out, looking Tilly up and down. 'It just isn't decent – some of us work a full day every day. The Butters must have taken leave of their senses, allowing you to run their business – and don't think I didn't notice the state of that window display this morning. You've brought shame on the high street.'

Tilly blinked. She was still half asleep and a little taken aback by Lavender's onslaught. She offered a smile and shut the door in the postmistress's face. Clutching the envelope she'd been given, she padded back to her blanket by the fire.

'Who on earth was that?' Hettie asked, sitting up in her armchair. 'I'm surprised we still have a back door after all that hammering.'

'It was Lavender Stamp. She brought this letter,' said Tilly, passing the envelope across to Hettie.

'It's not *just* a letter. It's a telegram, and it's for you.'

Tilly scowled at the envelope in Hettie's paw, treating it with great suspicion. 'I've never had a telegram and I'm not sure I want one now,' she said, shrinking back into her blankets. 'You open it, and if it's nasty I don't want to know.'

Hettie slit open the envelope with her claw and glanced at the telegram briefly before passing it back to Tilly. 'I think you'll be pleased, so you'd better read it for yourself.'

Tilly stared, trying to take in what it said before eventually reading it out loud:

'Matilda-(stop)- Urgent-(stop)- Come to tea-(stop)-Sunday at three-(stop)- Skrimshaw Priory-(stop)- Matilda and Matilda-(stop)- Not Dead Yet.'

Tilly threw the telegram down onto the hearthrug. It wasn't the reaction that Hettie had expected, and she could see that her friend was greatly troubled. 'Isn't that what you hoped for when you wrote that letter?' she suggested.

'That was before my nightmares. Now the thought of going there for real is just too frightening.'

'I think you've spent far too much time at the library going through this family tracing stuff and reading that book you brought home with you. You're just filling your head with nonsense. You don't have to take it any further – just burn the telegram on the fire and we'll stick a Miss Marble video on. I'm in the mood for a nice murder mystery to go with our steak and kidney pies.'

Hettie was trying hard to lighten the mood, but her efforts were in vain. 'You don't understand,' Tilly protested. 'I'm seeing cats and things I didn't know about in my dreams. I think Matthew Katkins was murdered by Matilda and it was covered up, but, in my dream, Matilda was me and I did it. It says he might have been murdered in that book, but I only read that bit after I'd had the nightmare.'

'Well, I'm really confused now,' said Hettie, 'and as far as I can see, there are way too many Matildas involved in all of this. I know what you're like – I think you've let your imagination get the better of you, and you're tired out from all these early mornings. The mind can play funny tricks when you're exhausted, and all this stuff you're talking about happened a very long time ago – if it happened at all.'

'But what should I do about that telegram? Do you think I should go to tea on Sunday?'

Hettie thought for a moment before replying. 'I think we should treat it as a day out. We'll get Bruiser to take us there in Miss Scarlet. If you meet up with your great-aunts, you'll probably feel better about all this – and they might not be connected to you at all. I just think it's quite funny that they are both called Matilda, unless it's a mistake on the telegram.'

Tilly was about to explain the significance of her ancestors being called Matilda, but realised that it was just another part of her dream, and she didn't want to appear sillier than she felt already. Hettie was right; she was exhausted, and what harm would it do to meet up with the two Matildas? It was some time since she and Hettie had had an adventure.

The two cats settled down with their pies and a video, in which a friend of Miss Marble's insisted that she had seen a murder on a train. It was one of Tilly's favourites, but neither cat got any further than the end of their pies before they were both fast asleep, leaving Miss Marble to draw her own conclusions.

****

January 6th 1666

Matilda had barely noticed Christmas. The servants did their best to garland the Priory, but there was no appetite for feasting or celebration. The plague, which had spread from London, had claimed so many cats. There were burial pits across the country and although the frosts had slowed the death toll, there seemed no end to the tragedies.

She shivered and pulled her shawl closer to her. The fire, although blazing in the grate, offered no warmth as her mother lay dying. She sniffed on the vinegar-soaked rag, which was supposed to keep the disease at bay, but now – as her mother's breath rasped in her throat – she didn't care if the plague took her as well.

For a while, life had been good under the new king. The Priory had blossomed, paths had been laid, and her mother had overseen the planting of gardens – beautiful places to retreat to on summer days with a book, or to paint the landscape that stretched for miles in every direction. As soon as Matilda had been old enough to understand, her mother had told her that all the land she could see would one day be hers. Cold comfort now, as the cat she most cared about would soon be carried to her grave, over by the mill where the father Matilda had never known slept on, waiting for the love of his life.

A gust of wind bellowed down the chimney, filling the bedchamber with smoke. When the air cleared, Matilda watched as her mother's spirit left her body, rose up and flew out through the window. The moment she had dreaded was over in a second. She stared down at the face on the pillow. The pain that had been etched there was gone, replaced by a peace she would cling to in her grief. The torch had passed to her, and now she must bring new life to the Priory and fulfil her destiny. She got up and stretched. It felt as though she'd been sitting in the same position for days – and she probably had. She crossed to the window and stared out at the windmill. The sails were turning as on an ordinary day, but for the first time in her life Matilda was alone.

****

Tilly awoke with a start. The video they'd been watching was rewinding itself noisily. She stumbled from her blankets and switched the machine off, then added more coal to the fire and returned to her bed. She was wide awake and her mind raced as she watched the flames lick at the chimney breast, hoping for some answers. Why was she being haunted by these shades from the past? What did they want from her?

Chapter Five

Saturday was one of Hettie and Tilly's favourite days of the week: when time allowed they enjoyed a lazy morning in their room with a Butters' breakfast bap, followed by a mixed grill at Bloomers for lunch and a stroll down the high street to Jessie's charity shop to browse the latest arrivals in clothes and bric-a-brac.

This Saturday was no different to any other and began with the heartwarming sound of the bread ovens roaring into life, confirming that the Butter sisters were safely returned from Prickly Brook and very much back at the helm of their own ship. Tilly had had very little sleep for fear of being transported back to Skrimshaw Priory. She'd distracted herself with one of her Christmas jigsaws – of *The Beverly Hillbillies*, one of her current TV favourites – and had heard the commotion of the Butters' arrival home just after midnight. They'd bumped their cases up the stairs to their flat, and Tilly had been tempted to greet them, but she knew they would only have a few hours' sleep before their day at the bakery began.

The night had seemed endless, but as soon as the bakery ovens came to life, Tilly fell into a deep and dreamless sleep, and would probably have slept through the day if it hadn't been for Hettie dangling a hot egg and bacon bap in front of her nose.

'Wake up sleepyhead,' she said, putting the bap down on the edge of Tilly's blanket. 'It's nearly eleven, and if we're to fit in a mixed grill at Bloomers, you'd better eat this now.'

Tilly struggled to a sitting position and rubbed the sleep out of her eyes with her paws. 'I can't believe it's so late,' she said, stretching her arthritic legs. 'That was the best sleep I've had in ages.'

Hettie was pleased to see her friend looking happier than the night before, and was determined to fill their day with nice things to distract Tilly from the darker side of her family history. 'I've booked Bruiser for our jaunt tomorrow,' said Hettie, settling into her armchair with her own breakfast bap. 'He's studying his maps to find us a scenic route. Betty and Beryl have offered to pack us up a picnic lunch for the trip, as Betty says Norfolk is further than you think, so we're all set for a jolly good day out.'

In her mind, Tilly doubted that there would be anything jolly about meeting her great-aunts Skrimshaw, but she appreciated Hettie's determination to make the day a nice one. She'd woken up refreshed and ready to deal with what the following day might bring and to prove it she took a healthy bite out of her bap, allowing some of the egg yolk to trickle down her chin and onto her pyjamas.

It was raining when they finally emerged into the high street and headed for Molly Bloom's café. Tilly had instigated a furious cleaning session in their room, with much shaking of blankets to remove crumbs from all the pies and pastries they'd enjoyed in recent days. Betty and Beryl had presented them with a peace lily, rescued from Clematis Wilt's garden centre, as a thank you for 'holding the fort'. Tilly was delighted, as she'd never owned a house plant before. She'd spent some time dusting the staff sideboard before putting it in pride of place, and called it Mrs White after a character in her favourite murder game. Even Hettie was pleased to see how neat and tidy their room was by the time Tilly had finished, especially as her only contribution had been to fill the coal scuttle from the stack in the Butters' backyard and fold some clothes away into the bottom drawer of the filing cabinet.

Bloomers was packed to the rafters with cats, all keen to get out of the rain. Molly kept a table for Hettie and Tilly at the back of the café, and they often used it for interviews connected with their detective work. Hettie was pleased to see that Bruiser was keeping it warm for them as they pushed through the tables of cats. 'I've ordered three mixed grills because Dolly's sayin' they might run out,' Bruiser announced as Hettie and Tilly slid into their seats. 'They've been rushed off their feet since it started chuckin' it down out there. I was 'opin' that Dolly could finish early, like they usually do on a Saturday – they're screenin' *Easy Rider* at the Kitema this afternoon, an' I thought I'd treat 'er.'

Bruiser had been sweet on Dolly Scollop since the day he'd met her at Agatha Crispy's holiday home in Devon, where she had been a maid of all work. He was even more smitten after he discovered that Dolly was the daughter of one of the country's most celebrated daredevil bikers. Billy 'the Bullet' Scollop, as he was known, eventually came to a sticky end, overshooting the wall of death at Padstow May Day Fair and landing head first on the doughnut stall, which killed him instantly. After her father's death, Dolly had left her native Cornwall for Devon, and it was there that she was persuaded by Bruiser to seek her fortune in the town as Molly Bloom's right-paw cat. The two cats hit it off immediately, and Dolly had moved in with Molly to share the flat above the café.

Bruiser and Dolly were a match made in heaven. They shared a love of anything to do with motorbikes and the cinema, and would often be found doing the crossword in *Bikers' Monthly* during quiet moments at the café. 'I've sorted out a route for our trip,' Bruiser continued, 'and I've found this Skrimshaw place – it's marked up as a point of interest.' He unfolded the map he'd brought with him, and Hettie and Tilly looked on as his paw pointed to a vast area of land. 'All these green bits is Skrimshaw land, as far as I can make out. That buildin' is the priory, right in the middle of all them fields. There's a campsite marked as well, so I s'pose it's a good place for a week away.'

'Is there a windmill marked on the map?' Tilly asked.

'Yup. Look – there it is, an' accordin' to me OS symbols, there's a burial ground right next to it. Odd sort o' thing to 'ave next to a windmill, but maybe there was a church there in the old days.'

Tilly shook her head. 'No, it's always been there,' she said, before she could stop herself.

Bruiser was about to ask how she knew, but Dolly arrived with the lunches and the map was hurriedly tidied away to make room for the plates. 'We're runnin' short on sausages, so Molly's put an extra chop on to compensate,' Dolly pointed out as she unloaded her tray. 'We've got treacle sponge, jam roly-poly or ginger tray bake, all with custard or ice cream – or both, if you've a mind – so what can I get you for your afters?'

Tilly chose the ginger sponge tray bake, as she said it sounded exotic. Bruiser and Hettie went for the jam roly-poly, and all three cats agreed that custard would be the perfect addition to their puddings.

Hettie and Bruiser cleared their plates in record time, but Tilly played with her food. Bruiser's map had upset her. The proximity of the priory to the mill and the burial ground was just the same as it had been in her dreams, and this feeling of déjà vu was beginning to frighten her. Hettie and Bruiser offered some practical help by eating what was left on her plate, and Tilly did much better with the ginger sponge tray bake, licking her bowl clean.

The rain had stopped and the café finally began to empty as the town's cats went about their business. Those who were left witnessed the arrival of a shiny silver E-Type Jaguar that pulled up outside. 'Blimey!' said Bruiser, 'someone's got a few quid.

Just take a look at that! You could buy one of them big 'ouses in Sheba Gardens for the price of that motor.'

Hettie wasn't impressed, but Tilly was rather taken with the long bonnet and huge headlights. The three cats left their table and moved towards the window for a closer look. The driver sat in his seat, staring ahead of him as if unsure of what to do next. Molly Bloom bustled out of her kitchen and joined them. 'Well now,' she said, putting her nose to the window, 'I think that might be Mr Spratt. He called me this morning about his poor mother's wake, so he did. Bugs Anderton thought he might like to be involved in the arrangements. I said for him to come over, as we've early closing, so we could talk sandwiches and the like. Looks like he's done rather well for himself, wouldn't you say?'

Tilly loved Molly's Irish accent. She found it mesmerising and so comforting. If it was Laxton Spratt sitting in his car, it occurred to Tilly that Molly Bloom would be the perfect sticking plaster for his grief.

'No wonder Lavender Stamp is cross all the time if he's the one that got away,' Hettie mumbled, mostly to herself.

The cat in the Jaguar finally got out of his car, causing the spectators to scatter from the window. Molly greeted him at the door, turned the café sign to 'closed' and led him to a table. He was an imposing figure and nothing like his mother. His clothes, like his car, shouted success in every stitch. There were rumours that he had gone into the film business after he'd left the town, but no one knew for sure.

As much as they would have loved to stay and listen in on Molly's conversation, Hettie and Tilly decided to make tracks for Jessie's charity shop and Bruiser went through to the kitchen to collect Dolly for their cinema date, leaving Molly to deal with wake bakes and Laxton Spratt.

The charity shop in Cheapcuts Lane was bustling with cats looking for a bargain when Hettie and Tilly arrived, and the general conversation was all about Marmite Spratt and her

Teasmade. One cat even suggested that Lazarus Hambone had sold it to her straight off the back of a lorry, but the veiled accusation was greeted with shocked denial by those who had benefitted from Lazarus's cut-price items.

Tilly announced to the bargain hunters that Laxton Spratt was currently planning his mother's wake at Bloomers, causing a stampede to pay up at the till before everyone headed up the high street to take a look at him. Jessie was pleased to be rid of them and turned the sign round on her door, inviting Hettie and Tilly into her back parlour for a cup of tea and a catch-up.

'It's been crazy today,' Jessie said, putting the kettle on. 'The rain brought them into the shop, but the gossip about Marmite kept them here. It's not even that she was well liked – bit of a shrew, really, although I shouldn't say that under the circumstances. Bugs Anderton was in here yesterday, saying she'd been lumbered with the arrangements as Marmite made her the executor to her will. She was lucky in tracing Laxton, but she said he wasn't even upset when she told him that his mother had died.'

'Well, it wasn't so long ago that we had her on our suspect list for the murder of Mavis Spitforce,' Hettie pointed out, remembering the Milky Myers case that they'd worked on. 'She took every opportunity to promote her books when the world's press descended on the town, giving interviews all over the place. She was more an obstruction than a help at the time. I can perfectly understand why there was no love lost between her and Laxton.'

'I've got a whole stack of her *Strange But Trues* in my second-paw book section that I never seem to be able to shift,' said Jessie, rescuing the tea bags from the mugs. 'I suppose they might actually sell now she's dead – and, looking on the bright side, at least there won't be any more of them.'

'Not unless her son finds one tucked under her bed and decides to publish posthumously,' Tilly suggested. 'I know she was planning a book launch at the library.'

'So come on – what's he like?' asked Jessie. 'I don't remember seeing him about. Did he ever visit her, I wonder?'

'All we know about him is that he walked out with Lavender Stamp when she was young and then dumped her,' said Tilly. 'He's just turned up at Bloomers in a lovely posh car, and he looks like something out of a James Blond movie. He's obviously very rich, but he's nothing like Marmite.'

'The funeral should be interesting then,' Jessie suggested, 'especially if Lavender turns up at St Kippers to pay her respects. She might catch him second time around and be whisked off to a Caribbean island for the rest of her days. At least we'd have someone decent at the post office at last, although I find it hard to believe that she's ever walked out with anyone.'

The three cats laughed at the prospect and Jessie changed the subject, bringing Tilly down to earth with an uncomfortable bump. 'So how are you getting on with tracing your family history?'

'It's all turned a bit nasty,' Tilly admitted. 'I wish I hadn't started it in the first place.'

Jessie listened while Tilly recounted her nightmares and the details she'd discovered in the book about Matthew Katkins, as well as their planned outing to Skrimshaw Priory. Jessie was fascinated. 'I think what you're describing is regression,' she said. 'I read about it in a book I had in the shop. The idea, as far as I can remember, is that the so-called nine lives a cat is given can be in front of or behind the life you have now. So you're going back into your past lives to revisit them, which is very exciting. You have the right sort of mind for it – you're supersensitive.'

'It's not exciting,' Tilly protested. 'It's very frightening and sad and I might even have been a murderer.'

'I think it's a load of nonsense,' said Hettie, 'and the sooner we visit these aunts the better, so we can clear all this silly business up. I could spit at Turner Page for causing such an upset with his genealogy workshops.'

'But surely there's nothing to get upset about?' said Jessie. 'Ghosts from the past are exactly that – they can't touch you now.'

Tilly shook her head. 'You don't understand. Everything is so real in my dreams, and I'm frightened that I might get stuck there and not find my way back. It's a bit like a film set. I'm drawn in, and I become one of the actual characters.'

Jessie could see that Tilly was getting more upset and Hettie more irritated, so she changed the subject again. They discussed the prospect of a summer book festival at the library, the Butter sisters' visit to Prickly Brook Garden Centre, and the pros and cons of running the bakery in their absence. By the time they'd drunk another cup of tea and raided a tin of Playbox biscuits that Jessie had been bought for Christmas, they were all in a much better mood.

Hettie and Tilly said their goodbyes and promised to call in the following week to let Jessie know how they had got on at Skrimshaw Priory. As they passed Bloomers, they noticed that Laxton Spratt was gone; there was no sign of his car either.

Betty and Beryl leapt on them as soon as they arrived home, announcing that they were treating them all to fish, chips and batter bits from Elsie Haddock's, and that Bruiser had kindly agreed to fetch them. Hettie and Tilly were delighted to be having a fish supper, and were both relieved that there had been no complaints regarding their two-day tenure of the bakery. The Butters seemed happy and grateful for their efforts, although Betty was slightly bewildered by a customer's request for an iced fancy fusion cake.

Bruiser looked extra smart when he delivered their supper. He'd combed his fur and was wearing his best waistcoat under his favourite leather jacket. 'Come and eat with us,' Hettie suggested, as she grabbed the hot parcels. 'We're going to watch *Columbo* on TV.'

Bruiser grinned, showing his lack of teeth. 'I've been invited round to Dolly and Molly's to watch it and I've got their fish suppers, so I'd better be on me way. I reckon we'd better make an early start tomorrow, so I'll 'ave Miss Scarlet ready for the off at ten if that's OK?'

'That's fine, but why don't you invite Dolly to come with us? You could make it a date and take her somewhere for tea while we deal with Tilly's great-aunts.'

Bruiser's grin was even wider than the first one he'd offered. The thought of spending the day on a motorbike with Dolly Scollop was his idea of heaven. 'Righto,' he said. 'I'll ask 'er. It is 'er day off, so I might be lucky.' He skipped out of the back door, leaving Hettie and Tilly to their evening. The cat in the shabby mac proved the perfect accompaniment to their fish and chip supper, and no sooner had Columbo caught his murderer than Hettie and Tilly fell fast asleep. Tilly's dreams took her no further than Elsie Haddock's chip shop, where she was accosted by a horde of batter bits, and both cats awoke refreshed – a little later than planned, but ready for their Norfolk adventure.

Chapter Six

The bright red motorbike and sidecar shone by the time Bruiser had finished polishing her chrome, and every cat who passed gave her an admiring nod as she waited for her passengers outside the bakery. Dolly was the first to arrive, having accepted Bruiser's invitation for a day out. She looked splendid in her leathers, and Bruiser wasted no time in telling her so. Betty and Beryl were next out into the high street, carrying a large picnic hamper. Hettie and Tilly, who had overslept, eventually joined the party on the pavement, both of them excited and looking forward to the day ahead.

They clambered into the sidecar while Bruiser crammed the hamper into the boot and swung himself onto the bike, offering his paw to Dolly. She pulled herself up behind him and the four cats sped off down the high street, waved off by the Butter sisters.

It was a bright morning, and not too cold for February. Miss Scarlet purred along the country roads, lapping up the miles with very little effort. Bruiser had studied his maps well, and within a couple of hours they were motoring through the middle of a vast forest, heading for the coast.

'I always think of bodies when we go through woods,' Tilly said.

'Why?' asked Hettie, keen to understand why Tilly had raised such an odd subject.

'Well, if you had a body you wanted to get rid of, it would be the best place to bury it. It might never be found, and even if it was, there probably wouldn't be much of it left. Foxes and wolves might dig it up and eat it, destroying the evidence, or big old black crows might rip it to shreds and peck its eyes out.'

Tilly was warming to her subject when Hettie interjected, 'But if you wanted to hide a body in a wood, you couldn't do it at this time of year because you can see right through the trees. There are no bushes or leaves to hide behind, so you'd have to do it at night, and then someone might see your car at the edge of the forest and wonder what you were up to. In this case, the road runs straight through the forest, so a parked car would give you away,' she pointed out.

'All right, where would you hide a body?' Tilly countered.

'I don't think I've ever thought about it, really. I suppose I might be tempted to burn it or throw it off a cliff and make it look like an accident. Most of the bodies we've had to deal with were in plain sight, left in the place where they were murdered. I think most killers want to leave the scene as quickly as possible. They don't want to lug a body around with them, let alone take it on a trip to the local forest. Why are you so interested in hiding bodies, anyway?'

'I was thinking about Matthew Katkins,' Tilly explained. 'If the Matilda in my nightmare did murder him, then it was a brilliant idea for the servants to feed him to the pigs.'

'Not if you ate bacon for breakfast or liked a nice pork chop for your dinner,' Hettie pointed out. 'That would be a clear case of cat eat cat with a piggy in the middle.'

Tilly screwed her face up at the very thought and licked her paw nervously before nibbling on a broken claw and spitting it out onto the tartan blanket they were sharing.

The forest turned into open countryside, punctuated by the occasional small village. Eventually even the villages were left behind, replaced by a stark, forbidding landscape. The sky had darkened to a moody black, flecked with angry-looking pink storm clouds.

They sensed the sea before it revealed itself, with marshes stretching out towards the coast, guarded by ever-present reed beds. Tilly stared in disbelief. Here was her nightmare again, and in her mind she could see the black form of Matthew Katkins galloping towards the priory. The land was familiar to her, and yet she had never been there. She shivered at what might be still to come.

Bruiser pulled off the road and parked Miss Scarlet in the entrance to a farm track to consult his map. Hettie threw the lid back on the sidecar. 'Looks like the weather is going to turn against us,' she said. 'I think we should stop here and break out the Butters' picnic.'

They all agreed and Bruiser pulled the hamper out of Miss Scarlet's boot. Tilly leapt out of the sidecar and lifted the lid on their picnic. 'Ooooh, lovely!' she said, before giving everyone a rundown of the contents. 'We've got pork pies, mini sausage plaits, salmon sandwiches with the crusts cut off, scotch eggs, crisps and cheese scones in savouries. They've packed Wagon Wheels, chocolate buns and flapjacks for sweets, and we've got a bottle of fiery ginger beer and a flask of tea – they've put a note on that saying that it's ready-sugared.'

There was plenty to go round and the four cats licked and chewed their way through their lunch. It was hardly picnic weather, so Dolly squeezed herself into the sidecar with Hettie and Tilly, while Bruiser sat on the bike to enjoy his food. By the time they'd finished, the wind was getting up and the sky looked even more threatening. 'I reckon we'd better push on,' said Bruiser, packing the hamper away in the boot. 'Accordin' to me map, we got another twenty miles before we come to the edge of the Skrimshaw land, as such.'

Dolly left the warmth of the sidecar and clambered back up behind Bruiser, who kicked the bike into life just as the rain began to fall. The countryside became more and more remote as they journeyed on, the sea now fully visible as a grey line on the horizon. The only sign of life was the occasional flock of birds rising from the reed beds and marshes.

'I hope there's a warm welcome waiting for us at the priory,' Hettie said, staring out at the bleakness that surrounded them. 'I'm looking forward to a crackling fire and a toasted crumpet served on a silver dish if your great-aunts are as rich as we think they might be. You've got to have a few bob to own your own priory these days.'

'It was a horrid, draughty place in my dreams,' Tilly pointed out.

'I think you should try and forget about your dreams,' Hettie suggested. 'Just think of it as an outing to visit a couple of lovely old cats. They must be quite ancient, because you're no spring chicken.'

Tilly could see the sense in Hettie's words and cheered up instantly, determined to make the best of things. They were having an adventure and she didn't want to spoil it for everyone by being upset and miserable. The road took them towards the coast, and, as the rain fell, a sea fret rose up and enveloped them. Bruiser slowed down and allowed Miss Scarlet to move slowly into the mist, taking care to keep her on the road, which was flanked by a ditch on either side. Hettie pulled back the lid on the sidecar, trying to improve their visibility, but she could barely see her paw in front of her face.

Tilly pulled the tartan blanket up to her chin. The sea fret had soaked her fur in an instant. She licked her lips nervously. Everything tasted of salt, and the muffled roar of Miss Scarlet's engine sounded a long way off. The mist had come down like a blanket, distorting everything as they moved nearer the sea.

To everybody's relief the sea fret eventually began to clear, leaving pockets of mist that swirled and danced around them like feverish ghosts, daring them to go no further. Bruiser killed the engine to take another look at his map, and they were instantly aware of the sea, listening to the sound of the incoming tide as it crept onto the shingle and sucked it back into the water. Hettie leapt out of the sidecar to get a sense of where they were and was more than shocked to discover that they were only a matter of yards from the water. 'It's a good job we didn't keep going,' she said, clambering back into the sidecar. 'We'd have driven straight into the sea.'

'I reckon we lost the proper road back there, just after the mist came down,' said Bruiser, studying his map closely. 'It's all these reed beds that's confusin'. There's paths through 'em and I think we picked up one of them by mistake.'

'What are all these reeds for?' asked Tilly. 'They smell horrible.'

'Them's for thatchin',' said Bruiser. 'When I was on the road, I used ta meet up with this old cat who travelled from village to village, thatchin' roofs. 'E told me some of the finest reeds come from 'ere – they grow it specially. Course, 'e's gone now, poor old boy.'

'What do you mean by gone?' Tilly asked.

'Gone as in dead,' said Bruiser. 'I 'eard 'e'd 'ad a barley wine too many an' slipped off a ridge in Cockily Cley, which accordin' to me map isn't far from 'ere.'

'Thatchin' can be naarsty work,' said Dolly, taking up the subject. 'My uncle was a thatcher, worked out of Cadgwith Cove in Cornwall. 'E was a real laarf – taught me to clog dance on a breadboard, 'e did, but 'e come unstuck when 'e slid off a thatch near Tintagel. Landed on 'is paws all right, but then got run over by the coach carryin' the Lostwithiel Juniors Town Band – they were out for a visit to Merlin's Cave. 'E 'ung on across that summer, but we knew 'e wouldn't make Christmas.'

'Sounds like you Cornish cats are accident-prone,' said Hettie, 'but I think we'd better move on as that tide is coming in, and unless Miss Scarlet can turn herself into a boat we could be in real trouble.'

Bruiser responded by folding up his map and kicking the bike into life. He turned around and headed back the way they'd come. After a few yards, the mist had cleared completely and the rain had stopped. Bruiser picked up the road he'd missed, which ran parallel to the shore; satisfied that they were now moving in the right direction, he pressed on.

The sun was now making a real attempt to burn a hole in the threatening storm clouds, but the endless reed beds did nothing to cheer up the landscape. The rain returned occasionally in short sharp showers, eventually creating an arcing rainbow across the sky, the only colour to be had in such bleak terrain. The reed beds eventually gave way to undulating heathland, and the ditches were replaced by a crumbling, ancient wall that marked the boundary to Skrimshaw land. In the distance, Tilly spied the unmistakable presence of a windmill and, behind that, a substantial shell of an old priory, looming large as they grew closer.

'It's a ruin,' said Tilly, more than a little disappointed. 'If that's Skrimshaw Priory, I doubt that my great-aunts are living there.'

'Well, maybe they have a nice little cottage in the grounds,' suggested Hettie. 'Why on earth would you want to live in that old place, even if it did have a roof? And look, Bruiser was right – in that dip there's a load of huts and caravans. That must be the campsite.'

'You don't think they live in a caravan?' Tilly said, rather indignantly.

'Possibly,' said Hettie, 'but as long as they put on a good tea and it's warm, I don't care where they live.'

Bruiser slowed right down, looking for a way in across the land. The crumbling wall began to rise in height, forming a side wall of a gatehouse. The entrance was arched, and – unlike the ruin of the priory – had been renovated to form a mini fortress. Bruiser was about to drive under the arch when a cat sprang down a flight of stone steps inside the keep and held up his paw to stop them. He was dressed in a bright red regimental jacket and wore a headband tied in a knot under his left ear.

'That's far enough, friend,' he said, positioning himself in front of Miss Scarlet. 'We're not open until Easter. We're not together enough for visitors. It's all a bit of a bad scene at the moment – too cold, too much mud, and the caravans are still in a mess from Christmas. We've got new followers still trying to enter our headspace, so we're not ready to pass on the love just yet.'

Hettie pulled back the lid on the sidecar and stood up to address the cat who stood in their way. 'We have been invited by Matilda Skrimshaw and are expected for tea – and we've come a very long way,' she pointed out.

'Wow, that's really far out. The Skrimshaws – or the Ancients, as we call them – never see anyone, so you'll have to tell me who you are before I let you go any further.'

Hettie was becoming quite irritated by the hippy cat and decided to turn the tables on him. 'Before we introduce ourselves, I'd like to know who you are.'

'Me?' he responded. 'Acrid Firestorm at your service. Leader of the Skrimshaw Pilgrims and keeper of this land.'

'But surely the Skrimshaws – or Ancients, as you call them – are the owners of the land?' argued Hettie.

'A debatable point, as we are two tribes descended from the great Viking warriors Ragland Firestorm and Matilda the Shield Maiden. Ragland had many sons, and I am descended from his line. Matilda had only daughters, and the Ancients are descended from her. The females have held this land for hundreds of years, but now there will be a new beginning as the land will finally pass to the sons of Ragland Firestorm.'

'Well, thank you for the history lesson,' said Hettie, somewhat dismissively. 'I'm sure that's all very interesting, but I think you should let us pass and direct us to the Skrimshaws.'

'Not until you introduce yourselves,' said Firestorm. 'We are the protectors of the Ancients and we serve them in everything and keep them from harm.'

Hettie spat out the introductions. 'I am Hettie Bagshot from The No. 2 Feline Detective Agency. These are my colleagues Bruiser and Dolly Scollop and this is Matilda Jenkins, great-niece of the Skrimshaws, and – if your history lesson is correct – descended from Matilda the Shield Maiden.'

Acrid Firestorm froze as if he'd been turned to stone. Bruiser broke the silence by noisily revving Miss Scarlet's engine, showing his intent to move forward. Firestorm recovered himself sufficiently to point his paw in the direction of the campsite. 'Ask for Serafin Parchment. She'll take you to the Ancients,' he mumbled, as if in a trance. Hettie had dealt a blow that shook him to his very core. As they drove towards the campsite, Tilly looked back at him, standing very still and glaring at her, his face as thunderous as the gathering storm clouds above his head.

Chapter Seven

The campsite reminded Tilly of a Saxon village she'd seen on TV, and if it hadn't been for the presence of several rather beaten-up caravans, she would have found it easy to believe that they had stepped back in time. The huts, on closer inspection, were constructed from mud and reeds. Bruiser parked Miss Scarlet on the edge of the site and the four cats waited to see if anyone would approach. There was a fire in the centre of the enclave, with several cats gathered around it clapping and chanting. They appeared to be roasting a pig on a spit and seemed oblivious to their visitors, possibly because they were all sharing a giant hubble-bubble pipe of catnip.

'I doubt we'll get any sense from that lot,' Hettie said. 'That stuff smells pretty strong to me. Maybe we should take a ride over to the priory and see if we can locate the Skrimshaws ourselves.'

Bruiser was about to start the engine again when a tall, gangly cat broke away from the group by the fire and glided over to them. 'Hi,' she said, gathering her long skirts to avoid the mud, 'that's a really cool machine you've got there. You could ride the universe on that.'

Hettie decided to get straight to the point. 'Actually, we're looking for Serafin Parchment. Mr Firestorm sent us and told us she could take us to the Skrimshaws. We're supposed to be having tea with them.'

The cat responded by doing a short dance, ending in a curtsey which almost left her face down in the mud as she slipped and briefly lost her balance. Recovering herself by hanging on to Miss Scarlet's bumper, and receiving a round of applause from the cats around the fire, she finally admitted to being Serafin Parchment. 'I'm not sure the Ancients will see you,' she said slowly, as if carefully selecting each word. 'They don't have visitors very often, as they're much too old. It's like they left the planet years ago but they're still here, if you see what I mean.'

Hettie, Tilly, Bruiser and Dolly had no idea what Serafin Parchment meant. In fact, it was taking them all their self-control not to break out into hysterical laughter. The situation was becoming more ridiculous by the minute. 'If you could just point us in the right direction, we won't trouble you any further,' Hettie said, with a definite edge to her voice.

'It's no trouble. I'll just get my tambourine,' Serafin said, disappearing into one of the mud huts and reappearing wearing a shawl and a circlet of flowers jammed on her head. 'Follow me,' she cried as she danced off across the field, banging her tambourine.

Bruiser started up the engine and turned the bike round slowly, following the cat across the field. There was no sign of a cottage or even a caravan in the direction she was taking – only the windmill, which stood in the middle of the field, surround-ed on three sides by a very old graveyard.

As they got nearer, Tilly's stomach did a somersault. She'd been here before and now she was about to revisit her nightmare in the cold light of day. 'I want to go home,' she whispered, but no one heard her.

Serafin stopped at the foot of the mill and proceeded to move into a full-blown performance, twirling and leaping in time to the beat of her tambourine. The dance went on for several minutes. Bruiser parked the bike at a safe distance and the four cats waited patiently for Serafin's frenzied activity to reach its natural conclusion.

'Why do you think she's stopped there?' Tilly asked. 'Surely the Skrimshaws don't live in that old windmill?'

'There's nothing else round here, but maybe it's all done up and lovely inside,' said Hettie, trying to remain positive for Tilly's sake.

'Wait a minute – look at that window up there! It's opening and there's a paw waving a black handkerchief,' Tilly said, at the same moment that Serafin stopped dancing. 'It must be some sort of signal.'

Tilly was right. Serafin put down her tambourine and entered the windmill by a heavy studded door. She was gone for some time and returned eventually to announce that the Ancients were at home to just two visitors as long as one of them was called Matilda.

Bruiser and Dolly were happy not to be included in the visit. They were keen to spend some time together in the sidecar, finishing off the Butters' picnic and a crossword that Dolly had cut out of the *Daily Snout*. Hettie and Tilly clambered out of Miss Scarlet and walked slowly towards the windmill, where Serafin waited for them.

The building was so much taller than it had appeared from the road. Its giant sails were still, waiting for a gust of wind to set them in motion. Except for the entrance, the ground surrounding the mill was wild with tangled briars that arched across time-worn stones and boulders. The occasional daffodil lifted its head from the dense thicket, reaching up to the light and refusing to be suffocated and robbed of a spring.

'There's a really bad vibe going on in there today,' Serafin said, pointing her paw towards the door. 'You're lucky that they'll see you at all. It's the ghosts, you see – they've had a really bad night with them. Paranoia big time.'

'What ghosts?' Tilly asked.

Serafin just smiled and danced off towards the campsite banging her tambourine.

'Well, it just gets better,' said Hettie. 'I can't wait to meet the Skrimshaws – nothing I like better than two reclusive, paranoid old cats. Shall we get this over with?'

Hettie lifted the latch on the door, which was solid oak, studded with iron. It gave some resistance, but the giant hinges announced their arrival before they had even stepped over the threshold, giving out a blood-curdling creak that would have been pure joy for a cat in charge of sound effects on a horror film set. Tilly tucked herself in behind Hettie as they moved into the mill. The entrance hall was no better than an outhouse – the old brick walls running with damp, a cold stone floor littered with dead and decaying leaves and evidence of mouse or rat droppings. A network of webs hung from the boarded roof, housing an entire colony of large and small spiders, all attending to their vast pantry of dead flies and other captured insects, bound up in their suffocatingly sticky gossamer threads.

Hettie paused for a moment, hoping for some sort of welcome, but the mill was totally silent. There was another door in front of them, slightly ajar. She pushed through it and was relieved to see that it opened into a much larger, less claustrophobic space, benefitting from arched windows, a boarded floor and an open wooden staircase which climbed to the next level. The room was almost round, taking on the contours of the windmill, with heavy beams, whitewashed brick walls and a substantial red brick fireplace that looked like it had been redundant for many years. The windows, although allowing a good amount of light, were heavily nailed shut. Except for a few old flour sacks, a coil of rusty chains from an abandoned pulley system and a bench in front of the fireplace, the room was empty.

'I think we should leave now,' Tilly whispered, but her voice was thrown back at her in an echo that reverberated around the room, signalling their presence to any ears that may have been listening. Hettie resisted a reply but moved swiftly to the staircase, pulling Tilly by the sleeve of her Sunday cardigan after her. Every stair they climbed announced their progress towards the next level, the time-worn treads responding as they had for hundreds of years to the workers and visitors to the mill.

The stairs opened out into a dimly lit space, and at first Hettie and Tilly thought it was unoccupied, but a sudden movement in the gloom drew their attention to the far side of the room. Hettie pushed Tilly forward to make the approach, but what confronted them was totally unexpected.

Two very old and seemingly blind cats sat side by side in front of a very small fire in a very large fireplace. Both cats sat in matching chairs, with crocheted blankets up to their chins. Both creatures had scabs across their eyes and, as Hettie and Tilly approached, moved their heads from side to side, sensing that they were no longer alone.

Tilly, seeing how utterly helpless the two cats were, found some courage and announced herself. 'Hello. I am Matilda Jenkins, although I'm really called Tilly, and this is my best friend Hettie. I think you might be my great-aunts and you invited us to tea.'

While Tilly was making the introductions, Hettie took in the room, and – to her considerable disappointment – there was no sign of an afternoon tea of any sort, nor any chance of one, looking at the general state of the elderly cats.

There was no immediate response from either cat. Tilly stepped a little closer and was rewarded by a swipe from one of them, claws fully extended and drawing blood to the side of her face. The swipe was followed by a blood-curdling, guttural growl from the other cat, which served as a warning for Tilly to stand back.

Nursing the scratch to her face, Tilly retreated to the top of the stairs, shaken by the assault. The old cats were now extremely agitated, and the one who had hit out at Tilly began to growl at her fireside companion, before leaping on her and lashing out with her claws. The catfight lasted seconds but the violence was extreme, leaving both elderly cats with bleeding ears. They crawled back into their chairs to lick their wounds, still grumbling and wary of each other.

Hettie and Tilly looked on, baffled by what had taken place. Serafin had talked of paranoia, but what they'd just witnessed was feral behaviour, savage and brutal in its execution.

They had come a long way and Hettie was now determined to get to the bottom of the circumstances surrounding these ageing cats and the odd set-up at the priory. The detective in her was taking over, and whether Tilly was related to the Skrimshaws or not, she sensed that there was something very dark about the priory and its inhabitants. There must be a reason why two seemingly fragile, elderly cats should have become so vicious to the world around them and to each other; Hettie's curiosity was fired up and ready to go.

Chapter Eight

Tilly had had enough. She couldn't get out of the windmill fast enough and away from the horror that lurked within. 'I'm sorry I ever started this,' she said, pulling the door shut behind her. 'I hope I'm not related to those creatures. They are monsters.'

Hettie had to agree, but was intrigued by the whole situation. 'There's something not right about any of this,' she said, staring across at the hippy campsite and the jagged ruins of the priory beyond. 'I honestly can't see either of those old cats being capable of sending a telegram to invite you to tea, so the big questions are – who sent the telegram, and why?'

'I hadn't really thought of it like that,' Tilly admitted. 'It was just such a shock to see them. I expected them to be very old, but why are they so nasty? And not just to me, but to each other?'

'Well, I think that's the point,' said Hettie. 'Something or someone has made them like it, and I don't think it would do any harm for us to ask a few questions down at the campsite before we leave.'

Tilly reluctantly agreed. 'Before we go down there, I'd like to take a look at this burial ground,' she said. 'It was so real in my dream and maybe if I look at it properly the nightmares might stop.'

'Or they might get worse,' Hettie pointed out. 'I'll go and let Bruiser and Dolly know what we're doing while you have a wander. I don't like the look of that sky so we'd better not stay too long – we've a long drive home.'

No sooner had Hettie mentioned the gathering storm clouds than a rumble of thunder sounded in the distance. Tilly pulled the hood up on her Sunday cardigan and moved into the burial ground, trying to avoid the long, vicious tendrils that choked the ground and encircled the stones. There was no formality in the way that the burials presented themselves: the stones were sporadically placed, some in circles and others standing alone. The inscriptions were mostly unreadable – faint impressions etched into the stone; where once they had recorded the memory of a life, now, blasted by centuries of weather, they were merely markers of what had once been.

As she moved round to the back of the windmill, she found more recent graves and could just about read some of the inscriptions. The dates were easier to decipher than the names. Many of them were attributed to the eighteen hundreds, a far cry from her nightmares, but as she got used to the faded lettering, it was clear that the name of Matilda cropped up over and over again, becoming even more distinct as the burials moved closer to the present day. The most recent grave was attributed to Matilda Skrimshaw and recorded her death as 17th August 1963. Tilly considered the fact that names ran through families, but she kept coming back to her nightmares and the edict seemingly handed down through generations that Skrimshaw land should always be presided over by a cat called Matilda. The great-aunts she'd met in the windmill that afternoon were incapable of protecting the land in any way. They appeared to be reclusive and had abandoned their land – or perhaps the land had abandoned them. Hettie was right: questions needed to be asked.

The thunder was coming closer and large droplets of rain had begun to fall. Tilly joined Hettie, Dolly and Bruiser and the four friends drove back down to the campsite, arriving just before the heavens opened. The hippy cats around the campfire scattered in every direction, escaping the downpour and seeking refuge in their huts.

Serafin Parchment, who'd been keeping an eye on the windmill and its visitors, came to the rescue and beckoned the four cats into her hut as lightning streaked across the sky in answer to the loud, angry rolls of thunder. From the outside, the hut seemed little more than a rather poor and basic dwelling place, but it was a very different story inside, offering a kaleidoscope of vivid colours in wall hangings, cushions and paw-painted bits of wooden furniture. Like the windmill, the space was circular and it included the comfort of a small log burner and a mattress piled high with cushions.

At Serafin's invitation, Tilly and Dolly made themselves instantly at home on the mattress, marvelling at the décor. Bruiser hopped from one leg to the other, looking awkward next to the log burner. Hettie, realising that they must head for home as soon as the storm had passed, decided to confront Serafin, hoping for an explanation regarding the state of the two elderly cats in the windmill.

'I have to say,' she began, 'that Tilly and I were really shocked on meeting the Ancients, as you call them. It seems to me that they should be somewhere where they can be looked after and kept from harm – to others, and to themselves. They're like prisoners living in their own asylum.'

'Yeah, you're probably right there,' said Serafin, putting a kettle to boil on top of the log burner. 'Fact is, they won't be helped. They're too far gone, so we just do what we can to keep them alive.'

'But how did they get in that state?' Hettie asked.

Serafin shook her head. 'I don't know. I've only been here a year. You need to talk to Acrid – he's our leader, and I guess he knows the history. He put me in charge of them when I moved in. I just take them food and clean up a bit. Some days, they even talk to me. They like me to read to them and they sing with me sometimes, but mostly they're on another planet.'

'You mentioned ghosts. What did you mean?'

'Well, that's all the bad vibes that come from the burial ground,' Serafin explained. 'The Ancients seem to think they're under siege from all their dead ancestors. Evidently they scratch at the walls at night, trying to get to them. It's been a really bad scene over who owns the land and who doesn't, and there's a lot of dead cats in those graves who have tried to steal the land and died for it. The bad stuff has been going on for hundreds of years. As far as I can make out from the Ancients, they've been driven mad by spirits attacking the mill and trying to kill them. All a bit cosmic, really. Now, I've got mint, dandelion, butterfly pea flower and catnip teas – what would you all like?'

Serafin's visitors sat speechless at the options and the clever way that she had seemingly changed the subject. It was Dolly who broke the silence. 'I don't mind tryin' your – what was it? Pea flower and butterflies? We're tryin' out some of them 'erbal teas at Bloomers, although I wouldn't say they were entirely successful as yet. Maybe a new flavour might perk things up sales wise.'

Serafin reached into one of her painted cupboards for a plastic box and spooned some of its contents into two mugs of hot water, passing one of them to Dolly and keeping the other for herself. Tilly and Bruiser passed on a hot drink, and Hettie decided to push on with her questions. 'My friend Tilly here has been tracing her family history and she discovered that she might have two great-aunts living at Skrimshaw Priory.'

Serafin interrupted Hettie by throwing her head back and laughing. 'Well, you're way off your astral route map there. As you can see, the priory is a ruin and has been for at least a hundred years. Although there have been sightings – we tell our summer visitors to look out for the Skrimshaw Nun and the Battered Friar. Lots of our visitors claim to have seen them, but I put it down to the exceptionally good catnip that Pilgrim Tabica grows here.'

'Who is Pilgrim Tabica?' Tilly asked, liking the sound of the name.

'She is the spirit of all knowledge and our head gardener. She is descended from Tabica, Queen of the Icecreamy tribe, or at least that's what we tell the tourists. Actually she moved in here when the Icecreamy replica village on the coast was shut down due to lack of interest. She does readings in her converted ambulance and runs an omens class for our summer residential courses. She takes them off into the fields and finds stuff that's supposed to mean something, like feathers or twigs. If you were staying longer, I'd introduce you. She gets strange feelings when she goes anywhere near the windmill. Laugh a minute, really, but she's on a much higher cosmic plane than the rest of us, and she grows a lovely far-out tomato.'

Hettie was beginning to think that she'd actually drunk a mug of catnip tea, as the conversation had taken a turn for the bizarre. The storm was now raging outside. It was late afternoon and they were miles away from home, sheltering in a hippy hut. Even Bruiser had chosen himself a cushion and was now settled on the floor next to the log burner. She grabbed her own cushion and sat on it next to the door, reinstating her original conversation with Serafin. 'As I was saying, we believed that Tilly's great-aunts lived here and Tilly wrote to them and received a telegram back inviting her to tea today, which is why we are here. But it's clear that the elderly cats living in the windmill are in no way capable of sending anything, let alone a telegram. It's all a bit of a puzzle. Do you know who could have sent it and why?'

Serafin shook her head. 'I see what you're saying, but that's just not in my orbit. You really need to share that with Acrid. He's in charge of all the happenings here.'

Serafin moved past Hettie to the door and peeped out, shutting it again quickly to keep the rain out. 'It's going to do this all night,' she said, referring to the storm. 'The roads out will be flooded by now. I think you're going to have to hang out here until morning. I'll go and see if there's a caravan you can sleep in. We're having Sunday supper in the big hut. You're welcome to share bread with us if you like, and you can speak with Acrid at our holding space session afterwards.'

'Will Tabica be there?' Tilly asked excitedly.

'Definitely,' said Serafin, pulling her shawl around her. 'She'll be leading the Pranayama before we eat.'

'What's that, then?' Dolly asked.

'Breathing,' Serafin replied as she ventured out into the storm.

'Well, I'm not sure how I feel about "hanging out",' said Hettie, 'and as for "holding space" with Acrid Firestorm, it's all beginning to sound as far away from my cosmic path as I can get.'

Tilly and Dolly giggled, but Bruiser put a positive spin on it. 'It might be worth it just to 'ave a proper supper,' he pointed out.

'I can only imagine what that might be,' said Hettie. 'Tabica's tomatoes crowning a meatless loaf of dandelion leaves and pea pods!'

'But they were roastin' up a pig when we got 'ere,' Dolly reminded them. 'It might be chops, mash and gravy, and a jam sponge for afters.'

'Or maybe they were just sacrificing the pig in some tribal ceremony dreamed up by Tabica, Queen of the Icecreamy,' said Hettie, employing as much sarcasm as she could muster. 'I think we should make a run for it in Miss Scarlet. We could be home in time for a burger from Greasy Tom's van.'

'But what about the two old cats in the windmill?' said Tilly. 'I'm beginning to feel sorry for them, even if they were nasty to me. Shouldn't we stay and find out a bit more about them?'

'I don't think we 'ave any choice,' Bruiser pointed out. 'We nearly ended up in the sea comin' – with floodin' as well, we don't stand a prayer.'

Hettie could see the sense in what Bruiser was saying, and she did find the mystery behind the two old cats tantalising. Before the conversation could continue, Serafin blew in through the door, soaked to the skin, the fur on her head standing up in points and making her look more like a porcupine than a cat.

'It's all sorted,' she said. 'Van number six is all yours for the night. The Christmas decs are still up from the visitors, but at least you'll be dry. Here's the key and Tabica kicks off her Pranayama at six in the big hut. We all meet up for that before we bless the food.'

Serafin began to remove her clothes and wring them out in a bucket. For decency's sake, Bruiser headed for the door, swiftly followed by Dolly, Tilly and Hettie. They were in luck, as the rain had stopped briefly, but the puddles it had left behind were almost deep enough to swim in. The four cats picked their way carefully across the campsite, aiming for a row of caravans beyond the enclave of huts. Parked beside the caravans was an old ambulance, highly decorated in Celtic signs and lettering, which they assumed belonged to Tabica.

Van number six was the last in the row and Hettie quickly unlocked it as the rain returned. By the time they were all inside, there was hardly any room to move; the decorated Christmas tree wasn't helping, or the paper chains strung across the roof. 'I think I'd better get some sleep in Miss Scarlet tonight,' Bruiser said. 'I'll be snug as a bug in 'er sidecar, and that'll give you three a bit more space in 'ere. I'm not 'appy leavin' 'er out there with all these weird cats about.'

There was no doubt that all four friends would have preferred to sleep in Miss Scarlet's sidecar, but as that wasn't possible, they agreed to Bruiser's plan.

The caravan bore no comparison to the comfort of Serafin's hut. It was sparsely fitted out with two bench seats doubling as beds, a central table, a small sink and a single ring burner attached to a gas bottle. 'I wouldn't want a holiday in one of these,' said Tilly, investigating the cupboard under the sink and finding nothing of interest. 'It's like living in a tin can, but there's a lovely view of the priory out of the back window.'

'I suppose Acrid Firestorm would describe that as a scenic experience,' mumbled Hettie, testing out the hardness of one of the benches.

'We always 'ad a van 'oliday when I was a kitten,' said Dolly. 'We travelled to lots of places where me pa was doin' 'is stunts – followed the fun fairs, we did. Always found a nice place by the sea, and none of your flat old coastlines like 'ere. Cornwall 'as proper seas with cliffs and rock pools, and proper sand and proper pasties and proper ice creams. Lots to do when you're small, an' stayin' in a van for the summer was so excitin'. Mind you, we 'ad a rough old time at Rinsey Cove one year. Storm raged for a week, with waves lashin' the van, and we were all kept inside. I ran out of colourin' books and me pa was down to 'is last bottle of Doom Bar, which wasn't a pretty sight.'

Dolly was becoming the life and soul of the party with her Cornish tales. Bruiser was in raptures every time she opened her mouth and Tilly loved to listen to her Cornish accent. Hettie, who rarely made any new friends, had welcomed her into their circle the moment she'd set eyes on her. In Hettie Bagshot's book, Dolly Scollop was a thoroughly good sort.

The rain was now hammering on the caravan roof, making conversation almost impossible. Dolly and Tilly spent time working their way through the lockers above the bench seats in hope of finding something interesting. The Christmas theme continued, with an abandoned box of mince pies going blue and a set of pink sugar mice that had stuck together in a sticky mess, briefly reminding Tilly of her fusion cake at the Butters' bakery. The real find was a box of 'proper' tea bags, as Dolly put it, and a kettle.

'At least we might be able to have a cup of ordinary tea,' Tilly said.

'Not without milk,' Hettie retorted, 'although I suppose we'd be expected to milk our own cow round here.'

Bruiser checked his pocket watch. 'I s'pose we'd better be makin' our way to this big 'ut Serafin was talkin' about. It's 'arf past five an' pitch black out there now. If you all wait 'ere, I'll fetch me torch from Miss Scarlet's toolbox and bring in what's left of the 'amper, just in case supper is disappointin'.'

'You'd better stick this over your 'ead if you're goin' out in this,' Dolly said, passing Bruiser an old plastic carrier bag that she'd found in one of the lockers. Bruiser appreciated the thought and dutifully placed it on his head before stepping out into the storm.

He was gone for some time and the three cats were becoming concerned that he might have slipped in the mud or even worse. Hettie was about to brave the weather to go and look for him when he turned up carrying supplies. 'I found the big 'ut,' he said, 'and a bottle of milk fell into me 'amper while no one was lookin'. They're all gatherin', so we'd better get goin', but there's lots of food. It's like one of them banquets all set out on a big long table.'

Bruiser put the hamper down and led his friends out into the rain, which was now little more than a drizzle, guiding them around the puddles with the beam of his torch. The scene that greeted them as they entered the big hut was more than a little strange. Several cats stood in a circle to one side of a table laden with food. They'd joined paws and were chanting responses to a cat in the centre of the circle. Her fur had been completely shaved from her head, leaving two pink ears that stood out, and the exposed skin was decorated with various tattoos, inked in blue.

'That must be Tabica,' Tilly whispered excitedly.

'There's no doubt about that,' muttered Hettie.

The chanting suddenly stopped and Serafin broke away from the group. 'Welcome, pilgrims,' she said. 'Come and join us for Pranayama in the presence of Tabica, Queen of the Icecreamy tribe and High Priestess of the Skrimshaw Pilgrims.'

Hettie was surprised that Serafin hadn't added 'head gardener' and 'grower of tomatoes' to Tabica's attributes, but she said nothing as the four friends were drawn into the circle, where the chanting resumed. Mercifully, it didn't last long and was followed by a bout of deep breathing, conducted by Tabica, before she seized a loaf of bread from the table and proceeded to incant over it. Once all the blessings had been bestowed on the uncut wholemeal offering, there was a stampede as the cats broke from the circle, taking up their places on benches at the long table. Acrid Firestorm sat at one end and Tabica at the other, making their exalted positions very clear to everyone.

Firestorm called the table to order, inviting Hettie and her party to sit with them. As soon as they'd settled themselves, he pointed his paw around the table, doing the introductions. Bod the Inhaler; Dryad the Oak Feller and Master Carpenter; Anger the Fox Slayer; Cambric the Weaver of Threads; Marjoram the Herbalist; Clawdelia, Provider of Feasts; Serafin Parchment, Keeper of the Ancients; Hathor, the Bringer of Music and Dance; and Tabica, Queen of the Icecreamy and Goddess of Enlightenment.

Hettie responded by offering their own names in brief. She left Tilly until last, calling her Matilda on purpose, which caused a heart-stopping moment as all the pilgrims looked in her direction. Their reaction spoke volumes and Hettie was even more determined to speak with Acrid after supper.

On Firestorm's signal, the cats around the table pitched in, passing bowls and plates of roasted meats, stews, chunks of freshly baked breads and savoury tarts to each other, all washed down with goblets of home-made wine. When the savoury course had been exhausted, the cat introduced as Clawdelia swept away the empty plates and replaced them with sweet pastries, giant fruit jellies and mountains of saffron cakes.

Even for Hettie, the eating was relentless, and Tilly gave up halfway through the puddings, passing the food she couldn't manage to Bruiser. Dolly was ecstatic about the saffron cakes, as they were native to Cornwall, and Clawdelia promised to give her the recipe when she'd finished clearing away.

It was nine o'clock, by Bruiser's pocket watch, before the feasting ended. The table was cleared and moved to the side of the hut, and cushions were placed in a giant circle on the floor. Dryad stepped forward to light a firepit bringing instant warmth to the gathering as the cats chose their seating and stretched themselves out for a communal licking and cleaning session after their meal.

Eventually Acrid Firestorm pulled his cushion into the centre of the circle to address the gathering. 'Pilgrims,' he began, 'it is time for you to raise any issues that may disrupt your peace in this place and to admit to any vows you may have broken and take your punishments.'

The cats all looked down at their paws in silence except for Clawdelia, who stood up from her cushion. Firestorm acknowledged her and she spoke. 'My Leader and Pilgrims, I must confess to breaking the fasting last Monday by baking and eating a loaf of bread. I offer no excuse except to say that I am hopeful of kittens in the next few days and I am constantly hungry.'

A murmur of surprise went around the circle and all eyes fell on Cambric, the Weaver of Threads. It was clear that he was responsible for Clawdelia's condition and Firestorm asked him to stand next to her. 'It is joyful news that new life is being nurtured,' he said, 'but the taking of food on fasting days is a crime committed against your fellow Pilgrims. Will you, Cambric, bear some of Clawdelia's punishment for this offence?'

Cambric reached for Clawdelia's paw before responding. 'I will,' he said, bowing his head.

Firestorm considered the two cats in front of him before offering his judgement. Hettie, Tilly, Bruiser and Dolly all held their breath, now caught up in the drama of the 'holding space' session. 'Clawdelia's crime carries a severe punishment. The survival of the Skrimshaw Pilgrims relies on truth and responsibility to others and kittens must be planned for,' Firestorm declared. 'Normally the penalty would be banishment from our land, but I will be lenient. Cambric, you will fast for a full five days without food or water. And you, Clawdelia, will work all the daylight hours to clean the caravans in addition to your work as provider of food.' Clawdelia and Cambric bowed their heads in deference to their leader and returned to their cushions in the circle. 'Are there any further matters before I call on Hathor to entertain us?' Firestorm asked.

This was Hettie's moment and she didn't squander it. She struggled off her cushion and stood up, commanding the interest of the whole company; she was a stranger in their midst and it was rare for Acrid Firestorm to be questioned by any cat. 'As visitors to this place, we are concerned by the state of mind we find Matilda and Matilda Skrimshaw in and would ask you to explain why they are virtual prisoners in the windmill. Under whose direction have you taken over their land?'

A hiss of shock and disapproval ran round the circle at Hettie's audacious challenge to their leader. Firestorm himself looked more than a little uncomfortable, but braved it out. 'As I told you when you arrived, I am descended from Ragland Firestorm. As the Ancients have no inheritors, the daughters of Matilda the Shield Maiden are soon to give up their line to the sons of Ragland.'

'If you don't mind my saying so, that is nonsense,' Hettie pointed out. 'Those two elderly cats in that windmill are still very much alive, and clearly frightened out of their minds by the set-up you have here, which in itself is ridiculous. What is all this rubbish about pilgrims, punishments and fasting? And what gives you the right to rule over these cats sitting here? This place is nothing more than a hippy holiday camp left over from Woodstock, but there's a much darker side to it than mud and music.'

Even Tilly was shocked by Hettie's outburst and Bruiser stiffened, ready to fight off any reprisals, but there were none. All eyes were on Firestorm and what he might do next, but it was Tabica who stood to defend him. 'We are rescued here from a world that rejected us – lost souls who have found peace and enlightenment in our leader. He has given us purpose, shelter and belief. You know nothing of our ways, as you come from a world of advantage and greed. You are outsiders, looking in and seeing what you want to see.'

Hettie stood her ground and was starting to enjoy herself. 'With great respect, you know nothing about us or the world we come from. I know what it's like to be homeless and without food. It is a cruel world out there and my friends and I spend our time trying to make it better. We don't join cults to be protected from real life. We don't surrender our freedoms to land-grabbing imposters and we don't lock our helpless elderly cats away in windmills.'

Tabica put her paws together in a silent prayer and resumed her place on her cushion, no longer wishing to engage. Acrid Firestorm finally found his voice and announced that the evening was over, instructing everyone to return to their huts. The pilgrims quickly dispersed, leaving only Hettie and her friends with the leader. Without witnesses, Firestorm's demean-our completely changed. He strode towards Hettie as if he was going to pounce on her, but Bruiser moved swiftly to her defence and the cat backed away. Tilly and Dolly left their cushions and stepped forward to flank Hettie in solidarity.

'I don't know who you really are or why you've come here,' Firestorm hissed, 'but I want you gone from my land by first light tomorrow – or you'll be sorry.'

Undaunted by his threat, Hettie decided to continue her conversation with the hippy cat; there were several questions to which she wanted answers. 'I think we have made our position clear,' she said. 'My friend Tilly was invited here by the cats whom we believe to be her great-aunts – which, incidentally, means that Tilly is very likely to be able to inherit all the Skrimshaw land after her aunts have died. Regardless of that, it is clear that the Ancients, as you call them, did not send out the invitation – so the big question is who did, and why? As a detective, might I suggest that one of your pilgrims isn't as happy with you as you might think and sent the invitation to muddy the waters a little? It seems that your so-called Viking heritage may be in question and if Tilly can prove that she is directly descended from this Matilda the Shield Maiden, then you my friend will be the one packing up and leaving.'

Firestorm seemed very unsettled by Hettie's words but the fight in him wasn't completely exhausted. 'The Ancients have already accepted me as their rightful heir in exchange for the care we give them. If we hadn't fed and looked after them, they would have died long ago. The Skrimshaw Pilgrims have worked the land and made it profitable and we will reap the benefits of true ownership in the fullness of time.'

'And what proof have you that you are descended from this Ragland cat? After all, the Vikings were here a very long time ago and at some stage the Skrimshaws got involved. You, I assume, are not a Skrimshaw? As I understand it, the title to this land can only be passed down the female line, and only by cats called Matilda, so I'm not sure where that leaves you, Mr Firestorm – if that's your real name. Unless you're planning on changing it to Matilda?'

The cat was now incensed, and Hettie decided for safety's sake to change the subject. 'You say that the two Matildas in the windmill have accepted you as the heir to this land in exchange for being looked after. Having visited them lately, they do seem in a very poor state – feral, in fact. Can you explain why they are so mentally fragile? They behaved like a couple of caged birds, beating their wings against an unseen terror.'

'I couldn't say why that is,' said Firestorm. 'I haven't seen them for over a year. Serafin looks after them. They passed the land to me three years ago and I haven't had much to do with them since. They have chosen to be reclusive and that's nothing to do with me. Now, I suggest that you go back to your caravan and sleep. I want you all out of here in the morning. You have disrupted our peace and your claim on the land is futile. You can bring as many cats called Matilda here as you like, but I will never give up my birthright. Like my ancestor Ragland Firestorm I would sooner die.'

Acrid appeared to have regained his composure, and Hettie was bored with him anyway. The four friends left him to his own thoughts and paddled across to the caravan with the help of Bruiser's torch. The rest of the camp was silent, as if brooding over the night's events, but the true horror of its consequences would not be revealed until the morning.

Chapter Nine

The caravan was cold and unwelcoming and Hettie was in two minds as to whether to brave the floods and head for home or stick it out until morning. She was keen to return to the windmill to try to understand the circumstances surrounding the two Matildas and how they had ended up the way they were, but there was Tilly and her feelings to consider. She'd been quiet since they'd arrived. The attack from the elderly cat had shocked her and she'd said very little since. Now she sat on a bench seat, staring out of the back window into the darkness and apparently in a very faraway place.

'Penny for them?' Hettie said, sitting down next to her friend. Tilly turned away from the window and Hettie could see that she had been crying. 'Cheer up,' she said. 'It might never happen.'

'It already has,' said Tilly, wiping her eyes with her paw. 'I hate this place. I hated it before we even got here. When I had those nightmares at home, even though they seemed so real, I convinced myself that they were just nasty dreams, but as soon as we arrived here it was like walking into my nightmare again. Everything is so familiar – the windmill, the burial ground, the priory. They're all in the right place and I'm so frightened that this is going to be my destiny.'

'What do you mean?' Hettie asked gently, troubled now by the sadness etched across Tilly's face.

'I mean that this is all about me inheriting these lands – and I don't want them. I was happy with our little room at the bakery, with all our friends in the town and the lovely lunches at Bloomers. Even Lavender Stamp seems bearable compared to all the nasty cats who live here. I feel very sad for those poor old cats in the windmill, but they were nasty too.'

Hettie suddenly felt responsible now that she understood how Tilly felt. She realised that she had started an unwanted war with Acrid Firestorm, and, in her keenness to depose his claim on the land, she had made Tilly even more unhappy. 'We really don't have to take this any further,' she said. 'By this time tomorrow, you'll be tucked up in your blankets by our fire, eating a Butters' pie and putting all this down to a dodgy day out. It's my fault for getting too involved with those ridiculous hippies and the way they've moved in and taken over.'

'But you're right,' said Tilly. 'Their treatment of those poor old cats is terrible, and I know we should try to help them because that's what we do. We try to put things right in all the cases we take on, and in my heart I know that really bad things have been happening here and we should do something about it before we leave. But I don't want it to be about me and the land. I want to live in our town and grow old there. I'm not Matilda. I'm just plain old Tilly Jenkins.'

'There's nothing plain about you,' Dolly said, putting the kettle on the hob as Bruiser turned on the gas bottle. 'You are the nicest friend a cat could 'ave – thoughtful, funny, sweet-natured, even if you are very messy with your food. What more could you ask for? I don't think this place would suit you at all. How would you survive without the bakery and what about all those murders you and Hettie solve? You couldn't give all that up for a ruin and a windmill.'

'Then there's Miss Scarlet,' Bruiser added. 'She wouldn't be 'appy livin' 'ere in all this mud, so I think you're right to stick with the town.'

Tilly was greatly cheered up by her friends and even managed a smile. They'd lifted the burden of the land from her shoulders, and now she was happy to visit the windmill again in the morning before they headed for home. Relatives or not, the elderly cats deserved better than the dire incarceration they found themselves in. If she and her friends could do anything to make their lives better, they should at least try.

The four cats enjoyed a hot cup of milky tea before Bruiser braved the puddles and made his way to Miss Scarlet's sidecar. Tilly and Dolly elected to share one of the benches, leaving Hettie a whole one to herself, as she was the bigger cat. Dolly had found some blankets under the benches, which brought a little more comfort to a cold and miserable overnight stay.

Tilly felt that she had hardly closed her eyes before her nightmares returned. This time, she faced an unimaginable horror.

****

May 1st 1060

Matilda awoke to a sea of carnage. The hut where she and her sisters slept had become a slaughterhouse and the deer skins that kept them warm all winter were now soaked in blood. All around her lay the bodies of her sisters, their throats cut as they slept. She wanted to cry out, but no sound came from her, just the fear that she would be next.

It was barely light. Embers from the central wood fire smouldered in the pit, but brought no comfort. She shut her eyes to block out the horror, hoping that when she opened them again all would be well and she would feel the warmth of her sister's body lying next to her. But there was no warmth, just a stiffened corpse whose spirit had flown, along with her other sisters. She no longer knew them in death. Their silence was alien to her – no laughter, no teasing, no joy to greet another day. Why had they left her so alone, and what of her mother and father? Were they lying slaughtered in their hut? Had they been raided by a wandering tribe at dead of night? There had been no fighting or she would have heard it. And why had she been spared? Perhaps the killer had been disturbed, but what would happen now?

The door swung open, flooding the hut with early morning light. Matilda hid under her deer skin, holding her breath for fear that the slightest movement would betray her. The scream, when it came, seared through her as if she'd been cut in half by her father's sword, but the voice that followed the scream was familiar. She dared to lift her head and was instantly snatched from her bed and carried out into the sunlight. Elswyth had been there from the moment she was born – a slave, but a cat who cared for her family: nurse, protector and a loyal servant to her mother, Matilda the Shield Maiden.

Elswyth's scream had been heard across the village. Cats came from their huts, rubbing the sleep out of their eyes, and gathered around Matilda. Some ventured into the hut to see for themselves; others stood in silence at the magnitude of what had happened.

Matilda's mother was at prayer in the Priory, oblivious to the fact that nearly all her kittens had been slaughtered. A messenger was sent and soon she came – a warrior Queen, loved by all who served her and now betrayed by the cat who slept at her side. Only the night before, little Matilda had heard her father declare that he would take her mother's lands and make them his own. He had sworn to rid her of her heirs, to wipe out the female line, but all who had witnessed his drunken threats had thought nothing of them as they went to their beds.

Now the warrior Queen wept and Matilda clung to her mother's robes as her dead sisters were brought out into the sunlight, away from their bloody tomb.

Ragland Firestorm was dragged from his bed, still bloodied from his night's work, and Matilda stared as he was bound and taken to the Great Hall. All were soon assembled, and Matilda watched from behind the great chair that her mother sat in. The Queen's judgement was swift as Firestorm begged for mercy. She raised her sword and cut off his head with one blow, then ordered that his body be taken to the burial pit beyond the huts.

There would be no Viking warrior funeral, no boat set ablaze with arrows, no welcome from Odin in the Halls of Valhalla. Ragland Firestorm's body and all his worldly goods were taken from the village and buried in a simple pit, where time would forget that he had ever existed.

****

Tilly awoke to her heart pounding in her chest. It took her several minutes to work out where she was, and why. Her fur was matted with sweat and she was cold, as her blanket had slipped to the floor of the caravan. Dolly was still fast asleep at the other end of the bench and Hettie was under her covers and snoring. Tilly clambered down from the bench and pulled the blanket around her. She was exhausted, her head ached, and even though the blanket offered some warmth she couldn't stop shivering. Her eyes were drawn to the old priory, framed in the back window of the caravan. It was just starting to get light and the ancient ruin looked as if it had been painted onto the glass. Everything was strangely unreal.

It was far too early to wake her friends, and in spite of the cold she needed some fresh air. She pulled on her cardigan and tiptoed out of the caravan, quietly closing the door behind her. She was relieved to see that the hippy camp hadn't changed since the night before, and that the windmill was still there across the field. There had been no windmill in her nightmare and, as the early winter sun rose above the priory, she put the night's terrors down to indigestion and Acrid Firestorm's behaviour at the Sunday supper. Soon they would be leaving this place and she would never have to return.

Feeling a little better, she decided to take a look around the priory ruins. She followed the line of the old wall until she came to an arch which was almost intact. In an open space beyond, a jagged low wall of footings was the only clue to the original accommodation. Some of the outside walls rose high into the sky, testifying to the rooms that had once made up the upper storeys and offering gashes in the stonework where once there had been windows. Tilly sat on one of the low walls and looked around her. On one side was evidence of a huge fireplace, which brought back the memory of her first nightmare and the murder of Matthew Katkins. She looked for any signs of a staircase but there was nothing – only fading scars intermittently marking out a memory where cats had once gone about their daily lives. She felt them now as she sat breathing in the history – her history, perhaps, but nothing she would swap her happy life for.

A sudden movement to her left made her jump. She stood up and cautiously approached one of the more complete dividing walls. Another archway led into a type of antechamber. She faltered briefly before entering, convincing herself that a bird had disturbed her. A murder of crows sat high up on the walls, watching her every move and challenging her not to overstay her welcome. The passing of time had given them secure tenure over the crumbling edifice, safe places to roost and build their nests away from the predatory nature of bloodthirsty cats.

The space that Tilly found herself in now was very different from the rest of the ruin. It was tucked away, protected by the outer walls from centuries of weather. The worn stones that made up the floor had been swept clean and cared for, and in the centre stood a large, rectangular altar stone, at least ten times bigger than Tilly. It was ornately decorated with cats of some ancient religious order dressed in flowing robes, their cowls mysteriously obscuring most of their faces. There was a peace about the stone and Tilly reached out to touch it, her claw tracing some of the images carved there.

'It's very beautiful, isn't it?' came a voice from behind her.

Tilly turned, expecting to see Serafin or one of the other pilgrims, but instead a nun presented herself in a shaft of sunlight, like some heavenly being. Tilly rubbed her eyes, expecting the vision to disappear, but the figure moved closer. 'Are you a ghost?' she whispered. 'I don't mind if you are, as long as you don't hurt me.'

'It depends what you mean by a ghost,' the cat replied. 'I am not dead, but I am a shade of who I should be.'

Tilly felt lost for words. She knew that she should be frightened, but the serenity of the figure before her felt comforting. Eventually she managed to pluck up the courage to ask the obvious question. 'Am I allowed to know who you are?'

'Of course. I am Sister Constance Surprise, keeper of the Skrimshaw Priory, from the Holy Order of St Matilda the Peace-Weaver. My ancestors are those you see on the altar stone.'

'And do you live in this ruin?' Tilly asked.

'Yes, and here I must stay, within these cloisters. I am banished from my lands.'

'By Acrid Firestorm?' Tilly suggested.

'No, by my sisters, who have disinherited me. I was firstborn to my mother in a litter of three, but after my mother's tragic death, my sisters wanted the land for themselves and cast me out when we were all very young. I was given to a religious order and as I grew older I just wanted to come home. I returned to this place and my sisters let me stay as long as I ventured no further than the priory – so this is where I live.'

'And are your sisters the old cats who live in the windmill, the two Matildas?' Tilly asked. 'You seem much younger than they are.'

Sister Constance smiled for the first time. 'That is because they are haunted by what they did. Time has ravaged them, and

91

insanity has claimed them, and they dwell in their own Tower of Babel, united in their confusion and hate for each other.'

Tilly knew nothing about Towers of Babel, but she did want to raise the Matilda question. 'I understood from the history of this place that the land has to belong to a cat called Matilda – and there are two Matildas in the windmill. If you are a Constance, how can they have cheated you out of your land?'

'Because, like you, I am a Matilda and they are not. My mother called them Romew and Remew, after the twin cats who founded the great city of Rome. Like many of my ancestors, she was a visionary and could see into the future while carrying the history of the past. She had dreams of things to come, but I was too young to understand her warnings. After her death, my sisters changed their names to claim the land.'

'But how do you know that I'm a Matilda?' Tilly asked.

'Because I read your letter. It was delivered here at the priory and I sent you a telegram to come.'

'But I thought you weren't allowed to leave the priory?' Tilly said. 'And why would you invite me?'

'My faithful friend Dikon brings me food and anything else I need. He lives in the woods beyond the wall. He sent the telegram for me, and I invited you because I believe that you are my great-niece. My sisters have allowed strangers to take over the land and Acrid Firestorm is an imposter. The ancestor he lays claim to committed a terrible crime against Matilda the Shield Maiden, murdering all but one of her kittens back in the eleventh century. Firestorm and his followers have no right to be here. You are the future of this land and I hoped you might fight for it.'

Constance's words hit home, forcing Tilly back into her nightmare and the horror of the bloodied bedchamber and the dead kittens. She felt her legs give way and tried to save herself from falling by reaching out to the altar stone, but hit her head against it.

Chapter Ten

Hettie woke to the sound of hammering on the door and for a few split seconds she expected it to be one of the Butter sisters offering breakfast. Coming to, she realised her mistake as she stared up at the festive paper chains on the roof of the caravan. The hammering came again. Dolly sat up, looking dazed, and Hettie staggered to the door. It was Serafin who greeted her, and with some urgency. 'You'd better come quickly,' she said, hopping from one foot to the other. 'Your friend is staggering about covered in blood.'

Hettie immediately thought of Bruiser, then looked back into the caravan and realised that Tilly was missing. 'Which friend?' she barked back at the hippy cat, but didn't wait for a reply. Pushing past her visitor, she ran towards the huts. There was no sign of Tilly in the campsite, but as Hettie looked towards the windmill, she spotted her weaving a very unsteady course across the field.

Bruiser, who was just stirring from the sidecar, followed Hettie's gaze and the two cats set off at speed. By the time they caught up with Tilly, she'd reached the burial ground. Serafin was right: Tilly's fur was matted with blood and she had a nasty gash to her head, which was still bleeding. She was talking nonsense and clearly concussed. 'Whatever have you been up to?' Hettie asked, more than a little out of breath.

Tilly stared back at her then collapsed at the door to the windmill. Bruiser immediately came to the rescue, picking Tilly up and carrying her back across the field to the campsite. Hettie was about to follow them, but was distracted by the noise of an unsecured open window swinging against the wall of the windmill, and then by a blast of wind that briefly set the giant sails in motion. She looked up and, to her horror, saw a cat dangling from one of them, suspended high up with a rope around its neck. It looked like an abandoned rag doll, its arms hanging loosely by its side. Hettie squinted, but couldn't make out the features as the head was turned towards the wall of the mill. The only thing she was sure of was that the cat was very dead.

She hurried across the field to raise the alarm and find out what had happened to Tilly, hoping that the two incidents weren't connected. Serafin met her halfway, carrying a basket of food and her tambourine. 'Your friend is lying down in the caravan. It looks like she's been involved in a bit of a bad scene and there's a nasty cut on her head. I'll bring some of Marjoram's special marshmallow cream to put on it after I've fed the Ancients.'

'That's kind,' said Hettie, 'but I wouldn't go any closer to the windmill at the moment. There seems to be a dead cat hanging from one of the sails. We need a ladder or something to get the body down.'

Serafin dropped her basket and the tambourine and started to run towards the mill. Hettie called to Cambric and Bod as she passed through the camp, and they followed on after Serafin. Tilly was sitting up on the bench when Hettie reached the caravan, and Bruiser was making tea while Dolly bathed her injury. 'Bad old cut this,' Dolly said. 'Looks like she's had an argument with a brick wall or a Cornish cliff face.'

'It was the altar,' said Tilly weakly. 'I must have fainted after what Sister Constance Surprise told me about the dead kittens that were in my nightmare. Firestorm murdered them in the hut and Matilda the Shield Maiden cut off his head.'

Hettie shared a look of concern with Dolly and Bruiser. 'I think the sooner we get Tilly home the better,' she said. 'All this nonsense is making her ill, and after what I've just seen hanging from one of the sails on that bloody windmill, we need to get out of here as fast as we can.'

Bruiser and Dolly looked puzzled but it was clear from Hettie's attitude that she was in no mood for questions. Bruiser passed a cup of hot milky tea to Tilly, and was about to go and get Miss Scarlet ready for the journey when Acrid Firestorm burst through the caravan door. 'So your plan is to claim this land by murder,' he hissed, looking across at Tilly. 'You won't get away with it. Better cats than you have tried and failed.'

Tilly began to sob and Hettie stood between her and Firestorm. 'What are you talking about?' she demanded. 'If you're referring to the body hanging from the windmill, I would look closer to home. Tilly had nothing to do with it, but if you'd like us to investigate, we could look into who did.'

Firestorm scowled at Hettie's suggestion. 'You, investigate? I don't need to look any further than her,' he said, jabbing his paw in Tilly's direction. 'Just look at her, covered in the blood of her night's work.'

'It was an accident,' Tilly protested.

'Well, why don't we all go and take a look at this "accident"?' Firestorm suggested. 'If you've the stomach for it, follow me.'

Bruiser was first out of the caravan and was instantly flanked by Bod and Anger, both carrying rough wooden clubs. Hettie and Dolly helped Tilly to her feet, and they joined the others outside. It was becoming very clear to them that they were under threat. Firestorm was last out, and took up a position at the back of the party while Bod and Anger escorted Bruiser across to the campsite.

All eyes turned on them as they were marched through the enclave and on up to the windmill. The dead cat was still hanging from the sail but Firestorm took no notice of it and pushed open the door of the mill. 'In you go, all of you – time to pay another visit to the Ancients,' he said, 'and if you're thinking of making a run for it, my two Pilgrims here will be obliged to cause you some pain.'

Bod and Anger stationed themselves at the door of the mill, making any escape impossible. Firestorm led the four friends upstairs to the room where Hettie and Tilly had met the two Matildas.

The scene was one of extreme horror. Dolly and Tilly retched at the sight before them and Hettie froze, taking in every minute detail. The two fireside chairs were on their backs and the fire itself smouldered in the grate, offering no warmth. There was food spilt on the floor, but it was the blood splattered across the walls that registered, even more than the dead cat lying on the rucked-up hearthrug; it was as if some maniac artist had gone berserk with a tin of red paint.

The body was only just recognisable as one of the Matildas. The attack had been vicious and prolonged, and lumps of blood-matted fur lay all around the corpse. There were puncture wounds in Matilda's neck and the dress she wore had been torn to shreds.

Eventually Hettie found her voice. 'Are you seriously suggesting that Tilly did this?'

'I'm not suggesting anything,' said Firestorm. 'The proof is here for all to see and the motive is clear. This cat you call your friend is covered in blood and was wandering around near the windmill early this morning. From the moment you all arrived here yesterday, it was obvious that you were on a mission to steal the land away from us – and all you thought stood in your way were the Ancients. You didn't bargain for me and the rest of the Pilgrims.'

Hettie decided not to challenge Firestorm's accusation but moved swiftly to the open window, still swinging on its hinges. There was blood on the sill, and – as she stretched her neck beyond it – she could see the other cat hanging by a rope. The wind had turned the sail just out of reach, but Hettie was close enough to the body to see that it was the other Matilda. She, too, was covered in blood and her head sat at a very strange angle; her neck had obviously been broken.

Hettie came away from the window and Bruiser moved from the top of the stairs to stand by her. 'I'm afraid this all looks a little too convenient,' she said, facing up to the hippy cat. 'Tilly had already made it clear to us that she had no wish to own or inhabit this land in any way, and it was only the storm that kept us from leaving last night. You, however, seemed to think that all this would be yours after the Ancients had died. As a detective, there are several conclusions I could come to, but one of them wouldn't be that Tilly was guilty of this carnage. You, or any one of your followers, could have done it. I suggest that you call your pilgrims together and start asking some questions before putting out wild accusations that make no sense at all.'

Acrid Firestorm shook his head. 'No. I'm satisfied I have the culprits right here and this is where you'll all stay. I shall announce several days of feasting to celebrate my inheritance and then I think we may offer you all a Viking funeral when my Pilgrims burn this windmill down. It's of no use to me, for I shall build a great house befitting the sons of Ragland Firestorm. Now I must leave you, as there is much to do.'

'But what about the bodies?' Hettie asked. 'Surely, as your benefactors, you owe them the respect of a decent burial.'

'Like I said, there's no higher honour than a Viking funeral pyre,' said Firestorm. Then he turned and hurried away down the stairs, banging the windmill door shut behind him.

Chapter Eleven

Hettie and Bruiser watched from the window as Bod, Anger and Firestorm crossed the field to the campsite. 'So what do we do now?' said Tilly. 'This is all my fault, and we're going to be burnt alive.'

'Of course we're not,' said Hettie. 'We just need a plan, but the first thing we have to do is check out the windmill to see if there's any possibility of escape. I'm assuming that Firestorm has locked the main door, but there may be other ways of getting out of here. We're only on the first floor and there must be more floors above us up those stairs. Perhaps there are windows we could climb out of.'

'I can't do heights,' said Tilly.

'And I'm not partial to a broken leg either,' Dolly agreed.

'Then I think we should try and make ourselves comfortable on the ground floor,' Hettie suggested. 'Bruiser and I will do a recce to check out the possibilities and sort out the mess in here. We need to find something to put this body in, if only for decency's sake.'

'What about the one 'angin out there?' Bruiser asked.

'I think we'll have to leave it. The sail has turned and it's out of reach now, but whoever did this must have used that window to put the cat out there. What I don't understand is why they didn't just leave it here with the other body.'

Tilly and Dolly made their way down the stairs, where there was very little comfort to be had, but both cats felt better being away from the carnage on the first floor. Hettie and Bruiser did their best to wrap the body in the hearthrug and clean up around it. There was nothing they could do about the walls. Bruiser dragged the two fireside chairs downstairs to make things a little more bearable on the ground floor, and Hettie took down some logs and a box of matches that she'd found.

Dolly and Tilly set about laying a fire while Bruiser and Hettie hunted round for anything useful in the room that the Matildas had lived in. The food that had been spilt on the floor was irretrievable, but Hettie found a packet of rich tea biscuits, a small jar of toffees, a very old tin of tea and some dried milk powder in a sewing basket next to the fireplace. She put them to one side and headed towards the second flight of stairs. 'I suppose we'd better get our bearings in this place and see what's on the next floor,' she said, climbing up with Bruiser close behind.

The second floor was similar to the first, but smaller and seemingly full of junk. There were bits of old furniture, a pair of deckchairs faded by sunnier days, a rusted bird cage and a rail of coats and dresses, suggesting that the two Matildas had once known a happier life. Like the other rooms, it was round with two very small windows that gave hardly any light. Bruiser tried both, but they were nailed shut. 'No chance of gettin' out there,' he said. 'That's too small even for Tilly t' squeeze through, and it's a sheer drop even if she could. We've got more chance with them ones below – they're a bit bigger, and maybe if we 'ad a good puff of wind one of us could grab onto one of them sails as it came round.'

'The trouble is we'd be seen from the campsite if we tried any sort of escape like that,' Hettie pointed out. 'And without Miss Scarlet, how would we get out of here?'

'I could try when it gets dark,' said Bruiser. 'If they're 'avin' a feast, they might not notice me. If I could just get to me bike, I could run 'em all down if I 'ad to.'

'You could try, but how would the rest of us get out of here if you failed? I can't see Tilly and Dolly leaping out of windows, and Tilly's still in shock from her accident. That head wound looks really nasty, and putting yourself in danger won't help any of us. I think we should sit tight and see what happens next. One or more of those cats is a murderer, but they're not all like Firestorm. Serafin, Dryad, Cambric and Clawdelia seem decent, so maybe we should keep our claws crossed for a rebellion. Acrid Firestorm says he intends to murder us by setting fire to the windmill, but maybe that plan won't go down very well with the rest of them.'

Bruiser could see the sense in what Hettie was saying, and he agreed that Tilly wasn't fit to do anything that would put her in even more danger. The two cats began to search the junk for anything useful. Bruiser found some old moth-eaten curtains that they could use for blankets, and put the deckchairs to one side. Hettie spent some time trying to get into an old trunk and eventually managed to break the rusted lock.

On first inspection, the trunk seemed to be full of crumpled bits of paper and photographs, but there were a couple of books too and a well-clawed old Bible. As they hadn't worked out a way to escape, Hettie decided to lug the trunk down to the ground floor for Tilly and Dolly to look through. She hoped it would serve as a welcome distraction from the fate that Firestorm was contemplating for them.

Bruiser struck lucky with an old first-aid tin. The tin itself was rusted but the contents were still intact; as well as plasters and bandages, it contained a tube of ointment for cuts and grazes which he pounced on for Tilly, hoping that it might help to fight any infection from her injury.

By the time Hettie and Bruiser brought their treasures to the ground floor, Dolly and Tilly had achieved a cheery blaze in the red brick fireplace and their situation looked far less bleak. Dolly pounced on the cream and plastered Tilly's cut with it, while Bruiser set up the deckchairs. The four friends sat round the fire to contemplate their situation.

'Firestorm said he was planning several days of feasting,' said Hettie, 'which gives us some time, but food is going to be a problem. We're going to have to eke out what we have between us. We've got a packet of biscuits, a jar of toffees, an old tin of tea and some powdered milk that probably lived through the Second World War.'

'An' I can offer a bag of Pengelly fruit drops,' said Dolly, pulling a bag out of her pocket. 'They're good thirst quenchers when you're stuck without a nice cup of tea.'

Tilly reached into her cardigan pocket and triumphantly pulled out two custard creams that looked as tired and worn out as she was. Bruiser added four liquorice allsorts to the pile of supplies. 'It's just like *The Wind in the Willows*,' Tilly pointed out, 'the bit when Mole finds his house again and they go through the cupboards looking for food for supper.'

'Oh, I love that book,' said Dolly, warming to the subject. 'That Mr Toad makes me larf with all them scrapes 'e gets in, although I'm not keen on them weasels an' stoats – good they got their comeuppance.'

Hettie was pleased to see that Tilly was back in the real world again. Kenneth Greyhair's masterpiece was her favourite book and a story she called on often to channel her own life experiences through. It was a good moment to leave her, comparing notes on the riverbank folk with Dolly, while Hettie and Bruiser completed their recce of the windmill. There was at least one floor left to explore.

Bruiser led the way. The stairs to the third floor of the mill were almost vertical and the hatch that opened into the space was small and quite claustrophobic to navigate. There was very little room, because the old machinery that had worked the mill was still in place. Giant cogs embedded in the roof beams and all manner of ironmongery gave testament to the days when the mill had been productive.

The windows were nothing more than slits in the walls, but the view from them was spectacular. Hettie looked out across the campsite and dramatic priory ruins to a substantial patch of woodland beyond. The window opposite offered distant reed beds, the sea and a clear view of the gatehouse where they'd first encountered Acrid Firestorm. Now, as far as Hettie was concerned, that gatehouse led to the road home. 'There's nothing here of any use to us,' she said, moving towards the stairs. 'No chance of escape and nothing to eat.'

Bruiser was about to follow her, but noticed a bucket which had clearly been strategically placed under a leak in the roof. 'I reckon if we boil this up on the fire we could 'ave a cup of tea, at least. Must 'ave filled up in the storm last night. I always used rainwater in me roamin' days ta brew up.'

Hettie was delighted with the find and remembered that she'd seen an old cracked tea set in the room on the second floor, thrown in a box with some rusted pans. With some difficulty, the two cats manoeuvred the bucket of water down the stairs, then Hettie collected the box of pots on their way back to Tilly and Dolly.

In their absence, there had been a major breakthrough on the ground floor. Dolly had been investigating the old discarded flour sacks and had found that one of them contained a few sprouting potatoes. 'Jacket spuds on the menu tonight!' she announced gleefully. 'I'm goin' to stick these in this old tin I've found an' put 'em in that fire, just like we do on bonfire night. Hot dinners all round!'

'An' a nice cuppa tea ta wash 'em down,' said Bruiser, filling one of Hettie's old pans with water from the bucket and placing it on the metal fret that ran along the front of the fire.

'Well, if we weren't locked in and under siege from Firestorm and his cronies, I'd say we were beginning to have a nice time,' Hettie pointed out. 'Except for the bodies, of course.'

It was already the middle of the afternoon, and they had had a long day. They all agreed that an early supper and a good night's sleep would be the best plan of action. Dolly prepared her potatoes and pushed the tin into the fire, giving them hopes of something hot to eat. Bruiser collected more wood from the first floor and Hettie allocated a toffee each to keep them going. Tilly dozed on and off by the fire, nursing her injury and trying hard not to fall into a deep sleep in case her nightmares returned.

Dolly's baked potatoes were a triumph, and all agreed that – even though they weren't drenched in butter – they were hot and tasty. Bruiser's tea was also acceptable, although the powdered milk insisted on floating on the top, but Tilly was allowed to sweeten hers with one of Dolly's fruit drops on account of her having sustained an injury. After supper, the four cats tucked themselves up in their chairs, swathed in the old curtains that Bruiser had found, and chatted over the day's events. Tilly didn't feel strong enough to talk about her encounter with Sister Constance Surprise and was beginning to doubt that it had ever happened, but she was pleased to be surrounded by her friends in relative comfort.

'I 'ope Molly is managin' OK at Bloomers,' Dolly said. 'She's got the line dancin' club supper tonight, an' Bunty Basham's cricket meetin' tomorrow. She'll be rushed off 'er feet, not to mention organisin' Marmite Spratt's wake.'

'I suppose the Butters will be wondering where we've all got to,' added Hettie. 'They would have expected us back last night.'

'Maybe they'll turn up in their Morris Minor ta rescue us,' Bruiser suggested hopefully.

'If they did, I think they'd give Acrid Firestorm a run for his money,' Hettie said, 'and speaking of Firestorm, I think we'd better barricade ourselves in tonight. We don't want to suffer the same fate as the two Matildas.'

'Romew and Remew,' Tilly corrected before she could stop herself, but no one heard her. Hettie and Bruiser were already halfway up the stairs looking for something to block the front door with and Dolly had her head in the potato sack, checking to see if there were enough left for another meal.

Minutes later, Hettie and Bruiser returned with an old sideboard they'd found in the room of junk. It was heavy and not the easiest thing to carry down two flights of stairs. At one point, it managed to trap Hettie against the wall, but Bruiser gave it an almighty shove, allowing it to freewheel and bump itself to the bottom of the stairs. The sideboard landed on its back, shedding one of its doors, but there was enough of it left to offer a substantial barrier between the occupants of the windmill and the outside world. Bruiser and Hettie dragged it into place, pushing it hard up against the outer door. 'That should keep those bloody hippies at bay and give us a peaceful night,' Hettie said, 'but god knows what tomorrow will bring.'

Chapter Twelve

If Hettie was hoping for a peaceful night, she was going to be disappointed. After Bruiser had built up the fire, the four cats settled down in their chairs to sleep. For fear of returning to the world of her nightmares, Tilly stayed awake for as long as she possibly could, but eventually gave in as tiredness washed over her. Hettie's mind was racing, and try as she might, sleep was impossible. She stared into the fire, searching for answers.

As darkness fell, the windmill became a very different place. There was no electricity and Hettie tried to imagine what it must have been like for the two elderly cats, shut away and totally reliant on the goodwill of Firestorm and his followers. Serafin had been kind to them and, if she was to be believed, they had responded to her. But why had they been so viciously murdered? By the state of their bodies, they had both put up a fight and it made no sense to lynch one of them in some sort of imaginative execution. Under the hippy leader's regime, he could have murdered them any time he wanted to after they'd passed the land to him – *if* that's what had happened. The question was – why wait until now? Was it Tilly's arrival and the threat she posed, or was there a bigger danger from within the pilgrim community? She had seen how Firestorm meted out justice towards Clawdelia and Cambric and the way that the wider community had accepted it – but maybe they weren't happy. Maybe one or more of the pilgrims had had enough of his dictatorship and had conspired to murder the elderly cats to frame Firestorm himself.

Hettie pondered on the possibilities late into the night and had only just closed her eyes when the whispering began. She looked across at her three sleeping friends but the noise she could hear wasn't made by any of them. It appeared to be coming from the walls and it was getting louder and louder. She threw off her cover and padded to one of the windows, staring out into total darkness, but the whispering persisted. The noise unnerved her and she was tempted to wake Bruiser, but decided to brave it out and climb the stairs to the first floor, feeling her way in the darkness. The whispering became even louder and was now accompanied by a rhythmic scratching noise which reverberated around the walls. She suddenly remembered what Serafin had said about the burial ground and how the Ancients had been terrorised by ghosts. But the Ancients were both dead, so if the disgruntled ancestors were still climbing the walls, was it now for Tilly's benefit? Hettie moved to the window where the dead cat was hanging just out of reach and opened it. The moon obliged her by throwing a shaft of silver light onto the outer wall of the mill and Hettie stuck her neck out, convinced that she would see a legion of long dead Skrimshaws clawing their way up the wall, clothed in their dirt-stained shrouds – but there was nothing. She closed the window. Instantly the noise stopped and the windmill fell silent again.

She felt her way back down the stairs, relieved to have the warmth of the fire and the closeness of her companions. She settled back into the deckchair she'd chosen to sleep in and pulled the old curtain up to her chin. She was shivering, but not with cold, and was now beginning to understand why the elderly cats had lost their minds: if they had been subjected to what she'd just experienced, it would have been enough to tip any well-adjusted cat into insanity.

She tried to rationalise what had just happened. She did believe in ghosts and had come across them in her detective work, but had found them to be mostly harmless. The town's medium, Irene Peggledrip, had made a lucrative profession out of them, but there was something different about the Skrimshaw Windmill. From the moment they'd arrived, Hettie had been aware of a dark malevolence, and not just in the mill. It was hard to nail it down, but it was almost as if the land itself was drenched in sorrow and regret from a terror that just kept on giving. Hettie considered the fact that Tilly had tapped into it with her vivid nightmares – it was as if some army of evil tendrils was reaching out to anyone with connections to the land to suffocate them into submission. But submission to what? What was so special about the Skrimshaw legacy? So many questions and no tangible answers.

The very first sign of daylight was filtering through the windows before Hettie finally gave in to sleep. It had been her dark night of the soul and the windmill had evoked more than just spirits; it had reinforced in her the conviction that evil really did exist, and no matter how far and fast you ran from it, it would catch up with you in the end. The only remedy was to face up to it, no matter how difficult the journey may be.

Chapter Thirteen

Hettie awoke to the sound of squawking crows and the clatter of domestic duties around her. Bruiser was filling a pan with water from his bucket, ready to make another round of teas; Dolly was picking some of the more advanced sprouting bits out of her stash of potatoes; and Tilly was counting out four piles of biscuits to gauge how many they could eat for breakfast. Hettie sat up and stretched. It felt late and she suddenly remembered how disturbed the night had been. She was in two minds as to whether to recount it all to her friends; it already seemed that their situation couldn't get much worse and she didn't want to add to their woes. Instead, she chose to be decisive. 'I think we should put our heads together and come up with a plan,' she announced, throwing off her covers and moving towards the fire to warm her paws. All eyes turned to her with nods of enthusiasm. 'As far as I can see, there are two things we need to achieve,' she continued. 'The first is to try and find a way out of this windmill and the second is to find out who murdered the two Matildas.'

'Romew and Remew,' Tilly corrected again, and this time everyone heard her.

'Who are they?' Hettie asked. 'Not more bloody hippies, surely?'

Tilly was feeling much better and had woken early. She'd lain awake, sifting through her early morning visit to the priory and her meeting with Sister Constance the day before. At first she had thought that it was another of her nightmares, but as her mind began to clear she'd realised that it had really happened and that what she had learnt was important. 'Romew and Remew are the real names of the two Matildas,' she said. 'They were imposters just like Acrid Firestorm.'

Jaws dropped all round as Tilly continued her story, recounting her conversation with Sister Constance and the impact that it might have on who should now claim the land. 'So you're saying that this Sister Constance Surprise is really a Matilda, and she got this other cat, Dikon, to send the telegram which brought us here?' said Hettie.

'I am, and there's more – Firestorm is definitely an imposter because Ragland Firestorm was executed by Matilda the Shield Maiden for murdering all but one of her kittens when this land was run by the Vikings and Saxons.'

'Hang on a minute,' said Hettie, getting confused. 'Did Sister Constance tell you all this?'

'Not exactly,' Tilly admitted, trying to protect her credibility. 'She confirmed what I'd already seen in my nightmare.'

Hettie was about to dismiss another of Tilly's fanciful regressions but suddenly remembered her own terrors of the night before. 'So what was your nightmare this time?' Hettie, Dolly and Bruiser listened intently as Tilly described the Saxon village, the murdered kittens and Ragland Firestorm's execution. 'So even if Acrid is related to Ragland Firestorm, he has no right to claim the land?' Hettie suggested.

'That's what Sister Constance said. She also said that she hoped I would be willing to fight for it.'

'Well, it's good to know we have an ally out there, but I don't see how she can help us if she's not allowed to leave the priory,' Hettie pointed out.

'But now 'er 'orrible sisters are dead, she can do as she likes as far as I can see,' chipped in Dolly.

'You've got a point there,' Hettie agreed, 'but she'll still have to get past Firestorm and his band of thugs, and anyway, if she's as reclusive as she sounds she won't even know that her sisters are dead.'

'I once knew a cat called Dikon,' said Bruiser, pouring hot water into four cracked cups. 'We travelled a bit together and got inta some scrapes. I saved 'im from drownin' once – 'e'd bin knocked inta a river, fightin' off an old farm cat. We 'ad some good times together, but 'e took off one day an' I never saw 'im again.'

'I'm not sure that's going to help us now, unless your Dikon is the one that lives in Skrimshaw Woods – and even if it is, how do we get to him? This windmill is like a fortress and time is running out if Firestorm sticks to his threat to burn it down with us in it.'

Dolly spooned tea and powdered milk into the cups while Tilly allocated two biscuits each for breakfast, and the four cats ate and drank in silence, allowing the crows to take over the dialogue. After breakfast, Hettie decided to take a closer look at the murder scene and Tilly was keen to accompany her to the first floor. Bruiser decided to investigate the lock on the main entry door to the mill and Dolly offered to assist him with some cheerful banter.

Climbing the stairs, Hettie was reminded of the whispering and scratching that had disturbed her in the night. In daylight, she refused to believe that she'd been under siege by thwarted ancestors from the burial ground and was determined to find a more tangible explanation.

The squawking crows were much louder on the first floor and Tilly opened the window to see what all the commotion was about. She drew back in horror at the sight of the elderly cat's body, hanging from the sail, being picked clean of any flesh as the crows delighted in their lucky find. 'That's just too horrible,' she said, shutting the window. 'They've come from the priory. They were watching me when I met Sister Constance.'

Hettie suddenly had an idea and bounded up the stairs to the room of junk, returning seconds later with a fishing net on a stick. 'I thought I'd seen this up there,' she said excitedly. 'This could be our way out of here!'

Tilly looked somewhat bemused as Hettie wielded the net around the room as if she was catching butterflies. 'Whatever are you going to do with that?' she asked.

'Crow catching,' Hettie replied, practising her technique. 'That old trunk I brought down had paper in it. See if you can find a blank bit and something to write with, and a bit of string or ribbon.'

'Well, one of those is easy as I've got a pencil in my cardigan pocket,' said Tilly triumphantly, bounding down the stairs to find some paper and string. She returned with an old notepad and an elastic band, hotly followed by Bruiser and Dolly, both keen to be involved in Hettie's plan.

'First we need to write a note,' said Hettie. Tilly responded by finding a clean page in the notepad, and waited for further instruction. 'Put "HELP" in big letters, then say "we are prisoners in the windmill and the two Matildas are dead".'

'But that's not their names,' Tilly protested. 'Sister Constance is a Matilda.'

'Well call them what you like. If Sister whatever-her-name-is knows her sisters are dead, she might be more inclined to leave the priory to help us get out of here,' said Hettie, a little irritated. 'But just hurry up before the crows finish their breakfast.'

Tilly scribbled the message and Dolly folded the paper, keen to play her part. Bruiser and Hettie moved towards the window. 'You'll 'ave ta be quick with that net,' Bruiser said. 'Soon as them crows sees what you're up to, they'll be off.'

Hettie took a deep breath to compose herself, knowing it was a make-or-break situation, then passed the net to Bruiser. 'You do it,' she said. 'You're much better at this sort of thing. I'll count to three and open the window.'

Bruiser reluctantly took the net firmly in his paw and waved it around to get the feel of it before nodding to Hettie. 'One, two, three,' she said, throwing open the window.

Bruiser was swift and accurate, reaching out and netting the biggest of the crows and pulling it back through the window. The bird fought for its freedom, viciously pecking at the net and its captors, and it was Dolly who stepped forward to calm it down; within seconds, the bird had become still in the net. Hettie attached the note to one of the crow's feet and Dolly took the bird to the window and released it. The crow flew high above the mill, squawking its dissatisfaction, and circled before flying away to join its companions on the priory wall.

'Wherever did you learn to do that?' asked Hettie, amazed at Dolly's skill with the bird.

'Ah well, you've got me old dad to thank for that. 'E 'ad pidgins, see – used to race 'em across to the Sillies an' back. We 'ad lofts of 'em in our back garden. 'E taught me 'ow to 'old 'em an' talk to 'em. Not a natural thing, cats an' birds, but it's all about trust. Me dad bred a champion racer – Pegasus Piecrust 'e called it. Broke 'is 'art when she came a cropper over Marazion, clipped by one of them 'elicopters out of Penzance. She was a good little flyer.'

'Well, we're very grateful to your dad,' said Hettie. 'We'll just have to wait and see if Sister Constance – or Matilda – has the same effect as you did on the crow.'

After the flurry of excitement, Bruiser reported that the door to the windmill was impossible to breach; he suspected that as well as being locked, it was most probably bolted from the outside. 'We're just going to have to keep our claws crossed that Mr Crow comes up trumps then,' Hettie said, closing the window and glancing across at the body of the dead cat rolled up in the hearthrug. 'All this is so frustrating. Here we are, standing in the middle of a murder scene with blood up the walls, and no chance of any investigation into whatever happened here.'

'We could do what we usually do now I've found a notepad,' Tilly pointed out. 'A list of suspects usually helps.'

'I love a list,' Dolly added. 'Probably one of my favourite things to do and even nicer when you can start crossin' stuff off it – makes you feel like you're gettin' somewhere.'

'All right, you two – go downstairs and make a suspects list,' said Hettie, 'and we'll discuss it over lunch – or should I say a toffee and half a custard cream. I want to take a closer look at this room with Bruiser. There must be some clues to this murder somewhere in here.'

The four cats went about their business. Tilly and Dolly built up the fire and settled themselves on the bench in front of it to work on their suspect list. The list didn't take long and they were soon amusing themselves with several games of noughts and crosses while Hettie paced the floor upstairs. 'The thing is,' she said, stopping in front of the fireplace, 'there's so much blood here and yet there are no traces of it on the stairs, the ground floor or around the main door. Whoever did this must have been saturated in blood if the state of this room is anything to go by.'

'Maybe they left by the window,' Bruiser suggested. 'There's blood on the sill. P'raps the sail was in the right place fer 'em ta climb down after they'd 'anged that cat. If it was done at night, no one would 'ave seen anythin'.'

Hettie agreed that it was a possibility, but she wasn't convinced. 'I think that would have been a really complicated manoeuvre, especially if the old cat was fighting for her life. The murderer would have been just as likely to break his or her neck as well as the victim's. It's quite some drop from here.'

'Maybe the old cat was dead already. Much easier ta 'ang it out there if it wasn't fightin' back,' Bruiser suggested.

'But if that's the case, why hang the body out there at all? Why not just leave it with the other one and escape by the front door? There's a trick I'm missing here and right now I just can't put my claw on it.'

'Unless the murderer is still in the windmill and never left?' suggested Bruiser, giving Hettie a heart-stopping moment.

'Right now I'd be willing to believe anything, but we've been over this place. The walls are round and there's nowhere to hide, nowhere even to wash the blood off – and, as we've already established, no chance of escape. It's all beginning to present itself as one of those Agatha Crispy locked room murders that Tilly thinks are so clever. Nothing in this room makes any sense, except possibly to the murderer. Another thing we shouldn't forget is that most of the cats out there in the campsite think Tilly is the killer, so as far as they're concerned it's case closed. It might have even got back to this Sister Constance – or she could be the killer herself. We don't know what happened after Tilly fainted and banged her head.'

Bruiser felt as defeated as Hettie. The two cats slunk down to the ground floor to join Tilly and Dolly and the prospect of a rather poor lunch.

Chapter Fourteen

The early spring sunshine had been replaced by a set of ominous black clouds, threatening heavy rain and doing very little to boost the spirits inside the windmill. The only silver lining was the prospect of Bruiser's bucket being replenished with rain-water, as his supply was running dangerously low. The scant lunch had gone nowhere and all four cats were beginning to feel permanently hungry. There was still plenty of wood for the fire but Dolly had warned that there were only enough potatoes for one more supper. Their outlook was bleak and, as every hour went by, they drew a little closer to Acrid Firestorm's plan to burn them alive.

'OK,' said Hettie, settling herself in one of the deckchairs by the fire. 'Let's have your list of suspects and any reasoning behind them.'

Tilly turned to her list and began to read the names out. 'I've put Acrid Firestorm at the top, as he had the most to gain from Remew and Romew's death – and we don't like him. Next come Anger and Bod, as they were quite nasty to us. If they were the murderers, I think they might have been acting on Firestorm's orders. I've put Tabica next, as she stuck up for Firestorm at the supper and she is a bit weird.'

'A *bit* weird?' interrupted Hettie. 'That's putting it mildly. Any cat who shaves her head and covers it in tattoos has got to be completely weird.'

'I think they call that Celtic art,' said Dolly, trying to be helpful, 'but that wouldn't suit me, specially not in the winter. If she bought 'erself a biker's jacket, she could 'ave 'er art put on that *an'* keep 'er fur.'

Bruiser nodded in agreement and Tilly pushed on with her list. 'Serafin Parchment comes next but I've only put her down because she looked after the old cats so she would have had access to them and it seems that they trusted her. But she was kind to us, and she didn't strike me as someone who would be capable of such a nasty double murder. Next there's Clawdelia and Cambric. I thought that after Firestorm's punishment they might be angry enough to frame him, but if they did they must have acted together – Clawdelia couldn't have managed the murders on her own with kittens on the way. I've put Marjoram the herbalist next, but I think she would have used poison if she was going to kill anyone. Finally I've got Dryad, who chops down trees, and Hathor, who we know nothing about except that she's supposed to be good at music and dance. That's it.'

'Not quite,' said Hettie. 'What about Sister Constance Surprise? Along with Firestorm, she has the best motive for wanting her sisters dead. You said they banished her and stole what should have been hers, and she arranged for us to be here. Maybe her plan was to have you blamed for their murders. We don't know what happened after your accident. She could easily have struck out for the windmill, committed the murders and left you in the field where we found you wandering about – or, for that matter, she could have been helped by this Dikon character she mentioned. We may have made a big mistake sending her that note; we've no idea who we can and can't trust at the moment.'

Tilly could see the sense in what Hettie was saying and reluctantly added Sister Constance and Dikon to her list.

'The trouble is,' Hettie continued, 'we can't take the list any further. Normally we would want to interview all those suspects to establish possible motives and alibis, but stuck in here we're on a road to nowhere.'

Hettie's musings were cut short by the sound of a tambourine, and all four cats stood up at once. 'Maybe Serafin has come to rescue us,' Tilly said excitedly as Hettie bounded up the stairs and opened the window.

Serafin stood at the foot of the windmill looking up at the window, her tambourine in one paw and a basket in the other. 'I haven't got long,' she said, 'but I thought you might need some food. I'll try and throw a rope up to you and you can pull the basket up, but Acrid will punish me if he finds out, so you have to promise to let me have the rope back so you can't use it to try to escape.'

'Why can't you just let us out?' asked Hettie. 'We've done nothing wrong and there's a killer on the loose out there. Don't you want to know who murdered the Ancients?'

'Not really,' said Serafin. 'This whole thing has turned into a really bad scene. I'm leaving as soon as I can slip away, but if Acrid finds out I've been helping you, he'll never let me go. They're all out of it down there, celebrating him getting the land, so I sneaked out to bring you some stuff.'

Without any further conversation, Serafin pulled a rope out of the basket and threw it up to Hettie. She succeeded on the third time of trying and quickly tied the basket to the rope for Hettie to hoist up. The basket was heavy, and Hettie struggled to pull it over the sill. She hesitated regarding the rope, but – as Serafin had already put herself in danger – she detached it from the basket and threw it back to her. 'Do you know what Firestorm intends to do with us?' Hettie asked.

Serafin shook her head. 'I really don't know, but last night at supper he said he was going to avenge the Ancients.' She looked up at the corpse still dangling from the sail, taking in the full horror of a cat she'd once looked after. 'And now I really need to go back to the campsite before I'm missed. I'm sorry I can't help you, but at least you've got some food.'

Hettie conceded defeat as far as an escape plan was concerned, not wanting Serafin to suffer for her kindness. She thanked the hippy cat and wished her well with her future plans, and watched her dance away from the windmill with the rope and her tambourine.

The rain began to fall in giant droplets and Hettie hurriedly shut the window. Bruiser, Tilly and Dolly were all waiting for her on the stairs, eager to see what was in the basket. The four cats returned to their fire and Tilly was given the task of unpacking the food, which she passed an item at a time to Dolly, who laid it out on the bench. 'We've got two loaves of bread,' Tilly began, offering a running commentary, 'a big piece of cheese, four chicken drumsticks, four pastry pies, although I'm not sure what's in them, some slices of ham, four boiled eggs, a bottle of milk, a packet of savoury biscuits, four bags of Wotsits and there's a cake tin at the bottom of the basket.'

Dolly assisted by taking the lid off. 'Well, that's a real treat – home-made flapjack. Nice!'

'And look what was under that tin,' said Hettie. 'The biggest bread knife I've ever seen. We owe Serafin a huge debt of gratitude. She must have taken a real risk to get all this lovely food together, and we've even got a weapon we could use if necessary.'

'That puts my 'umble baked potatoes in the shade,' Dolly said, as they marvelled at their tasty supplies. 'We're goin' to be spoilt for choice for tonight's supper.'

The food delivery had lifted everyone's spirits. The rain was now rattling at the windows, and Bruiser responded by taking his bucket up to the top floor to catch some more water. With their pantry looking considerably healthier, they treated themselves to an afternoon cup of tea with proper milk and a piece of flapjack before setting about the trunk that had so far supplied a notebook and an elastic band. Tilly decided to empty out the contents onto the floor and make separate piles of papers, photographs and books. Hettie took on the papers to sift through, while Tilly and Dolly pounced on the photographs. Bruiser ended up being stuck with the Bible and the other books. 'What are we lookin' for?' he asked, blowing the dust off.

'Nothing and everything,' said Hettie. 'I doubt we'll find anything to solve the murders, but at least we can try and understand more about the Skrimshaw history.'

'Well, these photos tell a story for starters,' said Dolly. 'There's some really old ones. I wonder who all these cats were? 'Ave you seen any family you recognise?'

'Not really,' said Tilly. 'The trouble is my grandmother had over twenty kittens in her lifetime. I remember my mother saying how many sisters she had, but as far as I know she didn't keep in touch with any of them. I left home when I was very young, after she took up with a nasty tomcat, and we lost touch, so I really don't recognise any of these cats and there's nothing written on the back of the photos to say who they are – or were, judging by how old-fashioned some of their clothes are.'

'There's some nice pictures of the windmill in this lot,' Dolly pointed out. 'Just look 'ow 'ansome it was inside once. Lovely furniture, bowls of flowers and there's them old curtains we're sleepin' in up at the windows, lookin' much nicer than they do now. An' 'ere's a snap of 'em all sittin' out the front in the sunshine in our old deckchairs. Looks like they were 'avin' a tea party, an' I bet that's them cracked cups we've got that they're drinkin' out of.'

Tilly looked closely at the photograph, which definitely told the story of sunnier days. Out of the four cats taking tea, she thought she recognised one of them. There was an older cat in the picture and three younger ones, all female and beaming at the camera, raising their teacups. 'I think that one is Sister Constance,' she said, pointing her claw at one of them, 'so maybe the others are Romew, Remew and their mother. They all look so happy and these ones inside the mill are just lovely. It looks like they made it into a proper home.'

'They're doin' that all over Cornwall now with the old tin mines,' said Dolly, 'callin' 'em bijou 'oliday lets, although they're little more than brick sheds with a log burner. Give me a guest 'ouse with 'ot an' cold water any day.'

'I wonder when it was that everything went wrong for them, and why?' Hettie said, looking at the photos. 'The story these pictures tell is of a happy life, prosperous even. Something bad must have happened to change everything.'

'I think it must have been when the mother died. She must have been my great-great-aunt,' suggested Tilly. 'Sister Constance should have inherited but her sisters joined forces to steal the land and sent her away.'

'But why didn't they keep themselves an' the windmill nice?' Dolly asked.

'Well, if Serafin is to be believed, they were haunted by the ghosts of the ancestors all clamouring for their birth rights and that sent them mad,' Hettie said.

'Thank goodness we're not bein' bothered by 'em,' Dolly said. 'I like a good 'orror film, but I'm not well disposed towards Zombies. My feelin' is once you're dead you stay dead. It's like you've 'ad your turn and that's your lot.'

At this point, Hettie was in two minds as to whether to mention the whispering and scratching she'd heard in the night, but she decided against it, reluctant to spoil the happy atmosphere that had descended after the delivery of Serafin's food basket. Instead, she began to sort through the raft of papers from the trunk. They were mostly old receipts, garden plans and estimates for repairs to the windmill and the priory, some going back over a hundred years, but there was one very old document that caught her eye. It was dated January 1st 1666. The writing was strange and almost unreadable, but it was a sort of will as far as

Hettie could make out. There were several references to a plague, but the most important part of the document was a bequest that all the lands belonging to the priory should be settled on Matilda Skrimshaw and her line in perpetuity, and that no male of that line should intercede in any way. It was signed at the bottom, and carried a wax seal with what looked like a crow's head on it. The signature was scratchy and almost unreadable, but the first name was clearly Matilda. 'Unless there's another document that leapfrogs over this one, Acrid Firestorm can have no legal claim on the Skrimshaw land,' said Hettie, passing it to Tilly. 'I'm not sure what the plague has got to do with it, though.'

'That's what Matilda's mother died of in my nightmare,' Tilly said, remembering in detail the sadness of the death bed scene. 'She must have had this drawn up just before she died.'

Bruiser looked across at the date and nodded. 'Spot on with the plague, 1665 to 1666. Started in London and spread across England. Fleas on rats caused it, an' over 100,000 cats died.'

All eyes turned to Bruiser. 'I'm impressed,' said Hettie. 'Where did you pick that gem of information up from?'

'I read it in one of them historical magazines while I was waitin' for a fry-up in a caf I used to call in at when I was out on the road. I 'aven't been near a rat since.'

'Wasn't that the same year as the great fire of London?' Dolly added. 'I always think of that when I'm stickin' a batch of scones in the oven – don't ask me why, but I just do. They must 'ave 'ad a right old time, what with the plague as well. I'm not sure what I'd 'ave preferred, dyin' of the pestilence or bein' burnt to a crisp.'

'Didn't that start in Pudding Lane?' Tilly asked. 'That's my favourite bit of the story.'

'I'm not sure we should be talking about being burnt alive,' Hettie pointed out, 'not with what we've got hanging over us.'

The conversation seemed to have moved away from the contents of the trunk, but Bruiser returned to the books, keen to lighten the atmosphere. 'This one looks good,' he said. 'It's called *Myths and Visions*. I bet there's some good stories in 'ere.'

'I've had enough visions to last me several lifetimes,' said Tilly. 'I think we should have something nice to eat. I'm starving.'

Everyone agreed that was the best idea, but there was some debate over the menu. Bruiser voted for a pie, Hettie was keen on the idea of a ham and cheese sandwich, but Dolly and Tilly won the day, reasoning that the pies and ham would keep but the chicken drumsticks needed eating. 'If we 'ad the chicken now, I could bake the laast of me potatoes for our supper – an' to keep our interest up, we could 'ave a slice of cheese on them as a toppin'.'

The chicken was tasty and went down well with a chunk of the newly baked bread and a cup of Bruiser's rainwater tea. If it hadn't been for their impending doom, their time in Skrimshaw Windmill could easily have been an interesting holiday adventure, especially now that the self-catering aspect had improved – but time was running out. Down in the campsite, the pilgrims were gathering wood and reed bundles, preparing for a Viking funeral.

Chapter Fifteen

'I know we shouldn't worry, but it's not like them not to get in touch,' said Beryl, dishing up two hefty portions of cottage pie. 'It was only supposed to be a day out on Sunday and now it's Tuesday teatime and there's still no sign of them.'

'Molly's worried, too,' added Betty. 'She was rushed off her feet when I popped in with the pies at lunchtime. She thinks they might have had an accident and that's why she hasn't heard from Dolly.'

'She could be right,' said Beryl. 'I've heard that Norfolk is a dark old place, full of strange villages and even stranger cats, and no proper roads to speak of. Mind you, they do a nice crab in Cromer – Malkin and Sprinkle had a load of them on their fish counter yesterday. I can't say I wasn't tempted.'

'I suppose if they don't turn up by tomorrow morning we should get the Morris out and go and look for them?' Betty suggested. 'If they're lying in a ditch somewhere, we'd never forgive ourselves. It's been three days without a word, and it's not like they were on one of their cases. It was only supposed to be afternoon tea with some old aunts that Tilly's found.'

'They've all clearly got themselves in a scrape of some sort. Tilly said these aunts live in an old priory, Scrumshaw or something similar – all sounded a bit far-fetched if you ask me.

Dangerous business, tracing relatives – you never know what's going to rise up and bite you. It didn't take Laxton Spratt long to turn up when he found out that Marmite had died and yet he never came near her when she was alive. That's no way to treat your mother, but I suppose he'll inherit her house now and all those awful books she wrote. Serves him right, really. What's that old saying Ma used to come out with? You can choose your friends, but you're stuck with your relatives.'

Betty had to agree. 'Just look at Clematis – she'd got herself in a right old mess at her garden centre and if Wisteria has her way she'll run that business into the ground with her Spanish hanging baskets and decorative patio pots that won't stand the frost. I wouldn't put it past her to arrange for bull fighting in the garden furniture and fancy goods section. The poor folk of Prickly Brook won't know what's hit them if Clematis doesn't get better soon.'

Beryl nodded before passing the gravy boat to her sister. 'If we did all the baking tonight, maybe Elsie would stand in for us tomorrow? She doesn't open on Wednesday lunchtime and she'll be finished in the bakery in plenty of time for her evening trade.'

'Good idea, sister. I'll give her a ring. I don't suppose there's much difference between selling bread and cakes or fish and chips when it comes down to it. We could drop off the pie orders to Molly and Malkin and Sprinkle's on our way out in the morning.'

The cottage pie was followed by a fruit sponge with double cream. While Beryl washed the dishes, Betty phoned Elsie Haddock, who agreed to hold the fort for them. The two sisters then returned to their preparation area to bake their breads, pies and cakes for the next day. By midnight, all was done and the bakery was fully stocked ready for Elsie to take over in the morning.

Betty and Beryl Butter fell into their beds. It had been a long day but tomorrow would be even longer.

Chapter Sixteen

Back in the windmill, Bruiser had been keeping his friends entertained with stories from his *Myths and Visions* book. Dolly had been delighted by the chapter that dealt with King Arthur and more especially Merlin, the magician, as there were several mentions of Tintagel. Tilly loved the story of Jason and his Argonauts and their search for the golden fleece. She'd watched the film several times over on TV to see the skeleton fight, which was her favourite bit.

Hettie dozed in her deckchair, catching only snippets of Bruiser's stories, but it was the penultimate one in the book that made everyone sit up and take notice. It was the story of Romew and Remew. 'Romew and Remew were the daughters of the God Mars,' Bruiser began. 'When the twin kittens were born they were in danger of being murdered, so their mother sent them down the river to escape from their wicked uncle. They nearly drowned, and were saved by a she-wolf and a woodpecker, who raised them. When they were fully grown, they journeyed back to the place of their birth, murdered their wicked uncle and argued about what to do next. Remew wanted to build seven hilltop cities with gardens, and Romew wanted to build one big city, so they decided to fight it out. Romew killed Remew and built her city, which became known as Rome. Romew ruled her city until she was killed by a tornado that lifted her up and carried her miles from the city she'd built. The cats in Rome thought she'd been called back to sit in heaven with her father, Mars the God of War, although some say she killed herself out of remorse for what she'd done to her sister Remew.'

'None of them myths ends well,' Dolly said, ''cept for King Arthur – that all turned out nicely with the round table an' all them lovely 'ansome knights, although Guinevere and Lancelot behaved badly. I s'pose they just couldn't 'elp themselves. I s'pose Arthur was too busy to notice what was goin' on right in front of 'is whiskers.'

'I wonder why their mother called them Romew and Remew?' Hettie said, still pondering over the story that Bruiser had just read to them.

'Do you mean my great-aunts?' Tilly asked.

'Yes. I can see that she might have been a fan of myths and legends, especially with the Viking and Saxon history of this place, but why would you call your kittens Romew and Remew?'

'Sister Constance told me that her mother was a visionary and that she could see into the past and the future. She told me that she had been too young to understand the warnings, or something like that.'

'Bit like you, then, with all your funny dreams,' Dolly pointed out. 'I'd like one of them time machines like that cat on the TV, although I wouldn't want to meet one of them Daleks. I hide behind Molly's sofa when they come on.'

'I sometimes wish Miss Scarlet was one of them time machines,' chipped in Bruiser. 'Visitin' all the biker exhibitions all over the world – I could look back at all them lovely old bikes and see what's comin' up in the future.'

'That'd be somethin',' said Dolly. 'I 'ope you'd take me with you. Maybe we'd meet a Dalek bike and sidecar along the way, although I might be a bit frightened and need protectin'.'

'I don't mind the Daleks but I'm really frightened by the Cybercats,' Tilly said. 'When I have one of my nightmares, it's just like going back in time, but the frightening thing is I become someone else, even though I'm still me. It's like watching a film with me playing a character, but it's just so real.'

'I'd be frightened of bein' stuck in the wrong time,' Dolly pointed out. 'I couldn't be doin' with all them Vikings and Saxons – no electricity, no shops, always fightin', an' worst of all, no Cornish ice cream. That's no way for a cat to live. It's bad enough 'ere in this old mill, but at least we're warm and dry.'

Hettie allowed the banter on the merits of time travel to float over her. Something that Tilly had said earlier troubled her. Suddenly she jumped up from her deckchair and bounded up the stairs to the first floor.

Bruiser followed, with Tilly and Dolly tumbling after him. Hettie had gone straight to the window and opened it. It was late in the day, but there was just enough light for her to see the corpse hanging from the sail. The wind had turned it slightly, and it was almost close enough for her to reach out and touch it. She stared down at the blood on the sill, then closed the window. As Tilly, Dolly and Bruiser watched, she paced across the room, once again taking in every detail of the crime scene. 'That's it!' she declared eventually. 'That's why she called them Romew and Remew – she could see into the future.'

'What do you mean?' asked Tilly.

'I mean their mother knew that this was going to happen. She must have had a vision in which they killed each other – that's why she called them Romew and Remew, from the story Bruiser has just read to us.' Hettie was excited.

'So are you saying that no one murdered them?' Tilly clarified.

'That's exactly it,' said Hettie. 'Romew murdered her sister, then hanged herself by attaching a rope to the sail and jumping out of that window. That's why there's no blood leading away from the crime scene. It's all self-contained in here with the two cats. My guess is that they had one of their fights, brought on by the whispering and scratching, and things went too far.'

'What whisperin' and scratchin'?' Dolly asked.

'The noises the dead ancestors make which drove the old cats mad,' explained Hettie. 'I heard it last night and it was enough to send any cat over the edge.'

'So we're locked up in this windmill, under siege from those nasty hippies who think I'm a murderer, surrounded by ghosts who scratch and whisper at night, and with the promise of being burnt alive any day now, and all for nothing?' said Tilly, trying hard to fight back the tears.

'But we 'ave got cheesy baked potatoes for supper and flapjack for afters,' said Dolly, hoping to cheer Tilly up by looking on the bright side.

The four friends returned to the ground floor, where Bruiser built up the fire ready for Dolly to push in her tin of potatoes. Tilly kept herself busy slicing cheese. Hettie's solution to the windmill murders had brought them very little comfort, and an air of doom descended as darkness fell. Being so isolated and cut off from any plans that Acrid Firestorm might be hatching was becoming desperately frustrating. They were powerless, and if Firestorm carried out his threat to burn the mill down, there was really nothing they could do to save themselves.

Although supper was tasty, there was very little conversation to go with it. All four cats were deeply entrenched in their own thoughts and even Dolly Scollop had finally run out of cheery things to say. They sat in their chairs, staring at the fire, until one by one they fell asleep.

****

August 17th 1963

Matilda was tired of all the fighting, especially on such a beautiful day. Her mother had made them a lovely tea and it was a real treat to sit outside the windmill and enjoy the food and the sunshine, but

Romew had to spoil it as she always did. The fight had started over a salmon sandwich and escalated into a war. Remew had stood her ground, initially hissing insults back at her twin, but their mother had intervened too late and the insults had turned into a full-blown cat fight. Matilda sought sanctuary in the burial ground, behind one of the giant stones, as Romew and Remew sliced through each other with their claws, biting off lumps of fur and spitting them out before going in for another attack.

Back and back they came at each other until Matilda's mother threw a bucket of water over Romew. Remew escaped into the windmill, followed by her mother. Romew shook herself and hissed at Matilda as she peeped out from behind the stone, then arched her back as if she was going to pounce, but at the last minute she changed her mind and bounded through the mill door. The fight continued inside the windmill, but it was her mother's voice Matilda heard crying out from the open window above her. It was over in seconds. Her mother lay broken across one of the ancient stones in front of Matilda, her eyes open, fixed and staring at the perfectly blue sky. Matilda looked up to see both her sisters at the window and they smiled at her, united at last in what they had done. Matilda screamed and screamed, but there was no one left to comfort her.

****

'Wake up! Wake up, you're having a dream!' Hettie said, as Tilly's screams reverberated around the mill. She sat up, confused, and continued to sob, rubbing her eyes to disperse the tears. Dolly and Bruiser, now both wide awake, looked on as Hettie tried to calm things down. 'Whatever has made you so upset?' she asked. 'Whatever it was, you're safe now. It was just one of your bad dreams.'

Tilly was inconsolable and sobbing even louder than before, her mind still full of the terrors that sleep had dealt her. Bruiser checked his pocket watch; it was only two o'clock, but there was no chance of any more sleep until Tilly was settled. He padded to the fire and added some more wood, putting a pan of water onto the fret to boil up for some tea. Dolly busied herself with the cups, and Hettie held one of Tilly's paws until she had stopped crying.

After a while, Tilly was able to come to terms with her nightmare and explain what had upset her. Her three friends listened as she described the cat fight and the death of Matilda's mother. 'I think the sisters murdered her,' she said. 'I think one of them pushed her out of that first-floor window. Sister Constance said her mother's death had been tragic, and it was. I just saw it happen right in front of me.'

'But did she say her mother had been murdered?' Hettie asked.

'Not exactly, but it makes sense. Their mother stood in the way of the twin sisters inheriting the land, and after her death it should have passed to Matilda, who's now Sister Constance – but Romew and Remew sent her away, changed their names to Matilda and stole the land.'

'This whole saga of Matildas is giving me a headache,' said Hettie, 'and why this Sister Constance thinks you'd be willing to fight for this godforsaken land I'll never understand. I mean, where is she? Why hasn't she left her bloody priory to come and find you?'

Tilly began to cry again, but quickly stopped as the whispering began. Just like the night before, it began quietly, but this time all four cats heard it. Bruiser's hackles rose and he bounded up to the first floor. Hettie followed him, telling Dolly and Tilly to stay where they were by the fire.

As before, the whispering became louder and louder and was soon joined by the scratching. Bruiser resisted the temptation to open the window as Hettie had done, but continued up to the second floor, with Hettie close behind him. It was dark, and it took the two cats a moment to accustom their eyes, taking care not to bump into any of the junk that was strewn around the room. The noise was now deafening and Bruiser signalled that he was going to climb the steps to the top of the mill.

The room they'd seen in daylight felt even more claustrophobic now. The giant machinery struck out at them as obstacles in every direction. Bruiser was more used to the space because of his visits to his rainwater bucket, but the two cats agreed that it was in this room that the whispering and scratching was the loudest. Bruiser began to feel around the walls with his paws and Hettie followed his example, realising what he was looking for. With a sudden triumphant movement, Bruiser gave an almighty tug on a wire he'd found. There was a crash as something tumbled from behind one of the giant cogs embedded in the beams on the ceiling, narrowly missing Hettie by inches. At this point, the noise stopped and all was silent.

'So that's the game,' said Hettie, looking at the smashed speaker at her feet. 'I bet this is Firestorm's work to frighten those old cats out of their wits. His little audio set-up was obviously doing a great job.'

Bruiser swung himself up into the roof, keen to find the rest of the equipment. Minutes later, after close investigation, he located a battery cassette machine which had been attached to the speaker hidden behind another one of the rusted cogs. He let it clatter to the floor and Hettie picked it up. 'Ingenious,' she said. 'Whoever put this together is a very clever cat. They've taken an ordinary cassette player and fitted a timer to go off at the same time every night. If that isn't an exercise in brain damage, I don't know what is – and those two old cats wouldn't have had a clue about what was really happening. Firestorm and his cronies may not have murdered them, but they are entirely responsible for their deaths.'

Hettie and Bruiser returned to the ground floor with the glad tidings that there would be no more whispering and scratching to disturb them. Dolly had done her best to cheer Tilly up, and they were both enjoying a toffee by the fire. Hettie and Bruiser helped themselves to one and joined them, pleased that two mysteries had been solved – or even three if they counted the murder that Tilly had witnessed in her most recent nightmare.

'So there are no ghosts?' Tilly said, as she picked some stubborn bits of the sweet out of her teeth with one of her claws.

'That's what it looks like, although I can't understand why anyone would want to build a windmill over a burial plot in the first place,' reasoned Hettie.

'Maybe it was ta cover up what was already 'ere?' Bruiser suggested.

'In my dream about Matilda the Shield Maiden, they were going to bury Ragland Firestorm here, but there was no windmill then.'

'So maybe we're sittin' on the tomb of a Viking warrior?' Dolly said excitedly. 'There might even be treasure, as them Vikings liked to be buried with all their stuff, just like them Pharaohs in pyramids. They even took their slaves with 'em. Bad luck if you worked for a Pharaoh and he was taken early to 'is grave. You'd 'ave to be bricked up with 'im in case 'e needed you in the afterlife. Miss Podger taught us all that stuff at our after school club in Lostwithiel – 'er favourite thing was to bandage us up like mummies. Frightened Mr Brittle, we did, when we went into 'is shop to buy lucky bags. 'E thought 'e was under attack from Zombies. I got a water pistol in me bag once – lasted me for ages till my ma confiscated it for dampin' down 'er washin'.'

Hettie had lost the thread of the conversation, as she often did when Dolly was talking, but she did find the prospect of a Viking warrior's grave interesting. 'Maybe we should start digging this floor up,' she suggested, mostly in jest, but her friends thought she meant it.

Bruiser was quickly on his feet, testing the floorboards. 'Even if there's no treasure under 'ere, there might be a way out. We could pull a few of these boards up an' see what's underneath.'

'Well, as none of us seems keen on going back to sleep, we've got nothing to lose, so let's take a look,' Hettie said.

The four cats moved their chairs closer to the fire to allow more space for their excavations. Bruiser jammed the bread knife into one of the gaps and levered the first board up enough for Hettie to get her paws around it. With Tilly and Dolly's assistance, they hauled the board up from the floor and leaned it against the wall. The room instantly filled with a blast of cold, damp, fetid air, and a certain amount of scuttling could be heard as mice and possibly even worse creatures looked for safety under the remaining floor area.

Bruiser stared into the void they'd created before pulling up another board, which snapped in half. The wood was clearly rotten in places, suggesting that the floor was the original, put down at the time that the mill was built. Once they had pulled several of the boards up, it was clear that there was another floor underneath – several feet down and much rougher than the planks they'd removed, made of split tree trunks laid out like a raft and roped together.

Bruiser jumped down into the hole to investigate, testing the ropes, which disintegrated in his paw. With a sudden crash, the tree planks gave way and Bruiser fell through them. 'Are you all right?' Hettie shouted, as Tilly and Dolly threw their paws up to their faces in shock.

There was no answer. Hettie carefully lowered herself into the hole, balancing on one of the tree planks that had remained intact. She was about to go further when Bruiser's head popped up, covered in dust and cobwebs. 'I think we got a tunnel,' he said, holding back a sneeze, 'but there's an old boat down 'ere as well. We need some light so I can take a proper look.'

Relieved and excited, Hettie clambered out of the hole, crossed to the fire and selected one of the larger sticks of wood that they'd found. She forced it into the flames until it was well alight and carried it back to Bruiser. He took the torch and disappeared from view for several minutes, before reappearing with triumphant news. 'There's definitely a tunnel, but there's a lot of dead cats down 'ere as well, all skeletons. I reckon it's some sort of ancient tomb.'

Hettie took the flaming torch from Bruiser and knocked it out on the grate. Bruiser hauled himself out of the hole and warmed his paws by the fire. 'It's as cold as the grave down there,' he said, without thinking, 'but I reckon that if Firestorm decides ta torch the windmill, we could easily escape into that tunnel. I didn't go far in, so I don't know where it leads to, if anywhere.'

'Sounds like an adventure waitin' to 'appen,' said Dolly, finally getting round to making the tea. 'I don't know about the rest of you, but I'm famished with all this excitement. 'Ow about some of that nice 'am and a slice or two off a cut loaf?'

There were no dissenters to the suggestion and Tilly sprang into action, wielding the bread knife while Hettie peeled off some ham slices from Serafin's basket. The extra supper was eaten in much better spirits than the last one. The prospect of escape was becoming a reality and the four friends were looking forward to exploring the tunnel that Bruiser had discovered. It was decided that they would wait until morning on the basis that being surrounded by dead cats at night was much more frightening than in the cool light of day, although Bruiser hastened to point out that these particular dead cats were always in the dark, and probably had been for hundreds of years.

Chapter Seventeen

The day dawned, offering a harsh ground frost. After the events of the night before, the four friends had managed little sleep. Hettie was first up and keen to investigate Bruiser's tunnel. She padded to the window and scraped the ice from it. The land around the windmill was completely white with frost; even the cobwebs hanging on the bushes were frozen, their spiders crystallised and hanging like diamonds as the winter sun touched them. Hettie glanced across at the campsite, where thin trails of smoke came from the chimneys of the huts. Was this the day they would burn the windmill down, she wondered?

Bruiser was next to wake and joined Hettie at the window. 'I 'ope Miss Scarlet's all right,' he said. 'I don't like 'er bein' out in the frost – plays 'avoc with 'er chrome. I don't s'pose any of them hippies 'ave thought to cover 'er up.'

'If your tunnel turns out to be an escape route, you'll be reunited with her by teatime, all being well,' said Hettie, determined to stay positive. 'I've been thinking about the connection between the burial ground and the priory and my guess is that's where your tunnel will come out.'

'Judgin' by the skeletons I've seen down there, they're in some sort of burial mound, all in their own enclosures. We're on a bit of an 'ill up 'ere, so maybe that's what it was before they built the windmill. If they carried their dead from the priory, that would explain the tunnel. It would 'ave 'ad to be secret 'cause there's grave goods with some of 'em.'

'My pa was buried with grave goods,' Dolly said, stretching in her armchair. 'We put three bottles of Doom Bar, 'is favourite tankard, all 'is wall of death trophies, and a giant sweet shop jar of barley sugars in 'is coffin. There was 'ardly room for 'im by the time we'd finished, specially as 'e was done up in 'is best leathers an' crash 'elmet. Took eight cats to carry 'im to 'is grave, but we 'ad a lovely wake afterwards. Town band turned out an' played all 'is favourites until the Proper Job started flowin' and one of them who shall remain nameless sicked up in 'is own trumpet!'

Tilly giggled for the first time in days, having woken from a deep sleep that contained no dreams of any sort. She loved Dolly's Cornish tales, and – regardless of the subject matter, which often chronicled the darker side of life – always felt uplifted by them.

'Time for breakfast,' Hettie announced, 'and then we'd better see where this tunnel goes.'

With a considerable hole in the mill's floor, their room was much colder. The firewood supply was dwindling, so Bruiser decided to raid the junk room on the second floor for anything that would burn to keep them warm while they made breakfast and be useful for making flame torches. Like most cats, they were able to see quite well in the dark, but extra light was a comfort when exploring new territory.

Bruiser returned with an assortment of chair legs that he thought would make slow burning torches and some woodworm-riddled drawers from an old dresser. He added one to the fire, hoping it would give enough heat to boil a pan of water for their tea. Tilly and Dolly sorted through Serafin's basket, offering the rest of the ham, a boiled egg, and a sizeable chunk of bread each for breakfast. 'I thought we'd save the pies for supper,' Tilly suggested. 'That still leaves us with bread, cheese, flapjack, biscuits and Wotsits.'

'We'd better pack those back into the basket and take it with us,' said Hettie. 'I'm hoping that we might just have seen the last of this windmill if things go well for us today.'

The tea was hot and the breakfast substantial. Afterwards the four cats scurried round collecting up their things and preparing to embark on what they hoped would be their bid for freedom. Hettie climbed to the first floor to take a final look around. She opened the window and instantly a giant black crow appeared and strutted in front of her on the sill, cocking its head to one side. Hettie stood back, shocked at the bird's arrival, and as she did so the crow opened its beak and a piece of paper dropped from it. Not waiting for any further engagement, the bird took off and circled the mill, squawking loudly before flying back to the priory wall.

Hettie was about to pick up the paper when she was distracted by what looked like a delegation from the campsite, led by Acrid Firestorm. On closer inspection, the pilgrims were all carrying bundles of wood and straw and as they got nearer it was clear that the moment had come to make a hurried exit from the windmill. She shut the window, grabbed the note from the floor and bounded down the stairs. 'Firestorm and his thugs are approaching,' she shouted, 'and they're equipped to start a bonfire, so we need to get into that tunnel now!'

Bruiser forced the chair legs into the fire, Dolly grabbed the food basket and Hettie helped Tilly into the hole. Dolly followed, passing the basket to Tilly; Hettie was next, and finally Bruiser, who passed the flaming torches and several of the floorboards down before leaping into the hole himself. With Hettie's help, he lodged the boards above him, filling the hole they'd made as best they could and hoping that if Firestorm entered the mill before he burnt it down he wouldn't notice their escape route.

Now lit by their torches, the chamber below the mill was a sight to behold. The small boat that Bruiser had mentioned was decorated and gilded in places, although the colours had faded. There was an impressive carved figurehead of a dragon at the helm, suggesting that this was indeed the tomb of a Viking warrior. The boat was sealed with planks of wood, but Bruiser couldn't resist pulling them away to look inside. Four pairs of eyes stared in amazement at the skeletal cat laid out. The most significant feature was that the body was headless, or at least the head wasn't where it should be. On a closer look, amid folds of shredded cloth and thick dust, it was just visible, tucked under one of the corpse's arms. The bottom part of the jaw had rotted away, leaving the top layer of teeth exposed and standing out from the skull. The eye sockets were now homes to spiders, giving the head a very different life to the one it had once known. The body had been laid out straight on its back, and a sword with an elaborately ornate hilt had been placed across it, running from the neck down to the feet. The weapon had sunk into the body where the disintegrated flesh and bone created a cavity. There were other things dotted around the corpse – tiny pots, a metal brooch and a small dagger.

'Do you think this is Ragland Firestorm?' Tilly whispered, shocked and fascinated in equal measure.

'That fits in with your dream,' said Dolly, 'on account of 'im 'avin' 'is 'ead chopped off.'

'And that sword belonged to an important warrior cat,' added Bruiser, who had a particular interest in old weaponry. 'If this is Ragland Firestorm, it's an amazin' discovery.'

'I hate to break up this moment in Viking history,' said Hettie, 'but if we don't get a move on, we're going to be toast or die of smoke. We need to get as far away from the windmill as possible.'

'But what about this body in the boat? That might get destroyed in the fire,' Tilly said.

'I don't see what we can do about that. It'll serve Acrid Firestorm right if he ends up torching his own ancestor,' Hettie replied. 'Now we really must get on.'

Bruiser reached into the boat and retrieved the sword and the small dagger. 'These might come in 'andy, an' at least there'll be somethin' left ta put in one of them museums if we get out of 'ere.'

Dolly was tempted to help herself to the metal brooch, but thought better of it. Bruiser replaced some of the boards over the body, and Hettie led them into the tunnel. The path was quite wide and, as Bruiser had mentioned, there were more bodies tucked into hewn-out crevices on either side. Each tomb seemed to have its own individuality, and from the fragments of clothing and jewellery it was clear that most of them held female cats. As with the first skeleton, they had all been laid to rest with weapons, either in their paws or laid across their bodies. It was a time tunnel of sorts, chronicling the different ages that the skeletons had lived through.

The four friends made slow progress, stopping every few minutes to take in yet another tableau of history that no cat had looked on for hundreds of years. The grave goods scattered around the bodies were no doubt priceless artefacts – pots, jewellery, coins, tokens from another life, and although tempted they left them alone.

'It's just like rooms in a doll's house,' observed Tilly. 'Every one of them is different, but they all look really important. I wonder if one of them is Matilda the Shield Maiden?'

'Judging by what we know already, they're probably all called Matilda,' said Hettie, rather sarcastically, 'but they certainly look like they were warriors with all those weapons around them. I wouldn't want to meet one on a dark night.'

'I think this must be one of them cattycoombs,' Dolly suggested. 'Miss Podger told us that they 'ave them for dead popes in Rome, all set up with their favourite furniture in proper room settins'. Makes sense, really, takin' your best chair with you to the afterlife, although I'd 'ave a preference for an 'ammock on account of its portability.'

'It's strange that none of them have coffins,' Tilly pointed out. 'Not like the crypt we visited last summer in London. That was a bit like this, but you couldn't see the bodies.'

'That's because those corpses were much younger than these,' said Hettie. 'This lot probably go back as far as the ninth century if any of them are Saxons or Vikings. I think there's something quite nice about not being bundled into a box. They look quite peaceful with all their treasures around them, and it looks like they've been laid out on deer skins or something similar.'

The tunnel began to narrow and the walls were now peppered with skulls set into the rock on either side. There was a definite change to their progress, as they now seemed to be going downhill, deeper into the earth. It was becoming quite claustrophobic and Hettie could detect a slight smell of smoke from behind them. The torches they carried were almost done, and as yet there was no sign of the tunnel coming to an end.

In their haste to get out of the windmill, Hettie had completely forgotten to look at the note that the crow had delivered. She pulled it out of her pocket to read before her torch ran out. The message was scribbled and brief.

'Cannot help, as Firestorm has me prisoner in the priory. Sister Constance Surprise.'

'Bloody marvellous!' said Hettie, passing the note to Tilly. 'If this tunnel does come out at the priory, we could be walking into a trap. Let's just hope they're too busy burning the windmill down.'

The four cats quickened their pace. One by one their torches gave out and the darkness closed in around them. They stumbled on, feeling the walls as a guide, trying hard not to panic as their breathing became more and more difficult.

Dolly was the first to give up. She slid to the floor, gasping for breath. 'I'm sorry, but I can't go any further. My 'ead's spinnin' and I might 'ave to be sick.'

Hettie realised that they were probably in more danger from suffocation than from Firestorm's bonfire at the windmill. The uncertainty of what was ahead and the reality of what they'd left behind was becoming a no-win situation. It was a gamble, but she decided to push on in hope that the tunnel would come to an end. 'I think it's best if Bruiser and I keep going and you two wait here,' she said. 'This tunnel can't go on forever and as soon as we find a way out we'll come back for you.'

Tilly welcomed the sit-down next to Dolly, but was fearful for Hettie and Bruiser. Part of her wanted to go with them, but Dolly was in a bad way so she agreed to stay with her. Hettie and Bruiser, armed with the Viking sword and dagger, disappeared into the gloom, leaving Tilly and Dolly to wait impatiently for their return, surrounded by the skulls, bones and treasures of long dead cats whose peace had been disturbed by visitors from another time.

Chapter Eighteen

Sister Constance Surprise struggled in her chair. The ropes that Anger and Bod had tied her up with were cutting into her paws. She'd been foolish to be caught writing the note, but the crow had been swift to carry it away before it could be intercepted. Now she was a prisoner in the cellar below the priory, a place she'd called home since her return. She'd made it comfortable, and her rooms were part of the old underground kitchens that had once been a hive of activity when the priory was home to religious orders carrying out the tasks of everyday life. They had been presided over by a succession of prioresses, all at the invitation of the descendants of Matilda the Shield Maiden. Over the years, plagues, wars and poverty had taken their toll and the building that had once stood tall in its magnificence had been allowed to fall into ruin. Only the ghosts of its glory days, the Skrimshaw crows, and Sister Constance remained to inhabit the skeletal walls of black flint.

When Firestorm had told her that her sisters were dead, she'd felt nothing: they'd been dead to her for years, but now she was a threat to him and had become his prisoner. He had no right to the land, she knew that, but it was a burden to which she no longer aspired, either. The cat who had come in search of her great-aunts had brought hope with her, but if Firestorm was to be believed, she had dealt the fatal blow to her sisters and was now being punished for it.

There was nothing she could do but wait and see what fate would deal her. She could pray, of course, but although she wore the clothes of the Order of Peace Weavers, her faith had melted away long ago. She had hidden her grief for her mother's death and the hatred for her sisters under the robes she wore. She had been content to move about in her solitary world and Dikon had been good to her. She'd wanted for nothing, but now that simple life was under threat.

The visitors who came every summer were told that she was a ghost, a restless spirit bound to the priory to walk its cloisters until the end of time. That's just what it felt like, but now there was a real threat to her existence and, as she sat bound in her chair, she realised that she just didn't care. She was tired of this life, and all the troubles it had brought her.

Chapter Nineteen

Hettie was beginning to think that their situation was hopeless. It had been several minutes since they'd left Tilly and Dolly, and their progress was slow as they tried to conserve the little air that did exist in the tunnel. Bruiser was wheezing, and Hettie was trying very hard to regulate her breathing at the same time as fighting off a panic attack. She was beginning to think they should cut their losses and go back towards the windmill where the path was wider, but suddenly the tunnel opened out into a type of anteroom. It was dark but there was air, which suggested that there might be a way out after all.

'I'll go back and fetch Tilly and Dolly,' Hettie said. 'At least we can breathe here. We could even sit it out until Firestorm has finished burning the mill down.'

Hettie left Bruiser investigating the room and retraced her footsteps. Her friends were greatly relieved to see her, but Dolly was now close to passing out. Hettie picked up the food basket in one paw, helping Dolly up with the other, and the three cats struggled on through the tunnel, gasping for breath but knowing now that there was hope at the end of it.

While Hettie was gone, Bruiser had busied himself running his paws around the walls. They were made of flint, which strongly suggested that they were underneath part of the old priory, but there was no sign of an exit. The roof was much higher than the tunnel had been, and Bruiser squinted up at it. 'I reckon we might 'ave more luck up there,' he said on Hettie's return with Tilly and Dolly.

'But it's much too high,' said Hettie. 'How could we reach it?'

'You'll 'ave ta get on me shoulders an' see what's up there,' Bruiser suggested.

Hettie was no acrobat and her waistline was a little bigger than she'd like, but needs must. With Tilly and Dolly's help, she clambered up onto Bruiser's bony shoulders. After the wobbling had settled down, she lifted her paws to the roof. 'Move a bit to your right,' she said. 'I think there's something sticking out up there.'

Bruiser did as he was asked and Hettie lunged for the object she'd spotted. 'I just can't reach it,' she said. 'It looks like an old iron ring sticking out of the ceiling, but it's hard to tell in this light.'

'Could you reach it with the sword?' suggested Tilly, waving the weapon about.

Hettie grabbed hold of it and forced the hilt into the iron ring, taking care not to injure herself on the blade, which was mercifully rusty. She clambered down from Bruiser's shoulders, leaving the sword hanging.

The four cats stared up at it, wondering what to do next, and it was Dolly – who'd finally managed to get her breathing under control – who drew a timely comparison. 'That's just like King Arthur's sword, 'cept 'is was magical. 'E gave it a good tug and out it came from that big old boulder.'

'We could give it a tug and see what happens, but it might bring the whole roof down,' said Hettie.

'If you all stand back, I'll 'ave a go at it,' offered Bruiser. 'That ring must be up there for some reason.'

Hettie, Tilly and Dolly all moved to the side wall, while Bruiser pulled a rather grubby, oil-stained handkerchief out of his pocket and wrapped it round one of his paws. He grasped the point of the sword and pulled on it with all his might. A shower of grey dust landed on him, making him sneeze; the impact dislodged something above, and a rain of flint stones tumbled down on Bruiser, knocking him to the floor. He sat up immediately and his friends were greatly relieved to see that he was still in one piece, if more than a little dusty. There was no doubt that he'd had a narrow escape, as the Viking sword had also been dislodged and was now embedded in the floor next to him.

It took a moment or two for the dust to clear, but when it did there was cause for a moderate celebration. Looking up, they could see that there was a hole big enough to get through, even though they had no idea where it would lead to. There was no sign of daylight, which suggested that the hole would come out somewhere inside the priory.

'So near and yet so far,' said Hettie. 'I don't see how we can get up there. We need something proper to stand on. If one of us could get through that hole, there might be a rope or something lying around to pull the rest of us up, but it's just too high.'

'I think we should 'ave a bag of Wotsits and a think,' Dolly suggested, pulling them out of the basket.

It was an odd moment to be sitting on the floor having a mid-morning snack, but it was a welcome respite from all the drama they'd put themselves through. They needed to gather their strength for the next stage of their escape, no matter how hopeless it was looking. The Wotsits were attacked with great enthusiasm but were soon finished and it was while they were licking and cleaning their paws that they suddenly became aware of a pair of bright eyes looking down on them from the hole above their heads.

The four friends froze, waiting to see what would happen next. Bruiser's paw moved to the dagger he'd pushed into his belt and Hettie eyed up the food basket, knowing that the bread knife was accessible if she needed it. 'And what or who 'ave we 'ere?' came the voice from above them. 'A little nest of burglars p'raps or more land stealin' 'ippies? Got yerselves in a fine mess down there, 'aven't you now.'

Bruiser stood up and addressed the hole in the roof. 'It's been a long time, but I'm so glad to 'ear that craggy old voice again!'

'Bruiser!' the voice shouted. 'Is that really my old mate Bruiser? 'Ow can that be after all these years? Whatever are you doin' down there?'

'Tryin' ta get out,' Bruiser replied, stating the obvious. 'This cat is my old friend, Dikon,' he said, pointing his paw up at the cat in the roof, 'and these are my friends Hettie, Tilly and Dolly.'

'Pleased to meet you all,' said Dikon. 'I see my old pal 'asn't lost any of 'is charm for the ladies, but I'm mighty impressed that 'e's netted three of you. I s'pose we'd better get you out of there. If you 'ang on, I'll be back with a rope.'

Dikon was gone for some time, but the feeling of relief was great and Hettie insisted that they all have a toffee followed by a Pengelly fruit drop to celebrate.

It wasn't the easiest of manoeuvres to get four cats to climb a rope. Bruiser shinned up with ease. Hettie made a valiant attempt and slid back down twice, burning her paws on the rope before claiming success on the third try. Tilly's arthritic paws wouldn't allow her to climb the rope at all and Dolly refused out of solidarity. The two cats allowed Dikon and Bruiser to haul them up on the rope, making sure that the food basket and the Viking sword went ahead of them.

When all the cats were safely on firm ground again, Hettie tried to make sense of their surroundings. They appeared to have come up into some sort of chapel, but there were no windows or any other form of light. There was something that looked like an altar, but it was in the centre of the space and there were worn stone benches all around the walls. 'What is this place?' she asked.

'In the olden days they called it the room of the dead,' said Dikon. 'I s'pose we'd call it the 'ouse of rest. It's where they laid out the corpse before buryin' it, so cats could come an' say their goodbyes. I keeps me 'ome brew in 'ere as it's nice an' cool. I was about to try me latest batch when the floor fell in an' there you all were.'

'I suppose it was convenient to have it so close to the burials,' Hettie said, and was about to enlarge on the subject of what they'd seen in the tunnel when Bruiser gently but meaningfully trod on her foot, giving her a look that suggested she should say nothing more to Dikon.

'I got ta say this was the last place I expected to run into you,' Dikon said, addressing his old friend. 'I know this priory like the back of me paw, but I had no idea there was anythin' below this room.'

Bruiser explained briefly about being held captive in the windmill by Firestorm and the death of Romew and Remew, deliberately missing out the treasure trove they'd discovered in the tunnel and its connection to Viking and Saxon history. 'Blimey!' said Dikon. 'I'd better let Sister Constance know. She's a nun – lives in the old kitchens under the priory. I look out for 'er in case them 'ippies try an' start somethin'.'

'You sent me the telegram that brought us here,' said Tilly. 'I met Sister Constance before we got locked up in the windmill and she told me how kind you'd been, but now she's a prisoner as well.'

Dikon's hackles rose and he stifled a hiss. 'What's that you say? Sister Constance a prisoner? I wondered why I 'adn't seen 'er takin' 'er walk in the cloisters yesterday, but I put it down to the bad weather. I must go an' look for 'er. It's time those bloody 'ippies got what's comin' to 'em. You can stay 'ere or follow me, but be prepared for a fight.'

Dikon swept out of the room of the dead in haste and Hettie, Tilly, Dolly and Bruiser followed on, with Hettie brandishing the

Viking sword with more than a little difficulty; it was as tall as she was, and almost as heavy. They emerged into the daylight to find the early frost had turned to pouring rain. The house of rest was just outside the main priory wall, and unless you knew it was there, it could easily have been mistaken for a pile of flint stones that had fallen from the wall. Dikon led them back into the cloisters and from there they had a clear view of the windmill. It was surrounded by Firestorm's pilgrims. They had clearly made an attempt to burn it down, but the rain was hindering their progress.

Dikon approached the corner of the cloister, where an old, windblown elder tree had planted itself. Behind the tree, some steps led down to what had once been the old kitchens. He paused to check that there was no one to challenge him, then led the party through a heavy oak door and down another set of steps into a warren of small, cell-like spaces, eventually coming to the room where Sister Constance spent most of her time.

She sat tied to her chair with her head bowed. The room was freezing and the fireplace – which took up half of one of the walls – offered no comfort, as the fire had long since gone out. Dikon bounded across the room, brandishing a substantial flick knife that he'd pulled from one of the leather gaiters he wore. With one swift movement, he sliced through the rope that bound Constance's paws behind her back.

She let out a piercing scream, thinking that she was under attack, and was shocked to find her room full of cats she didn't know. She had fallen into a deep sleep, having given up on any chance of being rescued, but after a few moments of recognition, she was joyful to see Dikon and Tilly. Tilly did the introductions and Dolly set about laying and lighting a fire to get some warmth back into the room. Constance, stiffened by her long incarceration, got to her feet with difficulty and stretched her limbs. Dikon, keen to keep the hippies at bay, bolted the outer door to give them time to come up with a plan.

Tilly and Dolly busied themselves in making tea. There were plenty of supplies, thanks to Dikon, who kept Sister Constance's cupboards well stocked. Hettie sat with Constance and explained her theory regarding the deaths of her sisters. Constance listened intently before responding. 'I'm grateful to you for bringing me this news,' she said. 'It was always going to be this way. My mother saw it in their future, as well as her own death.'

'And did they murder her?' Hettie asked as gently as she could.

'Oh yes, without a doubt. They pushed her from a window in the windmill, and she died instantly in front of me. The fall broke her back, but at least she didn't suffer. I'd like to think that they suffered much more than she did for what they'd done.'

By now Tilly had joined them, and she listened as Constance talked about her sisters and confirmed the details that had been so vivid in her nightmare. 'I'm sorry they gave you such a miserable life,' she said. 'It must have been hard for you, living here in this ruin all these years.'

'Ah, but I have been at peace, which is something Remew and Romew never knew. They were always at war – with each other, with my mother, and with me. Since I returned to the priory, I have found warmth and shelter and the company of the Skrimshaw crows. I have watched the seasons change and moved about in the confines of my own world. I have my books, I write my poetry, I even paint a little – and I have my loyal and devoted friend Dikon for anything else I need.'

Dikon puffed his chest out, pleased to be mentioned in such high esteem. Dolly passed the hot, sweet tea around, and shared out the four remaining pies from Serafin's basket, giving Dikon and Bruiser a whole one each and cutting up the rest for Constance, Tilly, Hettie and herself.

'But how do you manage for money?' Tilly asked, through a mouthful of pastry.

'I have to resort to begging,' Constance replied. 'To my shame, I put out a charity box for the summer visitors who come to look round the priory. They get very excited if they see me because they think I'm a ghost. I'm afraid I'm guilty of the deception, as I point in a ghostly way to the charity box. Dikon sometimes appears as the Battered Friar when the coffers are running really low. Most cats are frightened enough to be generous and I'm sure they dine out for many years on having seen the Skrimshaw Nun or the Friar.'

'What's your relationship with Acrid Firestorm and his so-called pilgrims?' Hettie asked.

Constance looked thoughtful before replying. 'Until now, they've left me alone, although Serafin Parchment often visits me. She's a sweet cat and quite troubled, I think. She had the unenviable task of looking after my sisters, but I think she made the best of it. She told me she'd run away from home after her mother died and Firestorm took her in. That's how most of his followers arrive here. By offering shelter to troubled or homeless cats, he's built himself an army of loyal subjects, but Tabica dominates them all, Firestorm included.'

'In what way?'

'Well, as far as I can gather, she started up a re-enactment village not far from here, setting herself up as some sort of tribal Queen of the Icecreamy. She hoped it would be a runaway success with tourists, but it floundered due to lack of funds and her inability to practise what she preached. She met up with Firestorm and convinced him that he needed a high priestess as part of the Skrimshaw community. She sets herself on a very high pedestal and no one dares to challenge the nonsense she talks, including Firestorm, who is besotted with her. They make a very dangerous combination.'

'What will you do now that your sisters are dead?' Tilly asked.

'I suppose I should fight for the land which is truly mine, but I have no strength against Firestorm and his followers, and no money to offer anyone else to do it for me. Firestorm is convinced that the land is his, based on a terribly distorted legend which

Tabica has filled his head with, and there's nothing I can do about it. When I got your letter, I was briefly filled with hope, but it's really a lost cause and I can see that you have already suffered enough at his paws. You must return to your life and forget about the Skrimshaw land – and me, for that matter.'

Dikon finished his pie and decided to take a closer look at what was happening at the windmill. Bruiser was keen to go with him for moral support, and took the Viking sword with him. The two cats left the old kitchens, making sure that Hettie bolted the door behind them.

Hettie returned to the fire, where Dolly was making another round of milky teas. Sister Constance looked much better after her ordeal, but was concerned about what she might do next. 'I suppose I could return to the religious order,' she said, 'but I will be sorry to leave my rooms here at the priory.'

'But why should you have to give them up?' Hettie asked. 'Firestorm has no right to this land; you said so yourself. If he could be got rid of, wouldn't you be tempted to take on the land and do something positive with it?'

'That's a big if, and what would I do with acres of grassland and a ruin?'

Hettie thought for a moment before replying, and when she did she chose her words carefully. 'Your family history is quite something,' she began, 'and I'm not sure that you realise what it is you're sitting on here. I don't know much about historic sights, but I think after what my friends and I have seen today you are possibly sitting on a gold mine of monumental importance.'

'What do you mean?' asked Constance.

Hettie explained in detail what they had discovered in the tunnel that linked the priory to the burial ground, including the small Viking boat that they suspected held the body of Ragland Firestorm.

Sister Constance listened intently and with a certain amount of disbelief. When Hettie had finished, the nun stared into the fire in silence. Eventually she spoke. 'So this is what my mother tried to tell me. All my life I have pondered over a conversation I had with her shortly before she died. She told me that this land was precious, and that it was my destiny to reveal its treasures to the world. Her words were lost to me over the years, as my sisters did little to look after the inheritance they murdered her for, and I doubt that they ever found any treasure. The priory lost its treasures centuries ago through wars and uprisings, stripped of its art and carvings, so my mother's premonition made no sense to me until now.'

'The first thing you have to do is get rid of Acrid Firestorm and his followers,' Hettie suggested. 'If they get wind of the Viking and Saxon tombs we've seen, they'll ransack them, taking anything of value and destroying the rest. He's probably setting fire to Ragland Firestorm's resting place as we speak, completely oblivious to the fact that he's the ancestor he claims to be descended from.'

'But how do I get rid of him? You've seen what he's capable of, and it's not just him. Tabica could prove to be a formidable enemy and there's the two who bound me to my chair, Anger and Bod. Serafin told me that she was frightened of them.'

'Hopefully Serafin has escaped by now,' said Tilly. 'She was very kind to us and brought us a whole basket of food, including the pies we've just eaten. I just hope that Acrid Firestorm didn't discover what she'd done.'

With all the talk of Firestorm's leanings towards violence, Hettie was beginning to get concerned for Bruiser. He and Dikon had been gone for some time, and she was tempted to go and look for them. 'I'm just going to pop my head out and see what's happening,' she said. 'One of you had better bolt the door behind me.'

Tilly wasn't happy about Hettie putting herself at risk and insisted on going with her, leaving Dolly to look after Sister Constance and bolt the door behind them. Hettie armed herself with the bread knife from the basket and Tilly selected a brass poker from the fireplace. By the time the two cats surfaced into the cloisters of the priory, the battle for the Skrimshaw land had already begun.

Chapter Twenty

It was clear that the element of surprise had initially worked in Bruiser and Dikon's favour. They must have decided to creep up on Acrid Firestorm and his mob as they gathered around the windmill. As Hettie and Tilly emerged from the safety of the priory wall, the distant sound of an almighty cat fight was the first thing they heard. Looking across to the windmill, there were indications that the battle had been raging for some time. Bruiser and Dikon were engaged in paw-to-paw fighting with Bod and Anger, as Firestorm and Tabica looked on with the rest of the pilgrims. Hettie was concerned to see that Firestorm was holding the Viking sword, which he had obviously taken from Bruiser.

'Things don't seem to be going our way,' Hettie said. 'It certainly looks like they could do with reinforcements, but I'm not sure what we can do. I don't think my bread knife and your poker are the weapons we need.'

Tilly looked down at her feet. 'I know what we could do,' she said. 'We could chuck stones at them.'

Hettie began to laugh, then thought better of it. It was such a simple plan of attack, but she had to agree that the sharp flint stones that peppered the ground around the priory would make excellent missiles. 'Come on, then – let's collect some of these.

If nothing else, we could create a distraction to give Bruiser and Dikon an advantage.'

They gathered as many stones as they could carry and took a circuitous route towards the windmill, hoping that they wouldn't be spotted before they were able to do some damage. The Skrimshaw crows obliged them by taking flight from the priory wall and noisily circling the fight, causing the onlookers to look up just as Hettie and Tilly struck. Hettie's aim was true and hit Firestorm on the back of his head, causing him to drop the Viking sword on his foot. At the same time, Tilly scored a direct hit on Tabica and threw another stone at her to make sure, knocking her to the ground. Bod turned away from Bruiser, sensing danger from the new assault, and Bruiser pounced on his back, gaining the advantage. Dikon wasn't so lucky. Anger had sunk his teeth into his throat and was now tearing at his flesh. Hettie responded immediately by bombarding the cat with her remaining stones until he finally rolled away from Dikon, who lay still in a pool of his own blood.

By now, Firestorm had recovered and turned on Hettie and Tilly, sweeping the Viking sword in front of him. Tilly threw the stones she had left, hitting her target several times, but Firestorm continued to come at them, his head bleeding from the cuts the flints had made. The rest of the pilgrims looked on, and Clawdelia broke away from them to attend to Dikon. It was no surprise that – in the commotion – no one noticed the Morris Minor driving at speed towards them across the field. It was a timely arrival, as Firestorm was raising the sword to despatch Hettie and Tilly. Betty Butter succeeded in accommodating him on her bonnet instead, sending the sword spinning through the air. Firestorm rolled off the car and collapsed in a heap at Bruiser's feet.

Tabica, still dazed, staggered to her feet and launched herself at Bruiser, who sidestepped her, allowing Beryl to finish her off with a saucepan she was wielding through the Morris's window. Tabica collapsed on top of Firestorm and the pilgrims responded by offering an energetic round of applause, which came as a great surprise to Hettie and Tilly. They were even more surprised to see Serafin Parchment sitting in the back seat of the Butters' car.

Dryad retrieved the sword and passed it back to Bruiser, who used it to round up Anger and Bod, marching them over to where Firestorm and Tabica cowered in a heap after the Butter sisters' onslaught. Bruiser stood over them, the Viking sword in his paw, ready to engage at the slightest encouragement.

Betty and Beryl stepped out of the Morris, pulling the passenger seat forward to allow Serafin out of the car. 'Well,' said Betty, 'that's a mighty fine pickle you've got yourselves in here. That's the last time we let you out for a Sunday afternoon tea. Where's Dolly?'

'She's safe with Sister Constance Surprise in a cellar below the priory, although she's really a Matilda,' Tilly said, realising how ridiculous she sounded.

'What's that?' asked Beryl. 'Dolly is really a Matilda?'

Tilly was about to reply with a much more comprehensive explanation, but Hettie intervened – there were more pressing issues to deal with. 'Why don't you take Betty and Beryl back to the priory, and Bruiser and I will sort the mess out here,' she suggested.

Tilly agreed and bundled into the Morris with Betty and Beryl. The car set off again and bumped across the grassland, coming to an abrupt halt at the priory wall.

'I didn't expect to see you again,' said Hettie, turning to Serafin.

'I met your landladies while I was hitching,' she explained. 'I managed to get out of here while Firestorm was busy trying to burn the mill down. I got a few miles down the road when this car stopped to ask directions to the priory. They were lost, so I said I'd show them the way. Actually, I felt bad about leaving you and I thought I might be able to do something better than running away. Betty and Beryl seemed really nice, and they told me how worried they'd been. I told them a bit about what had gone on and what was happening to the windmill, so Betty put her foot down and here we are.'

'I've seen a lot of films where the cavalry wins the day, but nothing compares to the Butters' Morris Minor charging down that hill. We owe you a debt which we will make sure is paid,' Hettie promised, 'but now it's time for some justice.'

She turned away from Serafin, leaving her to join the group of pilgrims who welcomed her like a long-lost friend. The big question now was what to do with Firestorm and his cohorts, but there was a more serious matter to attend to first. Dikon still lay injured and unconscious on the ground where Anger had attacked him. Clawdelia had removed her shawl and, on Marjoram's instructions, was pressing it into the wound in his neck to try to stop the bleeding, but he needed to be moved to somewhere more comfortable, where his injuries could be properly assessed and tended.

Hettie beckoned Cambric over to her. 'I want you to take over from Bruiser while he helps Dikon,' she said. 'I assume that you are on our side and not theirs, as you've taken no part in this fight?' She waved her paw in the direction of Firestorm.

'I'd be glad to,' Cambric said, taking the sword from Bruiser. 'I'd be happy to kill them all if you asked me to. They'd finally get what was coming to them.'

'That's one solution,' said Hettie, enjoying the fear in Firestorm's eyes, 'but I think we'd all like them to suffer a bit before we kill them. After all, we wouldn't want to rob them of the anticipation of their own deaths, would we? It was only a matter of hours ago that my friends and I were in a similar position, so we have a perfect understanding of how that one plays out.'

'Please,' said Firestorm, 'if you let us go, you'll never see us again. We'll leave this place and go where no one knows us.'

Tabica hissed at him, showing her disgust at his pleading. 'You stupid fool,' she said. 'You can't just walk away from your birthright. What would Ragland Firestorm think of you? These cats have no right to keep us prisoner and they are too cowardly to kill us.'

'And so speaks the all-seeing high priestess,' Hettie mocked. 'The sword that now hangs over you is the sword of a disgraced Viking murderer. It is the sword of Ragland Firestorm, and had the windmill been successfully burnt down, you would have destroyed his tomb as well, as it lies beneath the mill. I'm surprised that you didn't know that as a self-confessed mystic. I suggest your powers are dwindling and your games are over.'

Hettie walked away before Tabica could respond, leaving Firestorm, Anger and Bod nervously licking their wounds. She joined Bruiser at Dikon's side. 'I think I'll go an' fetch Miss Scarlet,' he said. 'I can drive 'im down ta the campsite in 'er sidecar.'

'You can put him in my hut,' Marjoram suggested. 'I can tend to his wounds much better there with all my herbs and salves.'

'I'll help you nurse him,' said Serafin.

Bruiser struck out across the meadow and returned minutes later with Miss Scarlet. He was joyfully reunited with her, but seriously worried about his old friend. With the help of Serafin and Dryad, they gently loaded Dikon into the sidecar and Bruiser drove slowly back to the campsite, followed by the pilgrims, all keen to help as much as they could.

Hettie stared up at the windmill. Romew's skeleton still hung off the sails, now picked clean of any flesh by the Skrimshaw crows. The base of the mill, where Firestorm had ordered the wood and reeds to be placed, was barely singed. The rain had come at the right moment to scupper his plans.

'So,' said Hettie, addressing Acrid Firestorm, 'how do you fancy a minibreak in a windmill? I can highly recommend it, and you will be closer to your ancestor than you could ever dream of. The facilities are a little limited and it gets very cold at night, especially without a fire. And then there are the ghosts, whispering and scratching at the walls – oh, and the bodies of the Ancients, of course. In fact, I think we'll put you all in the Ancients' sitting room – after we've nailed up the window, of course. We wouldn't want you to escape, would we? If you'd care to stay where you are while we prepare your accommodation, that would be most helpful.'

Having deposited Dikon into the care of Marjoram and Serafin, Bruiser returned on Miss Scarlet and helped Hettie to secure the mill with the aid of the trusty toolbox that he kept in the boot of the sidecar. To gain entry they forced their shoulders to the door and eventually, and with much effort, pushed the sideboard barricade out of the way. Hettie was relieved to see that there was no fire damage to the ground floor, and the two cats did their best to nail the boards back down over the tunnel. They moved the chairs back up to the first floor and secured the window. The door to Romew and Remew's sitting room looked like it hadn't been closed for years. Bruiser oiled its hinges and the two cats were satisfied that the first floor would make an ideal temporary place to keep Firestorm and his companions while they decided what to do with them.

Cambric assisted as the prisoners were marched into the windmill and up the first flight of stairs. It was with great satisfaction that Hettie slammed the door on them. Justice, she thought, was rarely poetic, but this time everything seemed to rhyme.

Chapter Twenty-One

As Hettie and Bruiser made their way back to the old kitchens beneath the priory, the Butter sisters and Constance were getting to know each other. There was much activity at the kitchen range, as Dolly and Beryl had decided that everyone deserved a proper meal after all the fighting. Beryl was rolling out pastry, while Dolly cooked up her special Cornish pasty mixture. Betty and Tilly sat drinking tea and dunking ginger biscuits with Sister Constance, listening as the nun told the story of her family and some of the history connected with it; Tilly chipped in occasionally with the details of her nightmares and Dolly recounted their time locked in the windmill for the benefit of the Butters.

Betty and Beryl were shocked by the revelations and fascinated by the history surrounding them. 'I have to say,' said Betty, 'that beats any story I've read by Katrin Cookpot, our favourite author from Lancashire. What do you think, sister?'

'I'm inclined to agree,' said Beryl, dusting the flour off her paws. 'I think Constance and Tilly should write it all down and make a book out of it. Those sagas are all the rage – we're enjoying that *Forthright Saga* as our TV preference on Sundays at the moment.'

'Me an' Molly's glued to *Poldark*,' chipped in Dolly. 'That's set around the time of Tilly's witchfinder, or thereabouts.

My favourite is Demelza. She always manages to smile, no matter what 'appens to 'er. She's got a proper Cornish attitude about 'er.'

Constance looked bewildered by all the TV talk. 'I have to admit, I haven't seen a television since the sixties. It was frowned upon by the Order of the Peace Weavers and I haven't engaged with it since, but I've clearly missed out judging by what you're saying.'

'You need to get Dikon to fix you up with a set,' Dolly suggested. 'It'd cheer your winter evenin's an' save you readin' all them books.'

Constance was about to point out that she loved reading books when a hammering on the outer door interrupted her. 'I'll go,' said Tilly, picking up the poker. 'Hopefully it's Hettie and Bruiser.'

It was, and the two cats were pleased to join in with the scene of contented domesticity overseen by the comforting presence of the Butter sisters.

'Where's Dikon?' Constance asked.

'I'm afraid he's not too good at the moment,' Hettie said, 'but he's in good paws. He's got Marjoram and Serafin looking after him.'

'I hope he'll be all right,' said Constance. 'He's been a true friend and I just couldn't bear it if anything happened to him.'

''E's made of tough stuff,' said Bruiser, 'and 'e's a fighter.'

'What have you done with that Firestorm creature and that ridiculous bald cat with the tattoos?' Betty asked. 'After what we've been hearing, there isn't a punishment good enough for them and their thugs. You could have all been killed in that windmill and goodness knows what they might have done to Sister Constance here.'

'Well, thanks to your timely arrival in the Morris we don't have to think about that any more,' said Hettie, gratefully accepting a hot, sweet, milky tea from Dolly and a ginger biscuit from Constance. 'We've got them locked away in the windmill for now, but there are much bigger decisions to make than what to do with them.'

'Like what to 'ave with these pasties,' Dolly pointed out, causing everyone to laugh out loud.

The pasties were very good indeed, helped down by a liberal serving of baked beans from Constance's pantry. When the food was finished, Bruiser went to check on Dikon and brought back good news. ''E's awake and sittin' up, an' enjoyin' all the attention from Marjoram an' Serafin. You can't keep an old cat like Dikon down fer long.'

Everybody was relieved at Dikon's progress and Hettie decided that it was time to make some plans. 'I think we need to get the decent pilgrims together and see what can be done to sort this place out,' she suggested. 'It seems to me that they would all be keen to stay on here at the priory without Firestorm and his henchmen, and to play a part in putting this place on the map.'

'I would be very happy if they stayed,' said Constance, 'but I have no funds to pay them and I'm not sure how we could make the most of what's here.'

'Ah well, I have an idea about that but Bruiser needs to take me to the nearest telephone box so that I can make a call,' said Hettie.

'And we'd better be making tracks for home,' Betty added. 'We've left Elsie Haddock looking after the bakery but she won't take kindly to doing another day in there.'

'I'll come back with you if that's OK?' said Dolly reluctantly. 'I can't leave Molly to struggle on 'er own in the café for much longer.'

'You're most welcome,' said Beryl, 'as long as you take over the map reading. I can't make head nor tail of these Norfolk roads, and if it wasn't for Serafin I think we'd still be stuck in those reed beds.'

'What about you three?' asked Betty. 'Sounds to me like you've got unfinished business here. I assume you'll be staying on for a day or two, but don't forget Marmite Spratt's funeral – it's on Saturday morning at St Kippers, and you won't want to miss that.'

Hettie nodded. 'We'll do our best to be there, but we won't leave here until we're happy that Sister Constance is safe and Dikon is out of the woods. We still have to deal with Firestorm and make sure that the remaining hippies can be trusted. I think it's also important not to tell anyone what we've discovered here until everything is secure. We don't want Sister Constance bothered by grave robbers.'

Constance offered a sigh of relief. 'I'm so very grateful to all of you,' she said. 'From living such a solitary life, I now find myself surrounded by friends, and the last few hours have been the happiest I've known since my dear mother died. Whatever the future holds, I will always remember your kindness.'

Betty, Beryl and Dolly said their goodbyes and piled into the Morris Minor. Bruiser kicked Miss Scarlet into life and Hettie jumped into the sidecar to go off in search of a telephone. Sister Constance and Tilly waved them off as they left in convoy and headed for the gatehouse. The Skrimshaw crows took flight en masse and followed them, forming an avian escort until the car and the motorbike were out of sight.

Hettie returned jubilant from finding a telephone box in a small village a few miles from the priory. Feeling a little lost without Dolly, Bruiser decided to go and check on Dikon and then spend the evening with Cambric, as he'd shown an enthusiastic interest in anything to do with motorbikes. Hettie was keen to share her news, but took Tilly to one side first to fill her in before telling Sister Constance about the phone call she'd just made. Tilly was as excited as Hettie once she'd learnt a bit more about what her friend had been up to and the two cats sat down with Constance to explain.

'I've arranged for you to have a visitor,' Hettie began. 'It's a cat we met while we were investigating a murder case in our town a couple of years ago. Her name is Binky Crustworthy. She's very rich and she runs an organisation called the National Crust. She goes around saving old buildings and investing in them. I took the liberty of telling her a little bit about your plight here and the Saxon and Viking treasures in the tunnel. She was very excited and couldn't wait to come and see you, so she's arriving tomorrow.'

'But what will it mean? Will I have to sell everything to her and what will happen to the treasures?' Constance looked fearful. 'I'm not sure my mother would have approved of me passing the land on to a stranger.'

'As far as I can tell, it would be more like a partnership, but you'll have to listen to what she's got to say and decide if you want to take it any further. She works with a whole legion of experts who will understand what you have here, and Binky will know how to turn that to your advantage if you want her to,' said Hettie, keen to put Constance's mind at rest.

'She is a very nice cat,' Tilly added. 'I think you'll like her.'

Constance could see the sense in the meeting that Hettie had set up for her. The day had been a very strange one, starting with the brutality she had suffered at the paws of Anger and Bod, followed by her rescue and the making of new friends; now, she had to face the realisation that – after all these years – she had finally succeeded her mother as keeper of the Skrimshaw legacy. She was exhausted, but sleep was impossible. Long after Hettie and Tilly had retired to the caravan for the night, Constance sat up, staring into the flames of her fire, thinking about her sisters and how much of her own life they'd stolen from her. Tomorrow might bring a fresh start, a new beginning that would make her ancestors proud.

Meanwhile, across the field, the windmill was under siege. As soon as darkness fell, the whispering began and then the scratching at the walls. Firestorm bounded to the top of the mill to disable the system he'd so effectively used to drive the Ancients mad, only to discover it in pieces on the floor. At that moment he knew true fear – centuries of dead Skrimshaws were crawling out of their tombs and scaling the walls, invading his mind with the tongues of angry, vengeful spirits.

Chapter Twenty-Two

Hettie and Tilly rose early, mainly because they were frozen and hungry. Their second night in the caravan had been no more comfortable than the first, and they wished that they'd swapped places with Bruiser, who'd spent the night tucked up in Miss Scarlet's sidecar. They'd slept in all their clothes for several nights and even Hettie, who cared very little for keeping up appearances, felt decidedly grubby.

'What's the plan for the day?' Tilly asked, trying really hard to stop her teeth chattering.

'The first thing is to find a hot breakfast,' said Hettie, 'then we'd better pay a visit to the windmill. I want to get Firestorm and his cronies out of the way before Binky Crustworthy turns up.'

'What do you think we should do with them?'

'That's a hard question to answer. If it was just Firestorm, I think we could kick him off the property and never see him again – he's essentially a coward hiding behind his ridiculous hippie persona. The trouble is Tabica. I wouldn't trust her not to stage a comeback with Anger and Bod as soon as we leave, and goodness knows what she'd do to Sister Constance. I think we need to assess the situation this morning when we see them.'

'What time are we expecting Binky Crustworthy?' Tilly asked, trying to smooth the fur on the top of her head in a cracked mirror which hung over the sink. 'I just feel so scruffy and she's so posh. I hope we don't put her off.'

'She's coming on her motorbike and hopes to arrive by lunchtime,' said Hettie. 'Judging by her excitement on the phone last night, I doubt she'll even notice us once she's clapped eyes on the tunnel – which reminds me, I need to get Bruiser to rig up some sort of ladder down into the tunnel from the priory end so we can give her the grand tour of the "cattycoombs", as Dolly calls them. I doubt that Binky Crustworthy or Sister Constance would appreciate being dangled from a rope.'

The thought made Tilly giggle as they struggled out into a frosty morning in search of breakfast. They decided to call in on Marjoram to see how Dikon was and were delighted, if a little envious, to see him sitting up and tucking into a bacon sandwich. He was swathed in bandages around his throat and two of his paws, but otherwise in very good spirits. He asked about Sister Constance, and Hettie assured him that she was safe and well after her ordeal with Anger and Bod.

Marjoram was busy mixing some ointment at a table in the corner of her hut. Tilly stared in amazement at all the bunches of herbs drying around the walls and the shelf of small bottles, all neatly labelled. 'How on earth did you learn about all these medicines?' she asked.

'I've got my ancestors to thank for that,' Marjoram said. 'I come from a long line of white witches. One of them was actually burnt at the stake back in the time of Matthew Katkins, who used to live here at the priory. He was the witchfinder, you know.'

Tilly felt a cold chill run through her but nodded and smiled back at Marjoram, not wishing to bring back the memory of Katkins' murder. Marjoram finished mixing her ointment and dipped her paw in it, gently wiping it on the side of Tilly's face where she'd been injured. 'That's healing nicely,' she said, 'but you must look after it.'

'That's very kind, thank you,' Tilly said as Hettie moved towards the door. They were about to leave when Serafin popped her head in.

'Ah, there you are,' she said. 'I looked for you in the caravan to see if you'd like some breakfast. Your friend Bruiser is already tucking in back in my hut.'

There was almost a stampede, as Hettie and Tilly didn't need asking twice. They made quick work of transferring from Marjoram's hut to Serafin's, where the smell of bacon was almost overpowering. Clawdelia had clearly been busy, as there was a pile of freshly baked baps and a frying pan loaded with bacon sitting on Serafin's table. Bruiser was on his second bap and third cup of what looked like milky tea.

'Help yourselves,' Serafin said. 'I'll make some more tea and don't worry – I've borrowed a box of ordinary tea bags from Sister Constance. I get the feeling that my herbals aren't that popular with you two either.'

'How is Sister Constance this morning?' Hettie asked, as she loaded a bap with bacon and passed it to Tilly, who'd settled herself on a cushion next to Bruiser.

'To be honest, I got a bit of a shock when I saw her,' Serafin admitted. 'I'd never seen her without that headdress thing she wears, and she's always looked like a nun in those black robes. When I went round there, it looked like she was in the middle of some sort of sixties fashion show. Pretty far out, really – lovely long, floaty dresses and flared jeans and T-shirts. She'd pulled them all out of an old chest. She was wearing a smart trouser suit which was a bit dated, but she looked fantastic. And she asked me to stop calling her Sister Constance. She said she was now going to be plain old Matilda Skrimshaw.'

Hettie smiled to herself. This was the best news and Tilly instantly felt that a huge weight had been lifted from her tabby shoulders. It was clear from what Serafin had described that the Skrimshaw legacy was in a safe pair of paws again with a Matilda at the helm.

After they'd finished their breakfast, Bruiser went off to enlist the help of Cambric, who was fast becoming a best friend. Hettie explained that she was keen to be rid of their prisoners in the windmill and Bruiser thought that an extra pair of paws would be useful if there was any resistance. Serafin pointed out that Tabica's old van might be helpful in the plan to expel them from Skrimshaw land. 'She used to live in it until she teamed up with Acrid,' she said. 'After that, she did her readings in there. I think it still drives OK, so maybe you could convince her to hit the road in it and take the other three with her. It's a shame about Anger and Bod, though – or should I say Sam and Jim. They were really nice cats when I first came here but Acrid and Tabica had this thing about turning them into Viking warriors and gave them new names. I think they went along with it so they could stay here. We all did really.'

Hettie and Tilly were beginning to understand the hold that Tabica and Firestorm had over the Skrimshaw community and they thought that packing Tabica off in her old van was a brilliant idea. When Bruiser returned with Cambric, Hettie sent him to check the van over and see if it started. Initially it coughed and spluttered, but after he'd given the spark plugs a once over with his oily handkerchief, it fired immediately, filling the place where it was parked with a cloud of blue-black smoke. Bruiser drove it round to the front of the campsite and Hettie, Tilly and Cambric jumped in the back to be driven across to the windmill.

All was silent as they entered the ground floor. Bruiser and Cambric went ahead and bounded up the first flight of stairs, leaving Hettie and Tilly to follow on. When they were all gathered at the top, Bruiser opened the door. They were immediately aware of a whimpering noise. It was Tabica. She sat in a space by the window with her paws in front of her face, as if trying to protect herself. 'Please don't let them get me,' she sobbed. 'I can still hear them. I'll do anything to stop them coming for me. Please just let me go and I'll never come back.'

Tabica's pleading was music to Hettie's ears, but she was confused about who exactly 'them' were. Bruiser and Cambric stood at the door in case anyone felt like making a run for it, but Firestorm, Anger and Bod all sat staring into space, not even responding to the fact that they had visitors. Firestorm appeared to be mumbling, but no sound came from him. The other two cats twisted their paws nervously, as if they were waiting for something bad to happen.

'Well, this is a sorry sight,' said Hettie. 'Anyone would think you'd all seen a ghost, and it's not the reception I was expecting. Thinking about it, we disconnected the ghosts before we left here so whatever can it be that has upset you so much?' The sarcasm in Hettie's voice did nothing to help the situation and Tabica began to rock backward and forward, issuing a high-pitched squealing noise. Firestorm got up from his chair and slapped her, bringing the bout of hysteria to an abrupt end.

He turned to Hettie. 'Whatever you're going to do with us, just get it over with. All I would ask is that we don't have to spend another night in this windmill.'

'I call that very ungrateful,' Hettie said, looking across at the body rolled up in a carpet, now attracting a battalion of flies. 'We thought you might like to join the Ancients. We could hang you all from the sails and let the Skrimshaw crows pick you clean, or we could lock you up in here and throw away the key, or we could burn down the mill with you all inside it.'

There was no fight left in Firestorm. He bowed his head and limped back to the chair he'd been sitting in, but Hettie hadn't quite finished with him. 'While you're deciding your fate, there are a couple of things I'd like to clear up with you. You accused my friend Tilly here of murdering the Ancients. You couldn't have been more wrong, as they actually killed each other – but you were responsible for their deaths because you drove them to it. It also seems that your illustrious ancestor Ragland Firestorm was a murderer and was executed by Matilda the Shield Maiden. He slaughtered her kittens and she cut his head off for it. As I mentioned before, we have his Viking sword, so perhaps it would be fitting to cut your head off with it as you're so keen to follow in his footsteps?'

'It's all a lie,' Firestorm blurted out. 'It was Tabica's idea. My real name is Nigel Small. I never meant for any of this to happen but Tabica said we could get away with it.'

Bod and Anger were now on their feet, hissing and spitting as they approached their deposed leader. Bruiser allowed them both a meaningful swipe before standing in their way, but Bod spoke in their defence. 'We've been tricked into this,' he said. 'We thought we were fighting to keep the land and our community together, but now we know the truth we'll do anything to put things right.'

Anger nodded in agreement and Cambric spoke up for them. 'Bod's right. We've all been hoodwinked by that pair,' he said, jabbing his paw at Firestorm and Tabica. 'We've all been made to do things we're not proud of but to stay here we had to live by their rules.'

'I'm calling a meeting of the Skrimshaw community later today,' said Hettie. 'You have a new leader now and I think Bod and Anger – or should I say Sam and Jim – should join us to see if they still have a future here.'

Sam and Jim beamed at Hettie, so pleased to hear their real names again. 'We'll do anything we can to make up for what we've done,' said Jim.

Hettie smiled back. 'I think you both have some apologies to make so get down to the campsite and see Marjoram to get your wounds attended to. You'll be pleased to know that Dikon is on the mend, but you need to make your peace with him

– and with Matilda Skrimshaw, of course.' Sam and Jim looked confused for a moment until Hettie explained. 'The nun you know as Sister Constance is the rightful heir to the Skrimshaw land. She has decided to shed her religious robes to assume her real name, Matilda Skrimshaw, and it is she who will inevitably decide whether you stay or go from here.'

Sam and Jim wasted no time in heading for the door to do what Hettie had asked of them and Cambric and Bruiser stood aside to let them pass. 'Now then,' said Hettie, addressing Firestorm. 'What's it going to be? Do we leave you here and throw away the key so you can starve and freeze to death? Or hang you both? Or shall we escort you to that Celtic monstrosity parked outside and let you drive away on the understanding that Sam and Jim will cut off your heads with the Viking sword if you ever set one claw onto Skrimshaw land again?'

Firestorm hesitated in disbelief. It took a moment or two for him to realise that they really were being offered their freedom, but eventually he spoke. 'I am truly sorry for all I've done, and, if you let us go, I promise I will never return to this place, and I will make sure that Tabica – or should I say Shirley – never returns either. You have my word.'

Hettie, Tilly, Bruiser and Cambric all sniggered together at the thought of Tabica being a Shirley. The name didn't seem to sit well with the shaved head and the tattoos. 'Well, if you and Shirley would care to get yourselves into the van and drive away immediately, the rest of us can get on with our day,' said Hettie, 'but if we see so much as one of your whiskers on this land again, then Sam and Jim will relieve you both of your heads and feed you to the Skrimshaw crows.'

Nigel and Shirley got to their feet and walked slowly to the stairs, where Cambric and Bruiser escorted them to the van. Nigel bundled Shirley into the back and settled himself in the driver's seat. The van spluttered into life and Nigel drove out at speed through the gatehouse entrance, narrowly missing a motorcyclist dressed in tweeds and an alarming pair of goggles who was driving in.

'Nice bike,' Bruiser said.

'Yes, but look who's riding it. It appears that Binky Crustworthy has made excellent time, so we'd better get down to the priory and introduce her to Sister... I mean, to Matilda Skrimshaw,' said Hettie. 'Could you and Cambric rig up a ladder or something so that we can take her on a grand tour of the tunnel from the priory end?'

'Righto,' said Bruiser. 'I'm sure we can sort somethin' out.'

The four cats made their way back to the priory, where Binky Crustworthy had just clambered off her motorbike. 'Ah, Miss Bagshot and Miss Jenkins – how lovely to see you both again, and in happier times,' said Binky, who had been grieving over her brother Bartlett's death when they'd last met. 'I just couldn't sleep last night after your phone call, so I got on the road at five this morning. Bit of a place to find, but what a magnificent ruin you've got here.'

Binky secured her motorbike and pulled her goggles off. She was dressed from head to toe in tweeds, and, as Tilly would comment later, resembled Margaret Rutherfur, the actress who had often played Miss Marble on the big screen. 'I think we'd better introduce you to Matilda Skrimshaw first,' said Hettie. 'The priory has been in her family for hundreds of years. Then we'll take you on a guided tour.'

'Splendid! Lead on!' said Binky.

Hettie and Tilly were as surprised as Serafin had been when Matilda Skrimshaw let them into the old kitchens. The transformation from Sister Constance to the cat in front of them was astonishing. She looked so much younger and carried an air of confidence about her that instantly impressed Binky. The two cats got on like a house on fire. Hettie and Tilly busied themselves making tea and raiding the biscuit tin while Matilda filled Binky in on her family's history and their connections to the Saxons and Vikings.

It was clear that Binky was impressed and she wasted no time in saying so. 'My dear Miss Skrimshaw, I can't wait to see what you have here. If the tombs Miss Bagshot mentioned are genuine, you probably have one of the most important collections of Saxon relics in the whole of our kingdom, and I would be delighted to be involved in securing it for you and the nation.'

Matilda was delighted with Binky Crustworthy's initial reaction; with all the enthusiasm swimming about, she was now keen to see the Skrimshaw treasures for herself. Hettie went to check that Bruiser and Cambric had managed to create a safe way of getting into the tunnel and returned with the good news that they'd rigged up a temporary chair and pulley system.

Binky was on her feet immediately and Hettie led the way to the house of rest, where Bruiser and Cambric stood ready to demonstrate their contraption. Hettie was the first to try it out. She sat on the chair and Bruiser gradually lowered her down into the room at the head of the tunnel. Cambric had collected several torches, and he lowered those down to Hettie next. Tilly followed, and then Matilda. Binky was last, as she was busy examining the stone catafalque in the centre of the floor.

Armed with torches, the four cats set out through the tunnel with Hettie leading the way and Tilly at the back. Almost immediately, Binky began to talk to herself, punctuating her words with gasps of delight and the occasional clap of her paws. Matilda was completely silent as they passed tomb after tomb of her long dead ancestors. Eventually they arrived at the small Viking boat underneath the windmill, which Hettie believed to be Ragland Firestorm's tomb.

Binky and Matilda stared in awe at the boat, neither cat daring to approach. Hettie and Tilly carefully removed the planks to reveal the body, and Binky summoned up the courage to step forward. 'I can honestly say I've never seen such an extraordinary find,' she said, 'and almost perfectly preserved.'

Matilda stared down at the headless skeleton with mixed feelings. Here was the cat who had tried to overthrow Matilda the Shield Maiden, a murderer executed for his crimes. Even if she hadn't known the story, she would still have felt the evil that she now sensed as she took in every detail of the skeleton, including the head tucked underneath one of his arms. To Binky, this was a priceless artefact, a window into the past, but to Matilda Skrimshaw it was much more personal, a painful reminder of all the cats who had died fighting for the land that had now been passed to her.

Hettie and Tilly replaced the boards over the body and the four cats retraced their footsteps, stopping occasionally to take in more details from individual tomb settings. 'There's a lot of work here,' Binky said. 'To do these treasures justice, I'd need to get an expert in to create an inventory of every item. For that reason, this find should be kept top secret until the work is done. It seems to me that the best way to display all these tombs is to leave them where they are and make them secure, rather than putting them all in a museum where cats will only visit them on rainy days. The whole thing is an experience of a lifetime, or several lifetimes if you count the skeletons down here.'

'I really wouldn't want them moved,' Matilda said. 'They are at peace, which is why they were put here in the first place. To move them would feel like desecration to me.'

'I totally agree,' said Binky, stopping at a particularly grand tomb setting. 'This is the skeleton of a female warrior – you can tell by the trappings surrounding her. She has coins and jewels as well as weapons, and if you look very closely under the deerskin she's lying on, there are smaller skeletons with her. My guess is that they are her kittens.'

It was Tilly's turn to gasp. 'I wonder if that's Matilda the Shield Maiden, buried with her murdered kittens?'

'Quite possibly,' said Binky. 'It makes perfect sense for the kittens to have been entombed together, and for her to join them when her time came. The whole thing is totally fascinating. I can hardly believe what I'm seeing, and it's all the richer for the story that goes with it.'

It was now some time since the bacon bap and Hettie was keen to move things along. 'Why don't we all return to the priory so that you two can discuss what to do next over lunch?' she suggested.

Matilda and Binky agreed and the four cats made their way back to where Bruiser was waiting patiently to hoist them up into civilisation again. Hettie and Tilly returned to the campsite with Bruiser, leaving Binky and Matilda with much to discuss in the priory kitchens over sandwiches and coffee. Hettie was concerned about how Sam and Jim had been received by the other hippies, but she needn't have worried. She found them in Marjoram's hut, plastered in ointment and playing a card game with Dikon, who had clearly forgiven them. There was no sign of Marjoram, and Dikon explained that she'd been called away in an emergency by Cambric.

'We've still got to see Sister Constance,' Jim said, 'but she wasn't there, so we'll go back later to apologise.'

'I hate to break up your game, but I have a little job for you both,' Hettie said. 'I need you to bury the Ancients as quietly and discreetly as you can. The body inside the windmill is fairly straightforward, but you'll have to get the other one down from the sail, which might be difficult as it's very high up. I suggest you bury them in the more recent part of the burial ground at the back of the mill. You can't be seen from the priory there.'

Sam and Jim jumped up, promising Dikon that they would return later to finish the game, and strode off, both keen to show Hettie that they meant what they'd said about making amends. Bruiser stayed with Dikon to talk over old times, and Hettie and Tilly went off in search of some food.

Serafin was hanging a line of washing out, which reminded Tilly of how nice it would be to wear something clean, but it was Cambric pacing up and down outside the hut next to Serafin's who caught their eye. 'I wonder what the emergency is that Dikon mentioned?' Tilly said. 'Cambric looks a bit upset.'

'So will I be if we don't find any lunch,' grumbled Hettie.

Serafin overheard and came to the rescue. 'I was just about to make myself a ham and cheese sandwich and a cup of one of my herbals,' she said. 'I could make you both a sandwich, and one for Bruiser and Dikon, as well, if you like? Thankfully Clawdelia got her baking out of the way just in time, so there's plenty of bread.'

'That would be lovely,' said Hettie, 'but just in time for what?'

Serafin was about to explain, but Marjoram suddenly appeared from the hut next door, her paws and apron covered in blood. Cambric looked horrified, but his mind was soon put at rest. 'You have four very beautiful kittens – two boys and two girls,' Marjoram announced. 'Clawdelia is absolutely fine, so you'd better come and meet your new family.'

Cambric skipped into the hut and Hettie, Tilly and Serafin gathered in the doorway to peep at the new arrivals. 'They're so tiny,' Tilly said. 'It's all a bit magical, really. I wonder what they'll grow up to be?'

'Who can say?' said Hettie. 'I'm just glad that they've been born into a world without Firestorm and Tabica dictating how their lives will be – or should I say Nigel and Shirley.'

Serafin burst out laughing. 'You are joking?' she said. 'Nigel and Shirley! That's as far out as it gets.'

Hettie, Tilly and Serafin left Cambric and his new family in peace and went off to have some lunch. Bruiser and Dikon were happy to stay where they were but the others sat to eat their sandwiches on a bench, and watched from a distance as Jim and Sam successfully managed to recover what was left of Romew's body from the windmill sail with the help of a long, extended ladder. Serafin shed a tear. 'I know they could be nasty, but I will miss them,' she said. 'This land has caused so much trouble. It's like it's cursed or something.'

'Let's hope that the curse is about to be lifted,' said Hettie, keeping her claws crossed that Matilda Skrimshaw and Binky Crustworthy had come up with a plan that would give the Skrimshaw land and its community a bright and meaningful future, especially now that there were four more tiny mouths to feed.

Chapter Twenty-Three

When Hettie and Tilly returned to the priory kitchens, they found Matilda and Binky pawing excitedly over a piece of paper spread across the table. It was a makeshift plan of how Binky saw the prospects for the future of Skrimshaw, and it appeared that her ideas had gone down very well with Matilda, who was totally animated.

They were keen to share their thoughts with Hettie and Tilly, and Binky gave them the guided tour of the plan so far. 'We'll obviously have to get one or two experts to make an inventory of the tombs, but I think with a bit of hard work we could have everything in place by the summer, so we can begin to recoup the costs of setting the whole thing up by letting paying visitors in. Now, if you look here, we should use the windmill as a visitor centre – and that would be at the end of the guided tour, so the last thing they'll encounter is the Viking boat tomb before spending their money in the centre's shop. I thought we could have miniatures of some of the artefacts for sale. You know the sort of thing – key rings, paper weights, et cetera. The schools will be an excellent source of income with group tickets, so we'll have to big up the stuff that kittens would find interesting – replica swords, colouring books, beads and coins. Anyway, where was I? Ah yes, the visitor centre here on the ground floor, and then a café on the first and second floors with views towards the priory. I don't know about you, but I won't go anywhere that doesn't have a café.'

Hettie and Tilly nodded in agreement as Binky batted on. 'As for the tombs, I think they should be left in situ, but to avoid any light-clawed visitors looking for treasure, we should erect glass screens in front of them on the principle of looking but not touching.' Binky pointed her claw at a rough sketch she'd done of the tunnel. 'The tour will start here in the house of rest. We'll have to construct a proper staircase down to the tombs, but that shouldn't be too difficult. I'm sure some of those hippies might be keen to help. It's going to be a case of all paws on deck to get us open by the summer, but I think it will be worth it.'

'I've called a meeting with the hippies for this afternoon,' said Hettie. 'Now that some of the more troublesome cats have left, I think a lot of them will want to stay on and help.'

'I hope they will,' said Matilda. 'I think it's important to have a community based here rather than hiring in cats we don't know, and some of them have skills we're going to need. We could put Serafin in charge of the visitor centre and Clawdelia could run the café, for instance.'

'That's an excellent plan,' said Hettie, 'and the cats you know as Bod and Anger are eager to walk through fire for you to make amends. Sam and Jim, as they are really called, will make very good maintenance cats, odd jobbers turning their paws to anything, and I gather Dryad is a carpenter by trade.'

'That's the spirit,' said Binky. 'I think it would be good if they dressed the part during opening hours as Saxons and Vikings to add a little colour to the proceedings. Maybe we could have a battle or two re-enacted on high days and holidays to add a bit of realism?'

'It would be nice to have a living village for them, too,' said Matilda. 'A place where they could raise their families and have a future – a proper Skrimshaw community.'

'I think that's already happening,' said Tilly. 'Clawdelia and Cambric have just had four kittens this morning.'

Matilda clapped her paws with delight. 'That is the most wonderful news – new life and a fresh start for us all.'

'What plans have you got for the priory?' Hettie asked.

'Well, the thing is, in my experience, everyone loves a ruin,' said Binky, 'and this one is outstanding. I think we should leave it just the way it is and spend some money on doing up Matilda's living quarters instead, as befits her status here. We've already discussed modernising the kitchen and adding a few more home comforts, and perhaps opening up some more rooms down here. The whole place will have to have electricity installed, including the windmill, obviously – we're not living in the dark ages, are we?'

Binky laughed at her own joke, having spent some time verbally reconstructing a period in history that many would regard as being very dark indeed. Tilly was more interested in the makeover of Matilda's accommodation. 'Will you have a TV?' she asked.

'Yes I shall,' she said. 'I've obviously been missing a lot of popular dramas and now I'm no longer Sister Constance I don't have to follow the Order of Peace Weavers' rules.'

Hettie and Tilly were very satisfied with the progress that was being made between Binky and Matilda. What had started as a Sunday afternoon tea had turned into an unimaginable nightmare of treachery and deceit, but, within days, Skrimshaw Priory and most of its inhabitants faced a much brighter future than the one Acrid Firestorm and Tabica had planned for them. Although the Skrimshaw affair hadn't been typical of their detective work, in time it would possibly prove to be one of their most impressive cases.

The meeting of the Skrimshaw community was well attended. Even Dikon managed to rise from his sick bed and the only notable exception was Clawdelia. Serafin and Hathor had spent the afternoon clearing out the hut that Firestorm and Tabica had shared, building a bonfire of all their things which now lit up the early evening sky. Now that the hut had been cleared, Hettie decided to hold the meeting there as it was warmer and cosier than the big hut where the feast had been held and Serafin provided cushions from her own collection for everyone to sit on.

Matilda and Binky attended as honoured guests, but it was Hettie who offered some opening remarks. 'Now that the old regime has been deposed and Matilda Skrimshaw has taken her rightful place as the owner and keeper of this land, you are all free to choose whether you stay or go. Those of you who stay will become part of a new enterprise created in a partnership between Matilda and Binky Crustworthy from the National Crust. If you stay, you will be expected to use your skills for the good of the priory and the land around it, and you will be guardians of possibly the most significant historical site in England. You will be expected to make your home here, raise your families here, and hopefully have a happy life. Before I ask Binky to outline the plans, I would ask that anyone who wishes to leave Skrimshaw will leave the meeting now, as there are things of great importance to be discussed.'

No one moved and Cambric raised his paw. 'I'd just like to say that you can count me and Clawdelia in if we're allowed to raise our kittens here. She's a bit busy at the moment feeding them, or she would have been here.'

'You are very welcome,' Matilda said, 'and congratulations. I look forward to seeing the new arrivals.'

Binky took to the floor next and went through the plans that she and Matilda had agreed upon, taking care not to give too many details regarding the treasures in the tombs until they'd been secured. By the time she'd finished, the hut was full of excited cats all keen to help in any way they could.

When Matilda got to her feet, she received a joyful round of applause and was so touched that she had to take a moment before addressing them. 'My friends,' she began, 'together we will make the Skrimshaw land something that the nation can be proud of – something to pass on to future generations to remind them of their history, and the cats who – through the centuries – have fought for their freedoms. I'm going to appoint Dikon as my steward and overseer of the land and the projects we need to undertake. Serafin will be the cat in charge of the commercial enterprise that Binky has just outlined. Sam, Jim and Dryad will work with Dikon, Marjoram will be head of health and safety and Hathor in charge of education and cultural projects. Cambric and Clawdelia will assume responsibility for public catering and for running a small bakery for our own needs. I know that many of you are aware that Tilly here is in line to succeed me, but she has made it clear that her life is busy enough already in her partnership with Hettie and The No. 2 Feline Detective Agency. She and Hettie will always be welcome here as part of our community. We owe these two cats and Bruiser a huge debt in helping to put me and the Skrimshaw land back on the map. The future, I'm delighted to say, is now guaranteed and in very safe paws: on my death, the land will pass to the National Crust to be kept for the nation. You and your descendants will all take a share in this prosperity as members of the Skrimshaw Community.'

Dikon offered three cheers and the room responded, adding a fourth for good measure. The meeting erupted into an excited forum of cats discussing their new roles. Matilda left first to visit Clawdelia and her new kittens and was delighted to learn that the two girls were to be called Matilda and Constance.

Binky Crustworthy was very satisfied with her day and full of appreciation for Hettie's quick thinking. 'I know that your business is usually murder,' she said, 'but by getting me involved in this project you have honoured the existence of so many extraordinary female cats who have fought to protect this land for centuries. The Shield Maidens, the Peace Weavers, and all those who took up arms to protect what is rightfully theirs. You and Tilly are the warriors of today, and for that reason I salute you both.'

Binky refused an overnight stay on the basis that she had much to plan, but promised to return the following week with her experts and the documents that would secure Skrimshaw's future. Everyone turned out to wave her off on her journey home. She made good progress through the Norfolk villages, but was delayed slightly by an accident once she'd reached the main road. It seemed that an old ambulance had driven into a tree, killing the male driver and his female passenger instantly. A witness at the scene said that the bald-headed cat with the tattoos had grabbed the steering wheel and forced the van off the road.

Chapter Twenty-Four

The Skrimshaw Community had much to celebrate and the feasting, singing and dancing went on well into the early hours. Eventually the cats crept away to their beds and Hettie, Tilly and Bruiser made themselves comfortable for the night on cushions in what had once been Firestorm's hut.

Matilda Skrimshaw rose early the next day. Pulling a warm shawl around herself, she walked through the frost to the windmill, escorted by a squadron of crows. The birds were silent except for the flapping of their wings, as if they knew what her purpose was. The windmill stood tall and formidable and she paused to look up at the sails where Romew had met her death. Her eye was then drawn to the stone where her mother had died. The burial ground was now alive with spring flowers – daffodils, primroses and tiny violets, all signs of a new beginning. She picked some daffodils and moved round to the back of the mill to lay them on the two fresh mounds of earth next to her mother's grave. She'd been taught by her holy order that forgiveness brought peace, and, as she walked back to the priory, she knew in her heart that it did.

Serafin had temporarily taken over the culinary duties, giving Clawdelia a chance to acclimatise herself to her new role as a mother. It was the smell of bacon that woke Hettie.

Tilly was just as keen to start her day, because at last they were going home. Bruiser had been up with the frost, polishing Miss Scarlet's chrome and making sure that she was ready for the journey. The three cats eventually gathered in Serafin's hut, where she had laid on a huge breakfast.

'I thought you'd need something substantial before your journey,' she said, filling three plates with sausages, bacon and eggs. 'It's the least I can do after all you've done for us. The plans for Skrimshaw are beyond our wildest dreams. I loved this place the first time I saw it, but until today I wasn't really happy here. I think I lost my way a bit after my mother died. I trusted cats I shouldn't and I got carried along by dreams that weren't mine.'

'You mean Acrid and Tabica?' Hettie said.

'Yes. I honestly thought they were good cats, but the one thing this has taught me is that good and evil live very close together. Like the Ancients, Romew and Remew – I spent a lot of time with them and mostly they were vile creatures, especially to each other, but there were moments when I could see a glimmer of hope or a genuine smile. I even got a thank you on rare occasions. I'm sad that they died, but I think it was almost a kindness, like putting them out of their misery.'

'In my experience, there's always a fight between good and evil,' Hettie said, mopping up her plate with a piece of bread. 'Like any battle, there's only one winner, but somehow it usually comes right in the end. A lot of cats have fallen by the wayside to get to where you and the community are today. Matilda Skrimshaw has sacrificed most of her life to make things right now. If Binky Crustworthy's brother Bartlett hadn't been murdered a few years back, I'd never have met her and she would probably never have known about this place. That's a perfect example of how evil comes good.'

'And then there's Matthew Katkins, the witchfinder,' added Tilly. 'If he hadn't been murdered, goodness knows what he'd have done, so his murder was a good thing.'

Hettie was pleased that Tilly had revisited her nightmare and put a positive spin on it. Now that the Skrimshaw burden had been lifted from her shoulders, she could put it all down to one of their many adventures. Something to tell Jessie about over a milky tea and a piece of flapjack, perhaps. The one thing Hettie was sure of was that Tilly would not be tempted to delve further into her family history, no matter how many books Turner Page threw at her.

Hettie, Tilly and Bruiser were given a heroes' send-off by the Skrimshaw Community. Matilda was quite tearful to see them go, and everyone promised to keep in touch. There was much waving until Miss Scarlet was out of sight, but the Skrimshaw crows stayed with them until they reached the coast road. It was a very fine spring morning. Once the sun had burnt off the frost, the day sparkled, which was more than could be said for the three bedraggled cats who eventually arrived back at the Butters' bakery, just as the sisters were wiping down their surfaces.

'Whatever do you three look like!' Betty said, giving them all a hug before passing them on to Beryl. 'Looks like you're all in need of a nice hot bath and some clean clothes.'

'That would be lovely,' Tilly said. She was used to taking a bath, as she was a messy eater, and even Hettie – who rarely immersed herself in anything – thought it a good plan. Bruiser was too tired to argue after such a long drive.

'Right then, sister!' said Beryl. 'I'll break out the tin bath and fill it while you stick the chicken in the oven. You'll be having your suppers with us tonight, unless you've other plans?'

Hettie shook her head vigorously. 'No, nothing planned at all, and that would be really nice.'

'Me and sister are dying to find out how you all went on after we left. Poor Sister Constance – got herself in a heap of trouble with those hippies, but I suppose you sorted it out like you always do. Dolly filled us in on the drive back, but that was only half the story,' Betty pointed out.

'And there's more excitement tomorrow, as we've got Marmite Spratt's funeral,' added Beryl. 'It'll be an early night – we don't want to miss any of the action. She's having a horse-drawn hearse according to Hilda Dabbit.'

Beryl placed the tin bath by the bread ovens and the three cats took it in turns, starting with Hettie and finishing with Bruiser. It was almost symbolic that they should wash away the dirt that had encompassed them. Hettie, later, likened their recent predicament to that of sin eaters, consuming the wrongs of the dead to wipe the slate clean for the living. Tilly was just looking forward to pulling on a clean pair of pyjamas and collapsing on her blanket by the fire after a roast chicken meal with all the trimmings in the Butters' flat. The sisters had been relentless in their questioning and were delighted at the prospect of a day out at Skrimshaw Priory once Binky and Matilda had set their plans in action.

It was only now, in the comfort of the Butters' sitting room, that the enormity of what Hettie, Tilly, Bruiser and Dolly had unearthed hit home to them. The tombs were a secret that had endured for possibly hundreds of years, and there was something that Hettie had been meaning to ask Bruiser. 'Why did you stand on my foot when I was talking to Dikon about the tunnel?'

Bruiser grinned and put down the chicken bone that he'd been chewing. 'Ah well, the thing is 'e was known on the road as Light-clawed Dick – slightest sign of anythin' valuable an' it was in 'is pocket before you knew it. I was just tryin' ta protect them grave goods until we knew what was 'appenin' with 'em. Don't get me wrong, 'e was a good mate an' 'e'd never 'ave stolen from me, but I was bein' cautious. 'E's fallen on 'is feet at Skrimshaw, though, and 'e's exactly the right cat for the job Miss Skrimshaw's given 'im.'

For Hettie, Tilly, Dolly and Bruiser, the Skrimshaw Saxon and Viking tombs had been a revelation – but nothing could have prepared them for Marmite Spratt's farewell journey.

Chapter Twenty-Five

The day dawned bright and frosty. Both Hettie and Tilly were
delighted to wake up in their own room. Tilly lingered in her
blankets, taking in all the things that were familiar to her. Her
books, the staff sideboard, the small sink, kettle and toaster,
the filing cabinet, TV and video recorder, and the clock on the
mantelpiece next to Hettie's catnip pouch and pipe. She was
relieved to see that Mrs White, the peace plant, was standing
proud on the sideboard where she had left her before their
so-called day out in Norfolk.

The book about Matthew Katkins had slid under the TV
stand. Tilly reached for it, tossing it rather disdainfully onto the
table to remind her to take it back to the library. She switched
on the kettle for their morning tea and prepared two mugs with
the milk that Betty had given them, adding two sugar lumps
each. She briefly remembered how strange her tea had tasted
sweetened by a Pengelly fruit drop, before loading the toaster
with two slices of bread. The bread had seen better days and she
clawed several small bits of blue mould off before pushing it into
the machine. She pulled the foil off two cheese triangles, poured
hot water into the mugs and spread the cheese on the toast. It
was these small rituals that brought her joy; after everything
they'd been through in the last few days, they meant even more

to her now, and had reinforced her decision not to let anything get in the way of her happy life. She had everything she could ever need – a home to share with Hettie, the Butters, Bruiser and Miss Scarlet, a host of friends in the town, and a job well paid enough to give her security for the rest of her life. As she stirred Hettie's tea, Skrimshaw Priory seemed a very long way away, and that was how she intended it to stay.

'Does one of those slices of toast have my name on it?' asked Hettie, sitting up in her armchair and stretching.

'It does, but I had to pick the mould off first. I think we'll have to fit a shop in at Malkin and Sprinkle later, as we've run out of basics.'

'I think we could leave that until Monday,' said Hettie. 'We'll get some treats from the bakery and eat out at Bloomers today and tomorrow – and anyway we've got Marmite Spratt's wake. I bet Molly and Dolly have pulled out all the stops for that.'

Tilly was pleased at the prospect of eating out. She sat and chewed her toast slowly, enjoying every mouthful and, in spite of Serafin's efforts, savouring the first decent cup of milky sweet tea that she'd had in days. Hettie demolished hers in record time. 'That toast went nowhere,' she said. 'I'm going to pull some clothes on and go and get us a Butters' breakfast bap to celebrate our homecoming, and a frothy coffee. How does that sound?'

Tilly clapped her paws, transferring cheese spread from one to the other. 'That would be lovely, but goodness knows what we're going to wear for Marmite's funeral. I don't think we've got anything in black, and there's no time to go to Jessie's charity shop to choose something. Betty said the procession starts at eleven and we don't want to miss that.'

'I can't believe that Marmite planned it down to the last nail in the coffin,' Hettie said. 'I mean, horse-drawn hearse, open casket in the church, gospel choir, doves and a fully paid-up plot in St Kipper's churchyard. She didn't leave much for Laxton Spratt to arrange. Maybe she didn't trust him to fulfil her wishes and that's why she appointed Bugs Anderton as executor. I bet she had menu cards printed for the wake as well.'

Tilly giggled at Hettie's irreverence. 'I wonder if Lavender Stamp will turn up to it? Just imagine – if her eyes meet Laxton's over the open casket, will their past romance be rekindled?'

'I just hope she stays off the sherry,' said Hettie. 'She's even nastier than normal after a couple of schooners. Anyway, you sort us out something to wear and I'll fetch the baps before the Butters shut up for the funeral.'

When Hettie returned Tilly had found a couple of black long-sleeved T-shirts at the bottom of the filing cabinet. They both carried band names that certainly wouldn't be appropriate for a funeral, but Tilly pointed out that if they wore them inside out nobody would be any the wiser. 'If we stick our macs over them, we should be fine. We'll just have to keep our coats on at the wake, and by then no one will care anyway.'

The cats enjoyed their second breakfast, changed into their T-shirts and struck out for St Kipper's at the bottom of the high street. There was quite a crowd forming when they got there, all pushing and shoving to get the best view. Betty and Beryl had closed the bakery after the breakfast rush and looked the part in their matching black maxi coats and hats with black feathers. Hilda Dabbit had gone for a double-breasted trouser suit in dark navy, which had fitted her once, and Elsie Haddock had broken with tradition, wearing a red military style coat trimmed in black, with a red pillbox hat perched precariously on her head at a rather jaunty angle. Bugs Anderton and several members of the town's friendship club lined the path into the church. Bugs' organisational skills were second to none and she ran the friendship club like a small army, ready to help and be involved in anything that presented itself.

Five minutes before the hearse was due to process down the high street, Lavender Stamp arrived dressed from head to toe in black crushed velvet. The outfit would have benefitted from being shortened, as she was walking with some difficulty. The veil she wore pulled down over her face was designed to give her an air of mystery, but Tilly pointed out that she looked more like Lily from *The Munsters*. Hettie added that she could easily have passed for a Stevie Nips lookalike if she'd had a tambourine with her.

Sadly, Marmite Spratt hadn't been well liked in the town, as she had spent her life poking her nose into other cats' family business. Unlike Hilda Dabbit, who loved a gossip, Marmite had been more secretive in her endeavours. She had systematically dug and delved into past lives, often coming to the wrong conclusions, then published her findings in her *Strange But True* series of books. It was no surprise that she had accumulated many enemies in the town – those she'd offended, and those whose family secrets had been exposed for all to read about. She'd done this work under the banner of being the town's local historian, but it was the fact that she was self-appointed in that role that rankled.

She'd managed to publish two books a year and her sales were strong, as the townsfolk felt obliged to buy them to see if their families had been subjected to Marmite's exposés. She would stop at nothing to sell a book and the more sensational she made them, the more her notoriety grew. Although a death should never be cause for celebration, the sigh of relief that reverberated around the town had been palpable when the *Daily Snout* announced her demise on its front page. Those whose paths she hadn't yet crossed regarded themselves as being off the hook, and those whose lives had been publicly exposed were heard to say that she'd got what was coming to her.

The funeral cortège left the recreation ground at exactly eleven o'clock. The glass horse-drawn hearse was driven by Mr

Trestle, accompanied by Mr Shroud, both looking splendid in their black top hats and tails. Morbid Balm led the procession on foot at the front of the horses, carrying a brass-topped walking cane. Morbid lived in black, as her out of office hours were spent as a Goth. She was numbered amongst Hettie and Tilly's closest friends; they were often thrown together on murder cases, and she had proved invaluable to them in her role as mortician at the town's undertakers. Today, she marched with the pride of her profession as the pavements filled on both sides of the high street to watch the spectacle pass by.

There could be no mistaking whose funeral it was. The name 'MARMITE' was written in white lilies on either side of the coffin, which – for a reasonably petite cat – was very large. The coffin, made of English oak, was gilded to match its brass handles. There was no doubt that Marmite had done herself proud in every respect; the sad thing was that she couldn't appreciate her own efforts, but the crowds that had gathered would remember the day for some time to come.

The procession was by no means silent. Laxton Spratt, Marmite's only son, followed behind the hearse in a funeral car, but behind him came the town's brass band in their bright red regalia, all wearing black armbands. They weren't what you might call seasoned performers, as they were only required twice a year for civic events. Several members had stepped down due to disputes with their conductor and musical director, or to the fact that they had been disqualified for bribing a judge with catnip at the regional brass championships. In spite of them being six players down, the musicians who were left were making a brave effort to escort Marmite to her final resting place, although those at the front seemed to be playing a very different tune to those at the back – which could easily be interpreted as a metaphor on life.

As the cortège passed down the high street, the crowds joined it behind the brass band. By the time the hearse came to a stop outside St Kipper's, it appeared that the whole of the town had turned out. The band struck up a rather confused version of 'Yellow Submarine' as Mr Shroud and Mr Trestle dismounted from their seats and gathered at the back of the hearse, with four other cats who regularly helped as bearers. Morbid stood at the front, holding on to the horses, who had begun to fidget when the crowd burst into song, accompanying the brass band.

The double glass doors were opened, the floral tributes removed, and the coffin was half out of the hearse when the horses took off with Morbid still hanging on to the reins. The bearers were taken by surprise and couldn't stop the extra-large coffin bumping to the ground. The crowd collectively gasped, and the band stopped playing as Mr Trestle inspected the casket, which mercifully was still intact. The problem now was how to get it into the church, as six bearers weren't enough to lift it up from the road. Laxton Spratt stepped forward and so did Bruiser, who had just arrived, and together the eight cats hauled the coffin onto the pavement. It was just too heavy to lift from pavement to shoulders, so Marmite was literally dragged into the church, where the Reverend Crispin Neeler offered a ramp from the vestry to slide the coffin onto the dais that had been prepared for it.

The congregation stampeded into the church, not wanting to miss anything. Hilda Dabbit led the surge of cats and Hettie, Tilly and the Butters followed her, making sure they had a good seat close to the front. Jessie slid in beside them, arriving later than she'd planned as she'd agreed to collect the doves as a favour to Bugs. Mr Shroud, satisfied that everything was back on track, unscrewed the fastenings and opened the casket, leaning the lid up against the pulpit.

It was instantly obvious why the coffin was so large and so heavy. Marmite lay, paws crossed, surrounded by her own books, and Hettie and Tilly were transported back to the Skrimshaw tunnel and the grave goods surrounding the Saxon corpses. 'She won't be short of reading where she's going,' Hettie muttered. 'It'll save Laxton taking them to your charity shop.'

'Don't even go there,' Jessie whispered. 'He delivered a mountain of beige twinsets belonging to her yesterday, and he's threatened me – in the nicest possible way – with her bric-a-brac for Monday.'

'Just make sure you refuse the Teasmade,' advised Hettie.

Tilly giggled and Betty dug her in the ribs. 'Behave yourself, or you'll start me and sister off as well.'

The funeral service went on for some time. Laxton Spratt offered a short, impersonal eulogy, as if he hardly knew his mother. The only cat animated by his words was Lavender Stamp, who nervously picked a hole in her veil with her claws as several pairs of eyes turned towards her. The Reverend Crispin Neeler took to the pulpit and, in accordance with Marmite's wishes, read a whole chapter from one of her books, furtively discarding it in her coffin when he had finished.

The gospel choir was probably the highlight of the service, and almost rivalled the open casket for visual entertainment. They swung and clapped their way through several songs featuring Jesus, and finished with a medley of Vera Lint classic wartime hits, ending with 'We'll Meet Again'. As Hettie pointed out later at the wake, the thought of meeting Marmite Spratt again on the astral plane was enough to make any cat want to live forever.

Those who had managed to squeeze themselves into the church then filed past the coffin before Mr Shroud screwed the lid down, bringing Marmite Spratt's final performance to an end. Morbid Balm, who'd missed the service entirely, arrived in time to lead the mourners round to the graveyard at the back of the church, having tethered the horses and the hearse in the undertakers' yard. The bearers staggered under the weight of the coffin, but manoeuvred it out of the church and round to the freshly dug grave.

Jessie collected the basket of doves from the church porch where she'd left them and passed them to Bugs, who set them free at the head of the grave. It was meant to be a dramatic gesture, but all but one of the birds stayed in the comfort of the basket, cooing to each other. The one that flew out circled the graveyard once before returning to join its friends.

The Reverend intoned the committal ceremony as the casket was lowered into the grave. The bearers strained every sinew as they took the weight, and all were greatly relieved when the job was done. Laxton Spratt stepped forward and threw a pawful of earth into the grave before pushing his way through the crowd and out onto the high street. A murmur of disapproval spread around the mourners at his lack of regret for his mother's death and his abrupt exit from the proceedings.

Hettie and Tilly thought they would get ahead of the crowd and followed him out through the lychgate. They were the only ones to witness him sharing a brief conversation with Lavender Stamp before walking back up the high street, leaving Lavender staring after him.

'Bugger!' said Tilly. 'If only we'd been a bit closer we might have heard what they were saying.'

'It certainly didn't look like the rekindling of a long-lost love affair,' said Hettie. 'Come on – let's get to Bloomers for the wake. I'm starving.'

Molly and Dolly had pulled out the stops for Marmite's wake. They had both stayed away from the funeral to put the finishing touches to the food. Tilly entertained them with the highlights as they set out the cups and saucers for the tea. Hettie had assumed that Laxton Spratt would be there already, but there was no sign of him; even stranger still, Lavender walked straight past the café towards her post office.

'That is a surprise,' Hettie said. 'No Laxton Spratt and no Lavender Stamp. It's all beginning to look a bit suspicious.'

Molly laughed. 'That's what you get for being away with those hippies, so it is. Your man cat has been visiting the postmistress since Sunday last. That car of his has been parked outside the post office at all hours of the day and night, so it has, and I'm not thinking he was after a postal order, if you get my meaning.'

'And 'e was in 'ere buyin' two bacon baps an' two milky coffees when we opened this mornin',' said Dolly. 'I watched 'im go, an' 'e was takin' them over there.'

Dolly pointed in the direction of the post office as a horde of mourners burst through the door. Hilda Dabbit led the pack and the Butters arrived a few minutes later, having taken the high street at a more sedate pace. Bruiser arrived through the back door of the kitchen, hoping for a catch-up with Dolly, but was immediately enlisted as wine waiter – and looked the part, as he was wearing his best waistcoat.

Hettie, Tilly and the Butter sisters retired to a table at the back of the café, where Dolly kept them supplied with sandwiches, pastries and cakes while the good and the great of the town demolished the wake bakes as if there was no tomorrow. That was true for Marmite Spratt, of course, but there seemed to be very little by way of tribute to her as the cats nibbled their way through the food she'd planned for them.

Hettie was keener to discuss Lavender Stamp than Marmite, especially after the bombshell that Molly had just dropped. 'Looks like the Lavender/Laxton thing is back on again,' she said, hoping that the Butters might be able to add to Molly's observations.

'She's playing with fire there,' said Betty. 'He'll be gone in a puff of smoke once he's sorted out his mother's affairs. She was walking on air when she came into the bakery yesterday for her plain iced bun. Took me and sister completely by surprise when she ordered two of our fresh cream éclairs and two of our large steak pies instead.'

'She's never ordered a cream cake in all the time we've known her,' added Beryl, 'and as for the steak pie, that was a real revelation. As far as we know, she never eats more than a meagre ham salad normally. She invited us over there to tea once – sad old plateful of lettuce and very little else. Sister and me found ourselves queuing at Greasy Tom's van afterwards for something with a bit of substance.'

'But what will happen to her if he leaves her again?' said Tilly.

'Well, I for one wouldn't want to have to pick up the pieces,' said Betty. 'He's ruined her life once and I'm sure he's about to do it again. I just hope I'm wrong.'

It was a rare thing for the Butters to be wrong about anything, but today was the day to pull the humble pie out of the oven, or so it seemed. There was barely a crumb from a funeral biscuit left when Laxton Spratt – freshly changed out of his mourning clothes – pushed his way into the wake to make an announcement. Lavender followed him, having shed her black crushed velvet for an almost cheerful twinset. He sprang up onto a table so that everyone could see him and clapped his paws to get the room's attention.

'I'd just like to thank everyone for coming,' he began, 'and a special thank you to Molly Bloom, Dolly Scollop and the Butters for the wonderful spread they've put on – and to Bugs Anderton, too, for all her efforts. I had a difficult upbringing in this town. My mother always had to take centre stage, and eventually she drove me away. I had fallen for the young cat at the post office and she wholeheartedly disapproved of that. She threw me out and told me never to return. I was forced to make my own way, and to leave behind the cat with whom I had hoped to spend the rest of my days. Now that my mother has gone, it is my intention to claw back some of those lost years in the company of my dear Lavender.'

Under normal circumstances, an announcement of such good news would have been cause for audible celebration, but it was met with complete silence. Too many angry and petulant exchanges had flowed under the town's bridge in the post office over the years and there wasn't one cat present whom Lavender Stamp hadn't insulted or humiliated in some way.

Laxton Spratt was visibly shaken by the silence and slowly got down from the table. It was now clearly up to Lavender to save the day; with Laxton's help, she clambered up onto the table. 'I can see that you are unwilling to share our happiness,' she said, 'and I don't blame you. All I can say in my defence is that since Laxton went away there has been nothing in my life that has made me happy. I've watched you all going about your business, enjoying the various chapters of your lives, and it has made me angry to think that I would never be able to feel that joy. My only defence was to make life difficult for anyone around me. At least by doing that I felt that I was making some sort of impact rather than being poor Lavender Stamp, jilted and unloved. I promise to try and change all of that and I apologise to anyone I've been unkind to. Please give me a chance to put things right.'

Lavender bowed her head as the tears rolled down her face and Betty stole the moment by getting to her feet. 'Three cheers for Lavender and Laxton!' she shouted, and the crowd responded with a raucous wave of clapping and cheering. Laxton helped Lavender down from the table and Molly sent Bruiser into the crowd with another round of sherries. It was noticeable that when he offered the tray to the happy couple, Lavender refused, saying she would prefer a nice cup of tea.

No one could say whether Laxton and Lavender would make a go of things, and it was impossible to predict how the future would pan out for them, but for now, as with all good stories, there was a definite possibility of a happy ever after.

****

The darkening skies closed in around Tilly as she returned to the windmill. What had brought her there was perhaps an irrational urge to lay to rest the ghosts that haunted her: Matthew Katkins and his evil pursuit of harmless female cats, blessed with healing powers that he refused to understand; the miller's son, so cruelly despatched by a Roundhead's sword; the tragic death of Matilda from the plague; the senseless killing of Romew and Remew's mother, and their own inevitable violent and bloody appointment with the justice they deserved. Too many cats had died protecting and fighting over the land, but none had evoked the horror of the vile crime laid at the Viking warrior Firestorm's door. To take the lives of his own kittens out of greed and a need for ultimate power was unforgivable, no matter how long ago their tiny bodies had been laid to rest. Now, under the protection of their mother, Matilda the Shield Maiden, their story would be told as generations of cats filed past their tomb, knowing that this was where the story began.

Tilly pushed the door open but didn't go in, distracted by the Skrimshaw crows who had taken flight from the priory wall. They circled above her, their deafening cries pleading with her to go no further. She put her paws to her ears to shut out the warning, knowing that she must face her demons; to allow them to continue to taunt her was more than she could bear. After all, she was descended from a Shield Maiden, a warrior whose fear was her strength. Now she must put that strength to the test.

The mill was quiet, waiting for something to begin. Tilly stood by the fireplace and followed the contours of the walls with her eyes, no longer seeing the prison she had so recently broken free from. She stared down at the ground and the broken boards covering the Viking tomb. Suddenly, one by one, they wrenched themselves from their fastenings and broke free of the floor, as if she was directing them to reveal the chasm below.

Ragland Firestorm rose from his tomb like a silent tornado. His headless body danced around the walls of the mill, changing shape as it filled the room and engulfing Tilly in a bitter-tasting mist of ectoplasm. She froze. There was no escape and all her strength had been drained from her, sucked out of her body by the satanic power that raged around her. She felt no fear, and realised that it was because she felt nothing at all; so this was what it was like to be dead, she thought.

The spectre suddenly shrank back and crouched low by the stairs as a rhythmic sound filled the air. Tilly stared down at the hole in the floor, and the noise grew louder until eventually she could see the tops of skeletal heads appearing in the void. One by one they clambered out, their grave clothes falling in folds around them, translucent and yet substantial. Tilly watched as they lined up around the walls, their spears and swords raised in some form of ceremonial salute. Finally came a beacon of light that filled the room, radiating from a golden gossamer staircase as Matilda the Shield Maiden emerged in full warrior regalia, magnificent and glorious. Tilly's heart leapt as she bowed her head, too overwhelmed to look upon such a powerful vision. She felt nothing but joy, and if she really was dead, this must truly be eternal peace.

The Shield Maiden turned to the lingering presence of Ragland Firestorm as the skeletons closed in a guard around her. Tilly lifted her head and watched as Matilda conjured up a giant fireball, directing it like a bolt of lightning at Firestorm. The apparition rose up against her, but undaunted she sent another strike to the heart of her adversary. This time the spectre shattered into tiny points of light, falling to the ground as their brightness dimmed and was eventually extinguished, leaving only dust on the windmill's floor.

The skeletons drew back from Matilda and she turned towards Tilly. This time Tilly looked into her face. She was beautiful – no longer the fleshless corpse but a living, breathing cat adorned in her robes of office, a warrior Queen risen from her tomb to execute her final judgement on the cat who had murdered her kittens centuries ago.

'You have done well to bring this sadness into the light, Matilda Jenkins,' the Shield Maiden said. 'All that was lost has been found, and you have brought the promise of a new age of understanding to our story. We are in your debt, and now offer you protection for *all the days of your earthly life. If fear should overtake you, then look to the sky and all will be well. May the blessings of peace and contentment rest with you.'*

The Shield Maiden was gone before Tilly could acknowledge her words and the windmill was as she had found it – silent and empty except, perhaps, for a little more dust on the floor. Tilly pushed the door open and stepped out into the daylight. She looked up at the sky, where the largest of the Skrimshaw crows circled above her, squawking its approval as she closed the door and left the windmill's secrets behind.

****

The tapping was insistent enough to wake Hettie from a deep sleep, brought on by considerable overindulgence of sherry, champagne and wake bakes from the night before. Marmite Spratt's after-the-funeral-gathering had turned into quite some party and they had crawled into their beds sometime after two o'clock in the morning. The fact that there was a giant crow pecking away at their window was the last thing Hettie needed to go with the hangover that she would probably be nursing for the rest of the day.

'Bloody birds!' she grumbled, as Tilly struggled to sit up in her blankets. 'You'd think after hundreds of years of animosity that birds would appreciate that we just don't like them.'

Tilly looked across at the window. The crow stopped tapping its beak against the glass and cocked its head on one side. She smiled. 'I think we're stuck with that one,' she said.

THE END

Acknowledgements

Writing this book was a fascinating journey. I was delighted to discover that the succession of the female line was very much alive and kicking in early English society in the shape of the Peace-Weavers and Shield Maidens. These women fiercely protected their families and territory and supported their male warriors whilst maintaining their own tribal independence. The idea of of female inheritance forms the basis for this story.

I would also like to thank my niece, Polly, for her detailed instruction on certain aspects of hippiedom, a state of mind I vaguely remember living through in the 1970s.

The location was very important and I would like to thank the owners of Cley Windmill in Norfolk for a spooky overnight stay; Castle Acre Priory for inspiration; and the wonderful West Stow Anglo-Saxon Village and museum for a window into the past. The research proved to be a time machine joy ride and reminded me of the struggles and battles women have fought through the ages, and to some extent are still fighting to this day.

About the Author

Mandy Morton was born in Suffolk and after a short and successful music career in the 1970s as a singer-songwriter – during which time she recorded six albums and toured extensively throughout the UK and Scandinavia with her band – she joined the BBC, where she produced and presented arts-based programmes for local and national radio. She more recently presents *The Eclectic Light Show* on Mixcloud. Mandy lives with her partner, who is also a crime writer, in Cambridge and Cornwall where there is always room for a long-haired tabby cat. She is the author of The No. 2 Feline Detective Agency series and also co-wrote *In Good Company* with Nicola Upson, which chronicles a year in the life of the Cambridge Arts Theatre.

Twitter: **@hettiebagshot** and **@icloudmandy**

Facebook: **HettieBagshotMysteries**

Also available

The No. 2 Feline Detective Agency begins

Hettie Bagshot has bitten off more than any cat could chew. No sooner has she launched her detective agency than she's thrown into her first case.

Furcross, home for senior cats, has a nasty spate of body-snatching, and three former residents have been stolen from their graves. Hettie and her sidekick, Tilly, set out to reveal the terrible truth. Is Nurse Mogadon involved in a deadly game? Has the haberdashery department of Malkin and Sprinkle become a mortuary? And what flavour will Betty Butter's pie of the week be?

In a haze of catnip and pastry, Hettie steers the case to its conclusion, but will she get there before the body count rises - and the pies sell out?

OUT NOW!

Also available

All aboard for the Summer of Fluff!

Meet Hettie Bagshot, a long-haired tabby cat whose whiskers twitch at the first sign of a mystery, and her best friend Tilly Jenkins. Together, they run The No. 2 Feline Detective Agency, and nothing will stop them from untangling each brain-teasing case that comes their way.

In scorching temperatures, Hettie Bagshot and her sidekick Tilly set out on a road trip to catch a killer cat amid a sea of entertainers. As Psycho Derek's bus lurches from one venue to the next, the killer strikes again. The big question for The No. 2 Feline Detective Agency is who will be next?

Will it be Patty Sniff, the ageing punk star? Or Kitty O'Shea from the Irish dance troupe? Or perhaps Belisha Beacon's days are numbered. As the fur flies and the animosity builds, Hettie and Tilly become embroiled in a world of music, mayhem and murder. As matters draw to a terrifying conclusion, will Magical Mystery Paws finally top the bill?

OUT NOW!

Also available

What mysteries lie beyond the gravy?

Psychic cat Irene Peggledrip is being visited by a band of malevolent spirits who all claim to be murderers. Not only is their message disturbing, but they cause chaos with indoor snowstorms, flying books and the untimely demise of a delicious Victoria sponge. Irene calls in Hettie and Tilly of The No. 2 Feline Detective Agency to help, but they're not sure how far their skills reach into the spirit realm.

Meanwhile, Lavender Stamp, the town's bad-tempered postmistress cat, has some good news to deliver to Tilly: she has won a competition to take afternoon tea with renowned mystery writer Agatha Crispy at her Devon home, Furaway House.

Will Hettie and Tilly finally lay the ghosts to rest? Can Molly Bloom's new café survive the seance? And will the moving claw give up its secrets before the gravy congeals?

OUT NOW!

Also available

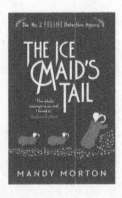

Do you believe in the Ice Maid's Tail...?

The town is gripped by a big freeze, and blizzard after blizzard has engulfed the feline community, leaving shops and business-es snowbound. Hettie Bagshot and her sidekick, Tilly Jenkins, have found sanctuary by their fireside but soon they are bucketed into a terrifying nightmare, called to investigate the disappearance of the town's kittens as – one by one – they are taken in the snow.

Who are the strange cats living in Wither-Fork Woods?

Will the ancient prophecy of the Ice Maid's Tail become a reality?

And can Hettie and Tilly defrost the fish fingers in time for tea?

Also available

Who will get to the crust of the matter?

As the Easter weekend approaches, feline detectives Hettie Bagshot and Tilly Jenkins are called to investigate the murder of local radio DJ Hartley Battenberg.

Bowled over by the prospect of a bake off competition, a cricket match and an outdoor screening of *The Sound of Music*, Hettie and Tilly struggle through a sea of trifle to catch out a killer. Will Bunty Basham's eleven be triumphant? Has Whisker FM played its final jingle?

And will celebrity cook Fanny Haddock get her just desserts?

OUT NOW!

Also available

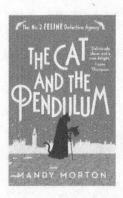

A claw-biting case

When the celebrated crime writer Agatha Crispy engages Hettie and Tilly in the search for a stolen manuscript, our feline detective duo is plunged into a world of Dickensian thieves and murderers.

Does the ghost of Jake the Nipper prowl the London streets of Kitzrovia? Will Madame Two Paws's exhibition wax or wane? And will the secrets in the crypt of the church of St Mavis and Cucumber finally be revealed?

Join Hettie and Tilly as they attempt to unravel yet another darkly humorous case for The No. 2 Feline Detective Agency.

OUT NOW!

Coming soon

Murder on the Santa Claws Express

Hettie and Tilly are invited to host a Christmas Eve murder mystery aboard the Santa Claws Express. No sooner has the train left the station at Mogbury-on-the-Tilt than our two feline detectives are caught up in a murderous family feud between the Shuttles and the Stokers.

Is the ghost of Hornby Stoker haunting the line? Are there enough sausage rolls in the Biscuit Jar Buffet? Who will hit the buffers at Hissingford Holt? And will Hettie and Tilly's Christmas be derailed?

Join our tabby heroes as they plough their way through red herrings, hot chestnuts and snowbound platforms in a hunt for a festive fiend who will stop at nothing.

Note from the Publisher

To receive updates on new releases in The No. 2 Feline Detective
Agency series – plus special offers and news of other humorous
fiction series to make you smile – sign up now to the Farrago
mailing list at farragobooks.com/sign-up.